A LIFE
FOR A LIFE

"I said whajadoin'?" growled West.

Morse looked at him, and in the young man's eyes there was something that made the murderer shiver.

"I'm making a tombstone."

"What?" West felt an icy fist clutch his heart.

"A marker for a grave."

"For—for Beresford? Maybe he won't die. Looks better to me. Fever ain't so high."

"It's not for him."

West moistened his dry lips with his tongue. "You will have yore l'il joke, eh? Who's it for?"

"For you."

"For me?" The man's fear burst from him in a shriek. "Whajamean for me?"

From the lettering Morse read aloud. "'Bully West, Executed, Some Time Late in March, 1875.'" And beneath it, "'May God Have Mercy on His Soul . . .'"

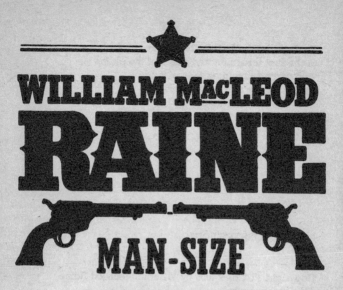

WILLIAM MacLEOD RAINE

MAN-SIZE

A WESTERN NOVEL

POPULAR LIBRARY

An Imprint of Warner Books, Inc.

A Warner Communications Company

To Captain Sir Cecil E. Denny, Bart.
of the first three hundred riders of the plains
who carried law into the lone lands
and made the scarlet and gold
a synonym for justice, integrity,
and indomitable pluck

POPULAR LIBRARY EDITION

Popular Library® and the fanciful P design are registered
trademarks of Warner Books, Inc.

This Popular Library Edition is published by arrangement
with Houghton Mifflin Company, One Beacon Street,
Boston, Mass. 02108

Cover illustration by George Bush

Popular Library books are published by
Warner Books, Inc.
666 Fifth Avenue
New York, N.Y. 10103

W A Warner Communications Company

Printed in the United States of America

First Popular Library Printing: May, 1987

10 9 8 7 6 5 4 3 2 1

CHAPTER I

In The Danger Zone

SHE stood on the crown of the hill, silhouetted against a sky-line of deepest blue. Already the sun was sinking in a crotch of the plains which rolled to the horizon edge like waves of a great land sea. Its reflected fires were in her dark, stormy eyes. Its long, slanted rays were a spotlight for the tall, slim figure, straight as that of a boy.

The girl's gaze was fastened on a wisp of smoke rising lazily from a hollow of the crumpled hills. That floating film told of a camp-fire of buffalo chips. There was a little knitted frown of worry on her forehead, for imagination could fill in details of what the coulée held: the white canvas tops of prairie schooners, some spans of oxen grazing near, a group of blatant, profane whiskey-smugglers from Montana, and in the wagons a cargo of liquor to debauch the Bloods and Piegans near Fort Whoop-Up.

Sleeping Dawn was a child of impulse. She had all youth's capacity for passionate indignation and none of the wisdom of age which tempers the eager desire of the hour. These whiskey-traders were ruining her people. More than threescore Blackfeet braves had been killed within the year in drunken brawls among themselves. The plains Indians would sell their souls for fire-water. When the craze was on them, they would exchange furs, buffalo robes, ponies, even their wives and daughters for a bottle of the poison.

In the sunset glow she stood rigid and resentful, one small fist clenched, the other fast to the barrel of the rifle she carried. The evils of the trade came close to her. Fergus McRae still carried the gash from a knife thrust earned in a drunken brawl. It was likely that to-morrow he would cut the trail of the wagon wheels and again make a bee-line for liquor and trouble. The swift blaze of revolt found expression in the stamp of her moccasined foot.

As dusk fell over the plains, Sleeping Dawn moved forward lightly, swiftly, toward the camp in the hollow of the hills. She had no definite purpose except to spy the lay-out, to make sure that her fears were justified. But through the hinterland of her consciousness rebellious thoughts were racing. These smugglers were wholly outside the law. It was her right to frustrate them if she could.

Noiselessly she skirted the ridge above the coulée, moving through the bunch grass with the wary care she had learned as a child in the lodges of the tribe.

Three men crouched on their heels in the glow of a campfire well up the draw. A fourth sat at a little distance from them riveting a stirrup leather with two stones. The wagons had been left near the entrance of the valley pocket some sixty or seventy yards from the fire. Probably the drivers, after they had unhitched the teams, had been drawn deeper into the draw to a spot more fully protected from the wind.

While darkness gathered, Sleeping Dawn lay in the bunch grass with her eyes focused on the camp below. Her untaught soul struggled with the problem that began to shape itself. These men were wolfers, desperate men engaged in a nefarious business. They paid no duty to the British Government. She had heard her father say so. Contrary to law, they brought in their vile stuff and sold it both to breeds and tribesmen. They had no regard whatever for the terrible injury they did the natives. Their one intent was to get rich as soon as possible, so they plied their business openly and defiantly. For the Great Lone Land was still a wilderness where every man was a law to himself.

The blood of the girl beat fast with the racing pulse of excitement. A resolution was forming in her mind. She realized the risks and estimated chances coolly. These men would fire to kill on any skulker near the camp. They would take no needless hazard of being surprised by a band of stray Indians. But the night would befriend her. She believed she could do what she had in mind and easily get away to the shelter of the hill creases before they could kill or capture her.

A shadowy dog on the outskirt of the camp rose and barked. The girl waited, motionless, tense, but the men paid little heed to the warning. The man working at the stirrup leather got to his feet, indeed, carelessly, rifle in hand, and stared into the gloom; but presently he turned on his heel and sauntered back to his job of saddlery. Evidently the hound was used to voicing false alarms whenever a coyote slipped past or a skunk nosed inquisitively near.

Sleeping Dawn followed the crest of the ridge till it fell

away to the mouth of the coulée. She crept up behind the white-topped wagon nearest the entrance.

An axe lay against the tongue. She picked it up, glancing at the same time toward the camp-fire. So far she had quite escaped notice. The hound lay blinking into the flames, its nose resting on crossed paws.

With her hunting-knife the girl ripped the canvas from the side of the top. She stood poised, one foot on a spoke, the other on the axle. The axe-head swung in a half-circle. There was a crash of wood, a swift jet of spouting liquor. Again the axe swung gleaming above her head. A third and a fourth time it crashed against the staves.

A man by the camp-fire leaped to his feet with a startled oath. "What's that?" he demanded sharply.

From the shadows of the wagons a light figure darted. The man snatched up a rifle and fired. A second time, aimlessly, he sent a bullet into the darkness.

The silent night was suddenly alive with noises. Shots, shouts, the barking of the dog, the slap of running feet, all came in a confused medley to Sleeping Dawn.

She gained a moment's respite from pursuit when the traders stopped at the wagons to get their bearings. The first of the white-topped schooners was untouched. The one nearest the entrance to the coulée held four whiskey-casks with staves crushed in and contents seeping into the dry ground.

Against one of the wheels a rifle rested. The girl flying in a panic had forgotten it till too late.

The vandalism of the attack amazed the men. They could have understood readily enough some shots out of the shadows or a swoop down upon the camp to stampede and run off the saddle horses. Even a serious attempt to wipe out the party by a stray band of Blackfeet or Crees was an undertaking that would need no explaining. But why should any one do such a foolish, wasteful thing as this, one to so little purpose in its destructiveness?

They lost no time in speculation, but plunged into the darkness in pursuit.

7

CHAPTER II

The Amazon

THE dog darted into the bunch grass and turned sharply to the right. One of the men followed it, the others took different directions.

Up a gully the hound ran, nosed the ground in a circle of sniffs, and dipped down into a dry watercourse. Tom Morse was at heel scarcely a dozen strides behind.

The yelping of the dog told Morse they were close on their quarry. Once or twice he thought he made out the vague outline of a flying figure, but in the night shadows it was lost again almost at once.

They breasted the long slope of a low hill and took the decline beyond. The young plainsman had the legs and the wind of a Marathon runner. His was the perfect physical fitness of one who lives a clean, hard life in the dry air of the high lands. The swiftness and the endurance of the fugitive told him that he was in the wake of youth trained to a fine edge.

Unexpectedly, in the deeper darkness of a small ravine below the hill spur, the hunted turned upon the hunter. Morse caught the gleam of a knife thrust as he plunged. It was too late to check his dive. A flame of fire scorched through his forearm. The two went down together, rolling over and over as they struggled.

Startled, Morse loosened his grip. He had discovered by the feel of the flesh he was handling so roughly that it was a woman with whom he was fighting.

She took advantage of his hesitation to shake free and roll away.

They faced each other on their feet. The man was amazed at the young Amazon's fury. Her eyes were like live coals, flashing at him hatred and defiance. Beneath the skin smock she wore, her breath came raggedly and deeply. Neither of them spoke, but her gaze did not yield a thousandth part of an inch to his.

8

The girl darted for the knife she had dropped. Morse was upon her instantly. She tried to trip him, but when they struck the ground she was underneath.

He struggled to pin down her arms, but she fought with a barbaric fury. Her hard little fist beat upon his face a dozen times before he pegged it down.

Lithe as a panther, her body twisted beneath his. Too late the flash of white teeth warned him. She bit into his arm with the abandon of a savage.

"You little devil!" he cried between set teeth.

He flung away any scruples he might have had and pinned fast her flying arms. The slim, muscular body still writhed in vain contortions till he clamped it fast between knees from which not even an untamed cayuse could free itself.

She gave up struggling. They glared at each other, panting from their exertions. Her eyes still flamed defiance, but back of it he read fear, a horrified and paralyzing terror. To the white traders along the border a half-breed girl was a squaw, and a squaw was property just as a horse or a dog was.

For the first time she spoke, and in English. Her voice came bell-clear and not in the guttural of the tribes.

"Let me up!" It was an imperative, urgent, threatening.

He still held her in the vise, his face close to her flaming eyes. "You little devil," he said again.

"Let me up!" she repeated wildly. "Let me up, I tell you."

"Like blazes I will. You're through biting and knifing me for one night." He had tasted no liquor all day, but there was the note of drunkenness in his voice.

The terror in her grew. "If you don't let me up—"

"You'll do what?" he jeered.

Her furious upheaval took him by surprise. She had unseated him and was scrambling to her feet before he had her by the shoulders.

The girl ducked her head in an effort to wrench free. She could as easily have escaped from steel cuffs as from the grip of his brown fingers.

"You'd better let me go!" she cried. "You don't know who I am."

"Nor care," he flung back. "You're a nitchie, and you smashed our kegs. "That's enough for me."

"I'm no such thing a nitchie," [1] she denied indignantly.

The instinct of self-preservation was moving in her. She

---

[1] In the vernacular of the Northwest, Indians were "nitchies." (W. M. R.)

had played into the hands of this man and his companions. The traders made their own laws and set their own standards. The value of a squaw of the Blackfeet was no more than that of the liquor she had destroyed. It would be in character for them to keep her as a chattel captured in war.

"The daughter of a squaw-man then," he said, and there was in his voice the contempt of the white man for the half-breed.

"I'm Jessie McRae," she said proudly,

Among the Indians she went by her tribal name of Sleeping Dawn, but always with the whites she' used the one her adopted father had given her. It increased their respect for her. Just now she was in desperate need of every ounce that would weigh in the scales.

"Daughter of Angus McRae?" he asked, astonished.

"Yes."

"His woman's a Cree?"

"His wife is," the girl corrected.

"What you doin' here?"

"Father's camp is near. He's hunting hides."

"Did he send you to smash our whiskey-barrels?"

"Angus McRae never hides behind a woman," she said, her chin up.

That was true. Morse knew it, though he had never met McRae. His reputation had gone all over the Northland as a fearless fighting man honest as daylight and stern as the Day of Judgment. If this girl was a daughter of the old Scot, not even a whiskey-trader could safely lay hands on her. For back of Angus was a group of buffalo-hunters related to him by blood over whom he held half-patriarchal sway.

"Why did you do it?" Morse demanded.

The question struck a spark of spirit from her. "Because you're ruining my people—destroying them with your fire-water."

He was taken wholly by surprise. "Do you mean you destroyed our property for that reason?"

She nodded, sullenly.

"But we don't trade with the Crees," he persisted.

It was on the tip of her tongue to tell him that she was of the Blackfoot tribe and not of the Crees, but again for reasons of policy she was less than candid. Till she was safely out of the woods, it was better this man should not know she was only an adopted daughter of Angus McRae. She offered another reason, and with a flare of passion which he was to learn as a characteristic of her.

10

"You make trouble for my brother Fergus. He shot Akokotos (Many Horses) in the leg when the fire-water burned in him. He was stabbed by a Piegan brave who did not know what he was doing. Fergus is good. He minds his own business. But you steal away his brains. Then he runs wild. It was *you*, not Fergus, that shot Akokotos. The Great Spirit knows you whiskey-traders, and not my poor people who destroy each other, are the real murderers."

Her logic was feminine and personal, from his viewpoint wholly unfair. Moreover, one of her charges did not happen to be literally true.

"We never sold whiskey to your brother—not our outfit. It was Jackson's, maybe. Anyhow, nobody made him buy it. He was free to take it or leave it."

"A wolf doesn't have to eat the poisoned meat in a trap, but it eats and dies," she retorted swiftly and bitterly.

Adroitly she had put him on the defensive. Her words had the sting of barbed darts.

"We're not talking of wolves."

"No, but of Blackfeet and Bloods and Sarcees," she burst out, again with that flare of feminine ferocity so out of character in an Indian woman or the daughter of one. "D' you think I don't know how you Americans talk? A good Indian is a dead Indian. No wonder we hate you all. No wonder the tribes fight you to the death."

He had no answer for this. It was true. He had been brought up in a land of Indian wars and he had accepted without question the common view that the Sioux, the Crows, and the Cheyennes, with all their blood brothers, were menaces to civilization. The case for the natives he had never studied. How great a part broken pledges and callous injustice had done to drive the tribes to the war-path he did not know. Few of the actual frontiersmen were aware of the wrongs of the red men.

The young man's hands fell from her arms. Hard-eyed and grim, he looked her over from head to foot. The short skirt and smock of buckskin, the moccasins of buffalo hide, all dusty and travel-stained, told of life in a primitive country under the simplest and hardest conditions.

Yet the voice was clear and vibrant, the words well enunciated. She bloomed like a desert rose, had some quality of vital life that struck a spark from his imagination.

What manner of girl was she? Not by any possibility would she fit into the specifications of the cubby-hole his mind had built for Indian women. The daughters even of the boisbrulés had much of the heaviness and stolidity of their native moth-

11

ers. Jessie McRae was graceful as a fawn. Every turn of the dark head, every lift of the hand, expressed spirit and verve. She must, he thought, have inherited almost wholly from her father, though in her lissom youth he could find little of McRae's heavy solidity of mind and body.

"Your brother is of the métis.[1] He's not a tribesman. And he's no child. He can look out for himself," Morse said at last.

His choice of a word was unfortunate. It applied as much to her as to Fergus. Often it was used contemptuously.

"Yes, and the métis doesn't matter," she cried, with the note of bitterness that sat so strangely on her hot-blooded, vital youth. "You can ride over him as though you're lords of the barren lands. You can ruin him for the money you make, even if he's a subject of the Great Mother and not of your country. He's only a breed—a mongrel."

He was a man of action. He brushed aside discussion. "We'll be movin' back to camp."

Instantly her eyes betrayed the fear she would not put into words. "No—no! I won't go."

His lids narrowed. The outthrust of his lean jaw left no room for argument. "You'll go where I say."

She knew it would be that way, if he dragged her by the hair of the head. Because she was in such evil case she tamed her pride to sullen pleading.

"Don't take me there! Let me go to father. He'll horsewhip me. I'll have him do it for you. Isn't that enough? Won't that satisfy you?"

Red spots smoldered like fire in his brown eyes. If he took her back to the traders' camp, he would have to fight Bully West for her. That was certain. All sorts of complications would rise. There would be trouble with McRae. The trade with the Indians of his uncle's firm, of which he was soon to be a partner, would be wrecked by the Scotchman. No, he couldn't take her back to the camp in the coulée. There was too much at stake.

"Suits me. I'll take you up on that. He's to horsewhip you for that fool trick you played on us and to make good our loss. Where's his camp?"

From the distance of a stone-throw a heavy, raucous voice called, " 'Lo, Morse!"

The young man turned to the girl, his lips set in a thin, hard line. "Bully West. The dog's gone back and is bringin' him here, I reckon. Like to meet him?"

[1] The half-breeds were known as "métis." The word means, of course, mongrel. (W. M. R.)

She knew the reputation of Bully West, notorious as a brawler and a libertine. Who in all the North did not know of it? Her heart fluttered a signal of despair.

"I—I can get away yet—up the valley," she said in a whisper, eyes quick with fear.

He smiled grimly. "You mean *we* can."

"Yes."

"Hit the trail."

She turned and led the way into the darkness.

CHAPTER III

Angus McRae Does His Duty

THE harsh shout came to them again, and with it a volley of oaths that polluted the night.

Sleeping Dawn quickened her pace. The character of Bully West was sufficiently advertised in that single outburst. She conceived him bloated, wolfish, malignant, a man whose mind traveled through filthy green swamps breeding fever and disease. Hard though this young man was, in spite of her hatred of him, of her doubt as to what lay behind those inscrutable, reddish-brown eyes of his, she would a hundred times rather take chances with him than with Bully West. He was at least a youth. There was always the possibility that he might not yet have escaped entirely from the tenderness of boyhood.

Morse followed her silently with long, tireless strides. The girl continued to puzzle him. Even her manner of walking expressed personality. There was none of the flat-footed Indian shuffle about her gait. She moved lightly, springily, as one does who finds in it the joy of calling upon abundant strength.

She was half Scotch, of course. That helped to explain her. The words of an old song hummed themselves through his mind.

"Yestreen I met a winsome lass, a bonny lass was she,
As ever climbed the mountain-side, or tripped aboon the lea;
She wore nae gold, nae jewels bright, nor silk nor satin rare,
But just the plaidie that a queen might well be proud to wear."

13

Jessie McRae wore nothing half so picturesque as the tartan. Her clothes were dingy and dust-stained. But they could not eclipse the divine, dusky youth of her. She was slender, as a panther is, and her movements had more than a suggestion of the same sinuous grace.

Of the absurdity of such thoughts he was quite aware. She was a good-looking breed. Let it go at that. In story-books there were Indian princesses, but in real life there were only squaws.

Not till they were out of the danger zone did he speak. "Where's your father's camp?"

She pointed toward the northwest. "You don't need to be afraid. He'll pay you for the damage I did."

He looked at her in the steady, appraising way she was to learn as a peculiarity of his.

"I'm not afraid," he drawled. "I'll get my pay—and you'll get yours."

Color flamed into her dusky face. When she spoke there was the throb of contemptuous anger in her voice. "It's a great thing to be a man."

"Like to crawfish, would you?"

She swung on him, eyes blazing. "No. I don't ask any favors of a wolfer."

She spat the word at him as though it were a missile. The term was one of scorn, used only in speaking of the worst of the whiskey-traders. He took it coolly, his strong white teeth flashing in a derisive smile.

"Then this wolfer won't offer any, Miss McRae."

It was the last word that passed between them till they reached the buffalo-hunter's camp. If he felt any compunctions, she read nothing of the kind in his brown face and the steady stride carrying her straight to punishment. She wondered if he knew how mercilessly twenty-year-old Fergus had been thrashed after his drunken spree among the Indians, how sternly Angus dispensed justice in the clan over which he ruled. Did he think she was an ordinary squaw, one to be whipped as a matter of discipline by her owner?

They climbed a hill and looked down on a camp of many fires in the hollow below.

"Is it you, lass?" a voice called.

Out of the shadows thrown by the tents a big bearded man came to meet them. He stood six feet in his woolen socks. His chest was deep and his shoulders tremendously broad. Few in the Lone Lands had the physical strength of Angus McRae.

His big hand caught the girl by the shoulder with a grip

14

that was half a caress. He had been a little anxious about her and this found expression in a reproach.

"You shouldna go out by your lane for so lang after dark, Jess. Weel you ken that."

"I know, Father."

The blue eyes beneath the grizzled brows of the hunter turned upon Morse. They asked what he was doing with his daughter at that time and place.

The Montana trader answered the unspoken question, an edge of irony in his voice. "I found Miss McRae wanderin' around, so I brought her home where she would be safe and well taken care of."

There was something about this Angus did not understand. At night in the Lone Lands, among a thousand hill pockets and shoestring draws, it would be only a millionth chance that would bring a man and woman together unexpectedly. He pushed home questions, for he was not one to slough any of the responsibilities that belonged to him as father of his family.

A fat and waistless Indian woman appeared in the tent flap as the three approached the light. She gave a grunt of surprise and pointed first at Morse and then at the girl.

The trader's hands were covered with blood, his shirt-sleeve soaked in it. Stains of it were spattered over the girl's clothes and face.

The Scotchman looked at them, and his clean-shaven upper lip grew straight, his whole face stern. "What'll be the meanin' o' this?" he asked.

Morse turned to the girl, fastened his eyes on her steadily, and waited.

"Nae lees. I'll hae the truth," Angus added harshly.

"I did it—with my hunting-knife," the daughter said, looking straight at her father.

"What's that? Are ye talkin' havers, lass?"

"It's the truth, Father."

The Scotchman swung on the trader with a swift question, at the end of it a threat. "Why would she do that? Why? If you said one word to my lass—"

"No, Father. You don't understand. I found a camp of whiskey-traders, and I stole up and smashed four-five kegs. I meant to slip away, but this man caught me. When he rushed at me I was afraid—so I slashed at him with my knife. We fought."

"You fought," her father repeated.

"He didn't know I was a girl—not at first."

15

The buffalo-hunter passed that point. "You went to this trader's camp and ruined his goods?"

"Yes."

"Why?"

The slim girl faced her judge steadily with eyes full of apprehension. "Fergus," she said in a low voice, "and my people."

"What aboot them?"

"These traders break the law. They sell liquor to Fergus and to—"

"Gin that's true, is it your business to ram-stam in an' destroy ither folks' property? Did I bring you up i' the fear o' the Lord to slash at men wi' your dirk an' fight wi' them like a wild limmer? I've been ower-easy wi' you. Weel, I'll do my painfu' duty the nicht, lass." The Scotchman's eyes were as hard and as inexorable as those of a hanging judge.

"Yes," the girl answered in a small voice. "That's why he brought me home instead of taking me to his own camp. You're to whip me."

Angus McRae was not used to having the law and the judgment taken out of his own hands. He frowned at the young man beneath heavy grizzled eyebrows drawn sternly together. "An' who are you to tell me how to govern my ain hoose?" he demanded.

"My name's Morse—Tom Morse, Fort Benton, Montana, when my hat's hangin' up. I took up your girl's proposition, that if I didn't head in at our camp, but brought her here, you were to whip her and pay me damages for what she'd done. Me, I didn't propose it. She did."

"You gave him your word on that, Jess?" her father asked.

"Yes." She dragged out, reluctantly, after a moment: "With a horsewhip."

"Then that's the way it'll be. The McRaes don't cry back on a bargain," the dour old buffalo-hunter said. "But first we'll look at this young man's arm. Get water and clean rags, Jess."

Morse flushed beneath the dark tan of his cheeks. "My arm's all right. It'll keep till I get back to camp."

"No such thing, my lad. We'll tie it up here and now. If my lass cut your arm, she'll bandage the wound."

"She'll not. I'm runnin' this arm."

McRae slammed a heavy fist down into the palm of his hand. "I'll be showin' you aboot that, mannie."

"Hell, what's the use o' jawin'? I'm goin' to wait, I tell you."

16

"Don't curse in my camp, Mr. Morse, or whatever your name is." The Scotchman's blue eyes flashed. "It's a thing I do not permeet. Nor do I let beardless lads tell me what they will or won't do here. Your wound will be washed and tied up if I have to order you hogtied first. So mak the best o' that."

Morse measured eyes with him a moment, then gave way with a sardonic laugh. McRae had a full share of the obstinacy of his race.

"All right. I'm to be done good to whether I like it or not. Go to it." The trader pulled back the sleeve of his shirt and stretched out a muscular, blood-stained arm. An ugly flesh wound stretched halfway from elbow to wrist.

Jessie brought a basin, water, a towel, and clean rags. By the light of a lantern in the hands of her father, she washed and tied up the wound. Her lips trembled. Strange little rivers of fire ran through her veins when her finger-tips touched his flesh. Once, when she lifted her eyes, they met his. He read in them a concentrated passion of hatred.

Not even when she had tied the last knot in the bandage did any of them speak. She carried away the towel and the basin while McRae hung the lantern to a nail in the tent pole and brought from inside a silver-mounted riding-whip. It was one he had bought as a present for his daughter last time he had been at Fort Benton.

The girl came back and stood before him. A pulse beat fast in her brown throat. The eyes betrayed the dread of her soul, but they met without flinching those of the buffalo-hunter.

The Indian woman at the tent entrance made no motion to interfere. The lord of her life had spoken. So it would be.

With a strained little laugh Morse took a step forward. "I reckon I'll not stand out for my pound of flesh, Mr. McRae. Settle the damages for the lost liquor and I'll call it quits."

The upper lip of the Scotchman was a straight line of resolution. "I'm not thrashing the lass to please you, but because it's in the bond and because she's earned it. Stand back, sir."

The whip swung up and down. The girl gasped and shivered. A flame of fiery pain ran through her body to the toes. She set her teeth to bite back a scream. Before the agony had passed, the whip was winding round her slender body again like a red-hot snake. It fell with implacable rhythmic regularity.

Her pride and courage collapsed. She sank to her knees with a wild burst of wailing and entreaties. At last McRae stopped.

17

Except for the irregular sobbing breaths of the girl there was silence. The Indian woman crouched beside the tortured young thing and rocked the dark head, held close against her bosom, while she crooned a lullaby in the native tongue.

McRae, white to the lips, turned upon his unwelcome guest. "You're nae doot wearyin' to tak the road, man. Bring your boss the morn an' I'll mak a settlement."

Morse knew he was dismissed. He turned and walked into the darkness beyond the camp-fires. Unnoticed, he waited there in a hollow and listened. For a long time there came to him the soft sound of weeping, and afterward the murmur of voices. He knew that the fat and shapeless squaw was pouring mother love from her own heart to the bleeding one of the girl.

Somehow that brought him comfort. He had a queer feeling that he had been a party to some horrible outrage. Yet all that had taken place was the whipping of an Indian girl. He tried to laugh away the weak sympathy in his heart.

But the truth was that inside he was a wild river of woe for her.

CHAPTER IV

The Wolfers

WHEN Tom Morse reached camp he found Bully West stamping about in a heady rage. The fellow was a giant of a man, almost muscle-bound in his huge solidity. His shoulders were rounded with the heavy pack of knotted sinews they carried. His legs were bow·ed from much riding. It was his boast that he could bend a silver dollar double in the palm of his hand. Men had seen him twist the tail rod of a wagon into a knot. Sober, he was a sulky, domineering brute with the instincts of a bully. In liquor, the least difference of opinion became for him a cause of quarrel.

Most men gave him a wide berth, and for the sake of peace accepted sneers and insults that made the blood boil.

"Where you been all this time?" he growled.

"Ploughin' around over the plains."

18

"Didn't you hear me callin'?"

"D' you call? I've been quite a ways from camp. Bumped into Angus McRae's buffalo-hunting outfit. He wants to see us to-morrow."

"What for?"

"Something about to-night's business. Seems he knows who did it. Offers to settle for what we lost."

Bully West stopped in his stride, feet straddled, head thrust forward. "What's that?"

"Like I say. We're to call on him to-morrow for a settlement, you 'n' me."

"Did McRae bust our barrels?"

"He knows something about it. Didn't have time to talk long with him. I hustled right back to tell you."

"He can come here if he wants to see me," West announced.

This called for no answer and Tom gave it none. He moved across to the spot where the oxen were picketed and made sure the pins were still fast. Presently he rolled his blanket round him and looked up into a sky all stars. Usually he dropped asleep as soon as his head touched the seat of the saddle he used as a pillow. But to-night he lay awake for hours. He could not get out of his mind the girl he had met and taken to punishment. A dozen pictures of her rose before him, all of them mental snapshots snatched from his experience of the night. Now he was struggling to hold her down, his knees clamped to her writhing, muscular torso. Again he held her by the strong, velvet-smooth arms while her eyes blazed fury and defiance at him. Or her stinging words pelted him as she breasted the hill slopes with supple ease. Most vivid of all were the ones at her father's camp, especially those when she was under the torture of the whip.

No wonder she hated him for what he had done to her.

He shook himself into a more comfortable position and began to count stars. . . . Ninety-five, ninety-six, ninety-seven. . . . What was the use of stressing the affair, anyhow? She was only a half-breed. In ten years she would be fat, shapeless, dirty, and repellent. Her conversation would be reduced to grunts. The glance he had had at her mother was illuminating.

Where was he? . . . One hundred eleven, twelve, thirteen. . . . Women had not obtruded much into his life. He had lived in the wind and the sun of the outdoors, much of the time in the saddle. Lawless he was, but there was a clean strain in his blood. He had always felt an indifferent contempt for a squaw-man. An American declassed himself when he went in for that sort of thing, even if he legalized the union by some form of marriage. In spite of her magnificent physical inheritance of health and vitality, in spite of the quick and passionate spirit that informed her, she would be the product of her environment and ancestry, held close to barbarism all her life. The man who mated with her would be dragged down to her level.

Two hundred three, four, five. . . . How game she had been! She had played it out like a thoroughbred, even to telling her father that he was to use the horse-whip in punishing her. He had never before seen a creature so splendid or so spirited. Squaw or no squaw, he took off his hat to her.

The sun had climbed the hilltop when Morse wakened.

"Come an' get it!" Barney the cook was yelling at him.

Bully West had changed his mind about not going to the buffalo-hunter's camp.

"You 'n' Brad'll stay here, Barney, while me 'n' Tom are gone," he gave orders. "And you'll keep a sharp lookout for raiders. If any one shows up that you're dubious of, plug him and ask questions afterward. Un'erstand?"

"I hear ye," replied Barney, a small cock-eyed man with a malevolent grin. "An' we'll do just that, boss."

Long before the traders reached it, the camp of the buffalo-hunters advertised its presence by the stench of decaying animal matter. Hundreds of hides were pegged to the ground. Men and women, squatting on their heels, scraped bits of fat from the drying skins. Already a train of fifty Red River carts [1] stood ready for the homeward start, loaded with robes tied down by means of rawhide strips to stand the jolting across the plains. Not far away other women were making pemmican of fried buffalo meat and fat, pounded together and packed with hot grease in skin bags. This food was a staple winter diet and had too a market value for trade to the Hudson's Bay Company, which shipped thousands of sacks yearly to its northern posts on the Peace and the Mackenzie Rivers.

The children and the sound of their laughter gave the camp a domestic touch. Some of the brown, half-naked youngsters, their skins glistening in the warm sun, were at work doing odd jobs. Others, too young to fetch and carry, played with a litter of puppies or with a wolf cub that had been caught and tamed.

The whole bustling scene was characteristic of time and

---

[1] The Red River cart was a primitive two-wheeled affair, made entirely of wood, without nails or metal tires. It was usually drawn by an ox. (W. M. R.)

place. A score of such outfits, each with its Red River carts and its oxen, its dogs, its women and children, traveled to the plains each spring to hunt the bison. They killed thousands upon thousands of them, for it took several animals to make a sack of pemmican weighing one hundred fifty pounds. The waste was enormous, since only the choicest cuts of meat were used.

Already the buffalo were diminishing in numbers. Vast hordes still roamed the plains. They could be killed by scores and hundreds. But the end was near. It had been several years since Colonel Dodge reported that he had halted his party of railroad builders two days to let a herd of over half a million bison pass. Such a sight was no longer possible. The pressure of the hunters had divided the game into the northern and the southern herds. Within four or five years the slaughter was to be so great that only a few groups of buffalo would be left.

The significance of this extermination lay largely in its application to the Indians. The plains tribes were fed and clothed and armed and housed by means of the buffalo. Even the canoes of the lake Indians were made from buffalo skins. The failure of the supply reduced the natives from warriors to beggars.

McRae came forward to meet the traders, the sleeves of his shirt rolled to the elbows of his muscular brown arms. He stroked a great red beard and nodded gruffly. It was not in his dour honest nature to pretend that he was glad to see them when he was not.

"Well, I'm here," growled West, interlarding a few oaths as a necessary corollary of his speech. "What's it all about, McRae? What do you know about the smashing of our barrels?"

"I'll settle any reasonable damage," the hunter said.

Bully West frowned. He spread his legs deliberately, folded his arms, and spat tobacco juice upon a clean hide drying in the sun. "Hold yore hawsses a minute. The damaged'll be enough. Don't you worry about that. But first off, I aim to know who raided our camp. Then I reckon I'll whop him till he's wore to a frazzle."

Under heavy, grizzled brows McRae looked long at him. Both were outstanding figures by reason of personality and physique. One was a constructive force, the other destructive. There was a suggestion of the gorilla in West's long arms matted with hair, in the muscles of back and shoulders so gnarled and knotted that they gave him almost a deformed appearance. Big and broad though he was, the Scot was the

21

smaller. But power harnessed and controlled expressed itself in every motion of the body. Moreover, the blue eyes that looked straight and hard out of the ruddy face told of coördination between mind and matter.

Angus McRae was that rare product, an honest, outspoken man. He sought to do justice to all with whom he had dealings. Part of West's demand was fair, he reflected. The trader had a right to know all the facts in the case. But the old Hudson's Bay trapper had a great reluctance to tell them. His instinct to protect Jessie was strong.

"I've saved ye the trouble, Mr. West. The guilty yin was o' my ain family. Your young man will tell ye I've done a' the horsewhippin' that's necessary."

The big trail boss looked blackly at his helper. He would settle with Morse at the proper time. Now he had other business on hand.

"Come clean, McRae. Who was it? There'll be nothin' doin' till I know that," he growled.

"My daughter."

West glared at him, for once astonished out of profanity.

"What?"

"My daughter Jessie."

"Goddlemighty, d'ja mean to tell me a girl did it?" He threw back his head in a roar of Homeric laughter. "Ever hear the beat of that? A damn li'l' Injun squaw playin' her tricks on Bully West! If she was mine I'd tickle her back for it."

The eyes in the Scotchman's granite face flashed. "Man, can you never say twa-three words withoot profanity? This is a God-fearin' camp. There's nae place here for those who tak His name in vain."

"Smashed 'em with her own hands—is that what you mean? I'll give it to her that she's a plucky li'l' devil, even if she is a nitchie."

McRae reproved him stiffly. "You'll please to remember that you're talking of my daughter, Mr. West. I'll allow no such language aboot her. You're here to settle a business matter. What do ye put the damage at?"

They agreed on a price, to be paid in hides delivered at Whoop-Up. West turned and went straddling to the place where he and Morse had left their horses. On the way he came face to face with a girl, a lithe, dusky young creature, Indian brown, the tan of a hundred summer suns and winds painted on the oval of her lifted chin. She was carrying a package of sacks to the place where the pemmican was being made.

West's eyes narrowed. They traveled up and down her slender body. They gloated on her.

After one scornful glance which swept over and ignored Morse, the girl looked angrily at the man barring her way. Slowly the blood burned into her cheeks. For there was that in the trader's smoldering eyes that would have insulted any modest maiden.

"You Jessie McRae?" he demanded, struck of a sudden with an idea.

"Yes."

"You smashed my whiskey-barrels?"

"My father has told you. If he says so, isn't that enough?"

He slapped an immense hand on his thigh, hugely diverted. "You damn li'l high-steppin' filly! Why? What in hell 'd I ever do to you?"

Angus McRae strode forward, eyes blazing. He had married a Cree woman, had paid for her to her father seven ponies, a yard of tobacco, and a bottle of whiskey. His own two-fisted sons were métis. The Indian in them showed more plainly than the Celt. Their father accepted the fact without resentment. But there was in his heart a queer feeling about the little lass he had adopted. Her light, springing step, the lift of the throat and the fearlessness of the eye, the instinct in her for cleanliness of mind and body, carried him back forty years to the land of heather, to a memory of the laird's daughter whom he had worshiped with the hopeless adoration of a red-headed gillie. It had been the one romance of his life, and somehow it had reincarnated itself in his love for the half-breed girl. To him it seemed a contradiction of nature that Jessie should be related to the flat-footed squaws who were slaves to their lords. He could not reconcile his heart to the knowledge that she was of mixed blood. She was too fine, too dainty, of too free and imperious a spirit.

"Your horses are up the hill, Mr. West," he said pointedly.

It is doubtful whether the trader heard. He could not keep his desirous eyes from the girl.

"Is she a half- or a quarter-breed?" he asked McRae.

"That'll be her business and mine, sir. Will you please tak the road?" The hunter spoke quietly, restraining himself from an outbreak. But his voice carried an edge.

"By Gad, she's some clipper," West said, aloud to himself, just as though the girl had not been present.

"Will you leave my daughter oot o' your talk, man?" warned the Scotchman.

"What's ailin' you?" West's sulky, insolent eyes turned on the buffalo-hunter. "A nitchie's a nitchie. Me, I talk straight.

23

But I aim to be reasonable too. I don't like a woman less because she's got the devil in her. Bully West knows how to tame 'em so they'll eat outa his hand. I've took a fancy to yore girl. Tha's right, McRae."

"You may go to the tent, Jessie," the girl's father told her. He was holding his temper in leash with difficulty.

"Wait a mo." The big trader held out his arm to bar the way. "Don't push on yore reins, McRae. I'm makin' you a proposition. Me, I'm lookin' for a wife, an' this here breed girl of yours suits me. Give her to me an' I'll call the whole thing square. Couldn't say fairer than that, could I?"

The rugged hunter looked at the big malformed border ruffian with repulsion. "Man, you gi'e me a scunner," he said. "Have done wi' this foolishness an' be gone. The lass is no' for you or the like o' you."

"Hell's hinges, you ain't standin' there tellin' me that a Cree breed it too good for Bully West, are you?" roared the big whiskey-runner.

"A hundred times too good for you. I'd rather see the lass dead in her coffin than have her life ruined by you," McRae answered in dead earnest.

"You don't get me right, Mac," answered the smuggler, swallowing his rage. "I know yore religious notions. We'll stand up before a sky pilot and have this done right. I aim to treat this girl handsome."

Jessie had turned away at her father's command. Now she turned swiftly upon the trader, eyes flashing. "I'd rather Father would drive a knife in my heart than let me be married to a wolfer!" she cried passionately.

His eyes, untrammeled by decency, narrowed to feast on the brown immature beauty of her youth.

"Tha' so?" he jeered. "Well, the time's comin' when you'll go down on yore pretty knees an' beg me not to leave you. It'll be me 'n' you one o' these days. Make up yore mind to that."

"Never! Never! I'd die first!" she exploded.

Bully West showed his broken, tobacco-stained teeth in a mirthless grin. "We'll see about that, dearie."

"March, lass. Your mother 'll be needin' you," McRae said sharply.

The girl looked at West, then at Morse. From the scorn of that glance she might have been a queen and they the riffraff of the land. She walked to the tent. Not once did she look back.

"You've had your answer both from her and me. Let that be an end o' it," McRae said with finality.

24

The trader's anger ripped out in a crackle of obscene oaths. They garnished the questions that he snarled. "Wha's the matter with me? Why ain't I good enough for yore half-breed litter?"

It was a spark to gunpowder. The oaths, the insult, the whole degrading episode, combined to drive McRae out of the self-restraint he had imposed on himself. He took one step forward. With a wide sweep of the clenched fist he buffeted the smuggler on the ear. Taken by surprise, West went spinning against the wheel of a cart.

The man's head sank between his shoulders and thrust forward. A sound that might have come from an infuriated grizzly rumbled from the hairy throat. His hand reached for a revolver.

Morse leaped like a crouched cat. Both hands caught at West's arm. The old hunter was scarcely an instant behind him. His fingers closed on the wrist just above the weapon.

"Hands off," he ordered Morse. "This is no' your quarrel."

The youngster's eyes met the blazing blue ones of the Scot. His fingers loosened their hold. He stepped back.

The two big men strained. One fought with every ounce of power in him to twist the arm from him till the cords and sinews strained; the other to prevent this and to free the wrist. It was a test of sheer strength.

Each labored, breathing deep, his whole energy centered on coördinated effort of every muscle. They struggled in silence except for the snarling grunts of the whiskey-runner.

Slowly, almost imperceptibly at first, the wrist began to turn from McRae. Sweat beads gathered on West's face. He fought furiously to hold his own. But the arm turned inexorably.

The trader groaned. As the cords tightened and shoots of torturing pain ran up the arm, the huge body of the man writhed. The revolver fell from his paralyzed fingers. His wobbling knees sagged and collapsed.

McRae's fingers loosened as the man slid down and caught the bull-like throat. His grip tightened. West fought savagely to break it. He could as soon have freed himself from the clamp of a vise.

The Scotchman shook him till he was black in the face, then flung him reeling away.

"Get oot, ye yellow wolf!" he roared. "Or fegs! I'll break every bone in your hulkin' body. Oot o' my camp, the pair o' you!"

West, strangling, gasped for air, as does a catfish on the bank. He leaned on the cart wheel until he was able to stand. The help of Morse he brushed aside with a sputtered oath.

His eyes never left the man who had beaten him. He snarled like a whipped wolf. The hunter's metaphor had been an apt one. The horrible lust to kill was stamped on his distorted, grinning face, but for the present the will alone was not enough.

McRae's foot was on the revolver. His son Fergus, a swarthy, good-looking youngster, had come up and was standing quietly behind his father. Other hunters were converging toward their chief.

The Indian trader swore a furious oath of vengeance. Morse tried to lead him away.

"Some day I'll get yore squaw girl right, McRae, an' then God help her," he threatened.

The bully lurched straddling away.

Morse, a sardonic grin on his lean face, followed him over the hill.

CHAPTER V

Morse Jumps Up Trouble

"THREW me down, didn't you?" snarled West out of the corner of his mouth. "Knew all the time she did it an' never let on to me. A hell of a way to treat a friend."

Tom Morse said nothing. He made mental reservations about the word friend, but did not care to express them. His somber eyes watched the big man jerk the spade bit cruelly and rowel the bronco when it went into the air. It was a pleasure to West to torture an animal when no human was handy, though he preferred women and even men as victims.

"Whad he mean when he said you could tell me how he'd settled with her?" he growled.

"He whipped her last night when I took her back to camp."

"Took her back to camp, did you? Why didn't you bring her to me? Who's in charge of this outfit, anyhow, young fellow, me lad?"

"McRae's too big a man for us to buck. Too influential with the half-breeds. I figured it was safer to get her right home to him." The voice of the younger man was mild and conciliatory.

"*You* figured!" West's profanity polluted the clear, crisp morning air. "I got to have a run in with you right soon. I can see that. Think because you're C. N. Morse's nephew, you can slip yore funny business over on me. I'll show you."

The reddish light glinted for a moment in the eyes of Morse, but he said nothing. Young though he was, he had a capacity for silence. West was not sensitive to atmospheres, but he felt the force of this young man. It was not really in his mind to quarrel with him. For one thing he would soon be a partner in the firm of C. N. Morse & Company, of Fort Benton, one of the biggest trading outfits in the country. West could not afford to break with the Morse interests.

With their diminished cargo the traders pushed north. Their destination was Whoop-Up, at the junction of the Belly and the St. Mary's Rivers. This fort had become a rendezvous for all the traders within hundreds of miles, a point of supply for many small posts scattered along the rivers of the North.

Twelve oxen were hitched to each three-wagon load. Four teams had left Fort Benton together, but two of them had turned east toward Wood Mountain before the party was out of the Assiniboine country. West had pushed across Lonesome Prairie to the Sweet Grass Hills and from there over the line into Canada.

Under the best of conditions West was no pleasant traveling companion. Now he was in a state of continual sullen ill-temper. For the first time in his life he had been publicly worsted. Practically he had been kicked out of the buffalo camp, just as though he were a drunken half-breed and not one whose barroom brawls were sagas of the frontier.

His vanity was notorious, and it had been flagrantly outraged. He would never be satisfied until he had found a way to get his revenge. More than once his simmering anger leaped out at the young fellow who had been a witness of his defeat. In the main he kept his rage sulkily repressed. If Tom Morse wanted to tell of the affair with McRae, he could lessen the big man's prestige. West did not want that.

The outfit crossed the Milk River, skirted Pakoghkee Lake, and swung westward in the direction of the Porcupine Hills. Barney had been a trapper in the country and knew where the best grass was to be found. In many places the feed was scant. It had been cropped close by the great herds of buffalo roaming the plains. Most of the lakes were polluted by the bison, so that whenever possible their guide found camps by

27

running water. The teams moved along the Belly River through the sand hills.

Tom Morse was a crack shot and did the hunting for the party. The evening before the train reached Whoop-Up, he walked out from camp to try for an antelope, since they were short of fresh meat. He climbed a small butte overlooking the stream. His keen eyes swept the panorama and came to rest on a sight he had never before seen and would never forget.

A large herd of buffalo had come down to the river crossing. They were swimming the stream against a strong current, their bodies low in the water and so closely packed that he could almost have stepped from one shaggy head to another. Not fifty yards from him they scrambled ashore and went lumbering into the hazy dusk. Something had frightened them and they were on a stampede. Even the river had not stopped their flight. The earth shook with their tread as they found their stride.

That wild flight into the gathering darkness was symbolic, Morse fancied. The vast herds were vanishing never to return. Were they galloping into the Happy Hunting Ground the Indians prayed for? What would come of their flight? When the plains knew them no more, how would the Sioux and the Blackfeet and the Piegans live? Would the Lonesome Lands become even more desolate than they were now?

"I wonder," he murmured aloud.

It is certain that he could have had no vision of the empire soon to be built out of the desert by himself and men of his stamp. Not even dimly could he have conceived a picture of the endless wheat-fields that would stretch across the plains, of the farmers who would pour into the North by hundreds of thousands, of the cities which would rise in the sand hills as a monument to man's restless push of progress and his indomitable hope. No living man's imagination had yet dreamed of the transformation of this *terra incognita* into one of the world's great granaries.

The smoke of the traders' camp-fire was curling up and drifting away into thin veils of film before the sun showed over the horizon hills. The bull-teams had taken up their steady forward push while the quails were still flying to and from their morning water-holes.

"Whoop-Up by noon," Barney predicted.

"Yes, by noon," Tom Morse agreed. "In time for a real sure-enough dinner with potatoes and beans and green stuff."

"Y' bet yore boots, an' honest to gosh gravy," added Brad Stearns, a thin and wrinkled little man whose leathery face and bright eyes defied the encroachment of time. He was bald, except for a fringe of grayish hair above the temples and a few long locks carefully disposed over his shiny crown. But nobody could have looked at him and called him old.

They were to be disappointed.

The teams struck the dusty road that terminated at the fort and were plodding along it to the crackling accompaniment of the long bull-whips.

"Soon now," Morse shouted to Stearns.

The little man nodded. "Mebbe they'll have green corn on the cob. Betcha the price of the dinner they do."

"You've made a bet, dad."

Stearns halted the leaders. "What's that? Listen."

The sound of shots drifted to them punctuated by faint, far yells. The shots did not come in a fusillade. They were intermittent, died down, popped out again, yielded to whoops in distant crescendo.

"Injuns," said Stearns. "On the peck, looks like. Crees and Blackfeet, maybe, but you never can tell. Better throw off the trail and dig in."

West had ridden up. He nodded. "Till we know where we're at. Get busy, boys."

They drew up the wagons in a semicircle, end to end, the oxen bunched inside, partially protected by a small cotton-wood grove in the rear.

This done, West gave further orders. "We gotta find out what's doin'. Chances are it's nothin' but a coupla bunches of braves with a cargo of redeye aboard. Tom, you an' Brad scout out an' take a look-see. Don't be too venturesome. Soon's you find out what the rumpus is, hot-foot it back and report, y' understand." The big wolfer snapped out directions curtly. There was no more competent wagon boss in the border-land than he.

Stearns and Morse rode toward the fort. They deflected from the road and followed the river-bank to take advantage of such shrubbery as grew there. They moved slowly and cautiously, for in the Indian country one took no unnecessary chances. From the top of a small rise, shielded by a clump of willows, the two looked down on a field of battle already decided. Bullets and arrows were still flying, but the defiant, triumphant war-whoops of a band of painted warriors slowly moving toward them showed that the day was won and lost. A smaller group of Indians was retreating toward the swamp on the left-hand side of the road. Two or three dead braves lay in the grassy swale between the foes.

"I done guessed it, first crack," Brad said. "Crees and Blackfeet. They sure enough do mix it whenever they get

29

together. The Crees ce'tainly got the jump on 'em this time."

It was an old story. From the northern woods the Crees had come down to trade at the fort. They had met a band of Blackfeet who had traveled up from the plains for the same purpose. Filled with bad liquor, the hereditary enemies had as usual adjourned to the ground outside for a settlement while the traders at the fort had locked the gates and watched the battle from the loopholes of the stockade.

"Reckon we better blow back to camp," suggested the old plainsman. "Mr. Cree may be feelin' his oats heap much. White man look all same Blackfeet to him like as not."

"Look." Morse pointed to a dip in the swale.

An Indian was limping through the brush, taking advantage of such cover as he could find. He was wounded. His leg dragged and he moved with difficulty.

"He'll be a good Injun mighty soon," Stearns said, rubbing his bald head as it shone in the sun. "Not a chance in the world for him. They'll git him soon as they reach the coulée. See. They're stoppin' to collect that other fellow's scalp."

At a glance Morse had seen the situation. This was none of his affair. It was tacitly understood that the traders should not interfere in the intertribal quarrels of the natives. But old Brad's words, "good Injun," had carried him back to a picture of a brown, slim girl flashing indignation because Americans treated her race as though only dead Indians were good ones. He could never tell afterward what was the rational spring of his impulse.

At the touch of the rein laid flat against its neck, the cow-pony he rode laid back its ears, turned like a streak of light, and leaped to a hand gallop. It swept down the slope and along the draw, gathering speed with every jump.

The rider let out a "Hi-yi-yi" to attract the attention of the wounded brave. Simultaneously the limping fugitive and the Crees caught sight of the flying horseman who had obtruded himself into the fire zone.

An arrow whistled past Morse. He saw a bullet throw up a spurt of dirt beneath the belly of his horse.

The Crees were close to their quarry. They closed in with a run. Tom knew it would be a near thing. He slackened speed slightly and freed a foot from the stirrup, stiffening it to carry weight.

The wounded Indian crouched, began to run parallel with the horse, and leaped at exactly the right instant. His hand caught the sleeve of his rescuer at the same time that the flat of his foot dropped upon the white man's boot. A moment,

30

and his leg had swung across the rump of the pony and he had settled to the animal's back.

So close was it that a running Cree snatched at the bronco's tail and was jerked from his feet before he could release his hold.

As the cow-pony went plunging up the slope, Morse saw Brad Stearns silhouetted against the sky-line at the summit. His hat was gone and his bald head was shining in the sun. He was pumping bullets from his rifle at the Crees surging up the hill after his companion.

Stearns swung his horse and jumped it to a lope. Side by side with Morse he went over the brow in a shower of arrows and slugs.

"Holy mackerel, boy! What's eatin' you?" he yelled. "Ain't you got any sense a-tall? Don't you know better 'n to jump up trouble thataway?"

"We're all right now," the younger man said. "They can't catch us."

The Crees were on foot and would be out of range by the time they reached the hilltop.

"Hmp! They'll come to our camp an' raise Cain. Why not? What business we got monkeyin' with their scalping sociables? It ain't neighborly."

"West won't like it," admitted Morse.

"He'll throw a cat fit. What do you aim to do with yore friend Mighty-Nigh-Lose-His-Scalp? If I know Bully—and you can bet a silver fox fur ag'in' a yard o' tobacco that I do—he won't give no glad hand to him. Not none."

Morse did not know what he meant to do with him. He had let an impulse carry him to quixotic action. Already he was half-sorry for it, but he was obstinate enough to go through now he had started.

When he realized the situation, Bully West exploded in language sulphurous. He announced his determination to turn the wounded man over to the Crees as soon as they arrived.

"No," said Morse quietly.

"No what?"

"I won't stand for that. They'd murder him."

"That any o' my business—or yours?"

"I'm makin' it mine."

The eyes of the two men crossed, as rapiers do, feeling out the strength back of them. The wounded Indian, tall and slender, stood straight as an arrow, his gaze now on one, now on the other. His face was immobile and expressionless. It betrayed no sign of the emotions within.

"Show yore cards, Morse," said West. "What's yore play?

31

I'm goin' to tell the Crees to take him if they want him. You'll go it alone if you go to foggin' with a six-shooter."

The young man turned to the Indian he had rescued. He waved a hand toward the horse from which they had just dismounted. "Up!" he ordered.

The Indian youth caught the point instantly. Without using the stirrups he vaulted to the saddle, light as a mountain lion. His bare heels dug into the sides of the animal, which was off as though shot out of a gun.

Horse and rider skirted the cottonwoods and disappeared in a depression beyond.

CHAPTER VI

"Something About These Guys"

WEST glared at Morse, his heavy chin outthrust, his bowed legs wide apart. "You've done run on the rope long enough with me, young feller. Here's where you take a fall hard."

The younger man said nothing. He watched, warily. Was it to be a gun-play? Or did the big bully mean to manhandle him? Probably the latter. West was vain of his reputation as a two-fisted fighter.

"I'm gonna beat you up, then turn you over to the Crees," the infuriated man announced.

"You can't do that, West. He's a white man same as you," protested Stearns.

"This yore put-in, Brad?" West, beside himself with rage, swung on the little man and straddled forward a step or two threateningly.

"You done said it," answered the old-timer, falling back. "An' don't you come closer. I'm liable to get scared, an' you'd ought not to forget I'm as big as you behind a six-shooter."

"Here they come—like a swarm o' bees!" yelled Barney.

The traders forgot, for the moment, their quarrel in the need of common action. West snatched up a rifle and dropped a bullet in front of the nearest Indian. The warning brought the Crees up short. They held a long consultation

32

and one of them came forward making the peace sign. In pigeon English he expressed their demands.

"He's gone—lit right out—stole one of our broncs. You can search the camp if you've a mind to," West replied.

The envoy reported. There was another long powwow.

Brad, chewing tobacco complacently behind a wagon wheel, commented aloud. "Can't make up their minds whether to come on an' massacree us or not. They got a right healthy fear of our guns. Don't blame 'em a bit."

Some of the Crees were armed with bows and arrows, others with rifles. But the trade guns sold the Indians of the Northern tribes were of the poorest quality.[1]

The whites, to the contrary, were armed with the latest repeating Winchesters. In a fight with them the natives were at a terrible disadvantage.

The Crees realized this. A delegation of two came forward to search the camp. West pointed out the tracks of the horse upon which their tribal enemy had ridden away.

They grunted, "Ugh! Ugh! Ugh!"

Overbearing though he was, West was an embryonic diplomat. He filled a water-bucket with whiskey and handed it, with a tin cup, to the wrinkled old brave nearest him.

"For our friends the Crees," he said. "Tell your chief my young man didn't understand. He thought he was rescuing a Cree from the Blackfeet."

"Ugh! Ugh!" The Indians shuffled away with their booty.

There was more talk, but the guttural protests died away before the temptation of the liquor. The braves drank, flung a few shots in bravado toward the wagons, and presently took themselves off.

The traders did not renew their quarrel. West's reasons for not antagonizing the Morse family were still powerful as ever. He subdued his desire to punish the young man and sullenly gave orders to hitch up the teams.

It was mid-afternoon when the oxen jogged into Whoop-Up. The post was a stockade fort, built in a square about two hundred yards long, of cottonwood logs dovetailed together. The buildings on each side of the plaza faced inward. Loopholes had been cut in the bastions as a protection against Indians.

---

[1] These flintlock muskets were inaccurate. They would not carry far. Their owners were in constant danger of having fingers or a hand blown off in explosions. The price paid for these cheap firearms was based on the length of them. The butt was put on the floor and the gun held upright. Skins laid flat were piled beside it till they reached the muzzle. The trader exchanged the rifle for the furs. (W. M. R.)

In the big stores was a large supply of blankets, beads, provisions, rifles, and clothing. The adjacent rooms were half-empty now, but in the spring they would be packed to the eaves with thousands of buffalo robes and furs brought in from outlying settlements by hunters. Later these would be hauled to Fort Benton and from there sent down the Missouri to St. Louis and other points.

Morse, looking round, missed a familiar feature.

"Where's the liquor?" he asked.

"S-sh!" warned the clerk with whom he was talking. "Haven't you heard? There's a bunch of police come into the country from Winnipeg. The lid's on tight." His far eye drooped to the cheek in a wise wink. "If you've brought in whiskey, you'd better get it out of the fort and bury it."

"That's up to West. I wouldn't advise any police to monkey with a cargo of his."

"You don't say." The clerk's voice was heavy with sarcasm. "Well, I'll just make a li'l' bet with you. If the North-West Mounted start to arrest Bully West or to empty his liquor-kegs, they'll go right through with the job. They're go-getters, these red-coats are."

"Red-coats? Not soldiers, are they?"

"Well, they are and they ain't. They're drilled an' in companies. But they can arrest any one they've a mind to, and their officers can try and sentence folks. They don't play no favorites either. Soon as they hear of this mix-up between the Crees and the Blackfeet they'll be right over askin' why-fors, and if they find who gave 'em the booze some one will be up to the neck in trouble and squawkin' for help."

West had been talking in whispers with Reddy Madden, the owner of the place. He stepped to the door.

"Don't onhook, Brad. We're travelin' some more first," he called to Stearns.

The oxen plodded out of the stockade and swung to the left. A guide rode beside West and Morse. He was Harvey Gosse, a whiskey-runner known to both of them. The man was a long, loose-limbed fellow with a shrewd eye and the full, drooping lower lip of irresolution.

It had been a year since either of the Fort Benton men had been in the country. Gosse told them of the change that was taking place in it.

"Business ain't what it was, an' that ain't but half of it," the lank rider complained regretfully. "It ain't ever gonna be any more. These here red-coats are plumb ruinin' trade. Squint at a buck cross-eyed, whisper rum to him, an' one o' these guys jumps a-straddle o' yore neck right away."

"How many of these—what is it you call 'em, Mounted Police?—well, how many of 'em are there in the country?" asked West.

"Not so many. I reckon a hundred or so, far as I've heard tell."

West snorted scornfully. "And you're lettin' this handful of tenderfeet buffalo you! Hell's hinges! Ain't none of you got any guts?"

Gosse dragged slowly a brown hand across an unshaven chin. "I reckon you wouldn't call 'em tenderfeet if you met up with 'em, Bully. There's something about these guys—I dunno what it is exactly—but there's sure somethiig that tells a fellow not to prod 'em overly much."

"Quick on the shoot?" the big trader wanted to know.

"No, it ain't that. They don't hardly ever draw a gun. They jest walk in kinda quiet an' easy, an' tell you it'll be thisaway. And tha's the way it is every crack outa the box."

"Hmp!" West exuded boastful incredulity. "I reckon they haven't bumped into any one man-size yet."

The lank whiskey-runner guided the train, by winding draws, into the hills back of the post. Above a small gulch, at the head of it, the teams were stopped and unloaded. The barrels were rolled downhill into the underbrush where they lay cached out of sight. From here they would be distributed as needed.

"You boys 'll take turn an' turn about watching till I've sold the cargo," West announced. "Arrange that among yoreselves. Tom, I'll let you fix up how you'll spell each other. Only thing is, one of you has to be here all the time, y' understand."

Morse took the first watch and was followed by Stearns, who in turn gave place to Barney. The days grew to a week. Sometimes West appeared with a buyer in a cart or leading a pack-horse. Then the cached fire-water would be diminished by a keg or two.

It was a lazy, sleepy life. There was no need for a close guard. Nobody knew where the whiskey was except themselves and a few tight-mouthed traders. Morse discovered in himself an inordinate capacity for sleep. He would throw himself down on the warm, sundried grass and fall into a doze almost instantly. When the rays of the sun grew too hot, it was easy to roll over into the shade of the draw. He could lie for hours on his back after he wakened and watch cloudskeins elongate and float away, thinking of nothing or letting thoughts happen in sheer idle content.

He had never had a girl, to use the word current among

35

his fellows. His scheme of life would, he supposed, include women by and by, but hitherto he had dwelt in a man's world, in a universe of space and sunshine and blowing wind, under primitive conditions that made for tough muscles and a clean mind trained to meet frontier emergencies. But now, to his disgust, he found slipping into his reveries pictures of a slim, dark girl, arrow-straight, with eyes that held for him only scorn and loathing. The odd thing about it was that when his brain was busy with her a strange exultant excitement tingled through his veins.

One day a queer thing happened. He had never heard of psychic phenomena or telepathy, but he opened his eyes from a day-dream of her to see Jessie McRae looking down at him.

She was on an Indian cayuse, round-bellied and rough. Very erect she sat, and on her face was the exact expression of scornful hatred he had seen in his vision of her.

He jumped to his feet. "You—here!"

A hot color flooded her face with anger to the roots of the hair. Without a word, without another glance at him, she laid the bridle rein to the pony's neck and swung away.

Unprotesting, he let her go. The situation had jumped at him too unexpectedly for him to know how to meet it. He stood, motionless, the red light in his eyes burning like distant camp-fires in the night. For the first time in his life he had been given the cut direct by a woman.

Yet she wasn't a woman after all. She was a maid, with that passionate sense of tragedy which comes only to the very young.

It was in his mind to slap a saddle on his bronco and ride after her. But why? Could he by sheer dominance of will change her opinion of him? She had grounded it on good and sufficient reasons. He was associated in her mind with the greatest humiliation of her life, with the stinging lash that had cut into her young pride and her buoyant courage as cruelly as it had into her smooth, satiny flesh. Was it likely she would listen to any regrets, any explanations? Her hatred of him was not a matter for argument. It was burnt into her soul as with a red-hot brand. He could not talk away what he had done or the thing that he was.

She had come upon him by chance while he was asleep. He guessed that Angus McRae's party had reached Whoop-Up and had stopped to buy supplies and perhaps to sell hides and pemmican. The girl had probably ridden out from the stockade to the open prairie because she loved to ride. The rest needed no conjecture. In that lone land of vast spaces

36

travelers always exchanged greetings. She had discovered him lying in the grass. He might be sick or wounded or dead. The custom of the country would bring her straight across the swales toward him to find out whether he needed help.

Then she had seen who he was—and had ridden away.

A sardonic smile of self-mockery stamped for a moment on his brown boyish face the weariness of the years.

CHAPTER VII

The Man In The Scarlet Jacket

MORSE ambled out at a road gait to take his turn at guard duty. He was following the principle that the longest way round is the shortest road to a given place. The reason for this was to ward off any suspicion that might have arisen if the watchers had always come and gone by the same trail. Therefore they started for any point of the compass, swung round in a wide détour, and in course of time arrived at the cache.

There wasn't any hurry anyhow. Each day had twenty-four hours, and a fellow lived just as long if he didn't break his neck galloping along with his tail up like a hill steer on a stampede.

To-day Morse dropped in toward the cache from due west. His eyes were open, even if the warmth of the midday sun did make him sleepy. Something he saw made him slip from the saddle, lead his horse into a draw, and move forward very carefully through the bunch grass.

What he had seen was a man crouched behind some brush, looking down into the little gorge where the whiskey cache was—a man in leather boots, tight riding-breeches, scarlet jacket, and jaunty forage cap. It needed no second glance to tell Tom Morse that the police had run down the place where they had hidden their cargo.

From out of the little cañon a man appeared. He was carrying a keg of whiskey. The man was Barney. West had no doubt sent word to him that he would shortly bring a buyer with him to the rendezvous.

The man in the scarlet jacket rose and stepped out into the open. He was a few feet from Barney. In his belt there was a revolver, but he did not draw it.

Barney stopped and stared at him, his mouth open, eyes bulging. "Where in Heligoland you come from?" he asked.

"From Sarnia, Ontario," the red-coat answered. "Glad to meet you, friend. I've been looking for you several days."

"For me!" said Barney blankly.

"For you—and for that keg of forty-rod you're carrying. No, don't drop it. We can talk more comfortably while both your hands are busy." The constable stepped forward and picked from the ground a rifle. "I've been lying in the brush two hours waiting for you to get separated from this. Didn't want you making any mistakes in your excitement."

"Mistakes!" repeated Barney.

"Yes. You're under arrest, you know, for whiskey-smuggling."

"You're one of these here border police." Barney used the rising inflection in making his statement.

"Constable Winthrop Beresford, North-West 'Mounted, at your service," replied the officer jauntily. He was a trim, well-set-up youth, quick of step and crisp of speech.

"What you gonna do with me?"

"Take you to Fort Macleod."

It was perhaps because his eyes were set at not quite the right angles and because they were so small and wolfish that Barney usually aroused distrust. He suggested now, with an ingratiating whine in his voice, that he would like to see a man at Whoop-Up first.

"Jes' a li'l' matter of business," he added by way of explanation.

The constable guessed at his business. The man wanted to let his boss know what had taken place and to give him a chance to rescue him if he would. Beresford's duty was to find out who was back of this liquor running. It would be worth while knowing what man Barney wanted to talk with. He could afford to take a chance on the rescue.

"Righto," he agreed. "You may put that barrel down now."

Barney laid it down, end up. With one sharp drive of the rifle butt the officer broke in the top of the keg. He kicked the barrel over with his foot.

This was the moment Morse chose for putting in an appearance.

"Hello! What's doin'?" he asked casually.

Beresford, cool and quiet, looked straight at him. "I'll ask *you* that."

"Kinda expensive to irrigate the prairie that way, ain't it?"

"Doesn't cost me anything. How about you?"

Morse laughed at the question fired back at him so promptly. This young man was very much on the job. "Not a bean," the Montanan said.

"Good. Then you'll enjoy the little show I'm putting on— five thousand dollars' worth of liquor spilt all at one time."

"Holy Moses! Where is this blind tiger you're raidin'?"

"Down in the gully. Lucky you happened along just by chance. You'll be able to carry the good news to Whoop-Up and adjacent points."

"You're not really aimin' to spill all that whiskey."

"That's my intention. Any objections?" The scarlet-coated officer spoke softly, without any edge to his voice. But Tom began to understand why the clerk at the trading-post had called the Mounted Police go-getters. This smooth-shaven lad, so easy and carefree of manner, had a gleam in his eye that meant business. His very gentleness was ominous.

Tom Morse reflected swiftly. His uncle's firm had taken a chance of this very finale when it had sent a convoy of liquor into forbidden territory. Better to lose the stock than to be barred by the Canadian Government from trading with the Indians at all. This officer was not one to be bribed or bullied. He would go through with the thing he had started.

"Why, no! How could I have any objections?" Morse said.

He shot a swift, slant look at Barney, a look that told the Irishman to say nothing and know nothing, and that he would be protected against the law.

"Glad you haven't," Constable Beresford replied cheerfully—so very cheerfully in fact that Morse suspected he would not have been much daunted if objections had been mentioned. "Perhaps you'll help me with my little job, then."

The trader grinned. He might as well go the limit with the bluff he was playing. "Sure. I'll help you make a fourth o' July outa the kegs. Lead me to 'em."

"You don't know where they are, of course?"

"In the gully, you said," Morse replied innocently.

"So I did. Righto. Down you go, then." The constable turned to Barney. "You next, friend."

A well-defined trail led down the steep side of the gulch. It ended in a thick growth of willow saplings. Underneath the roof of this foliage were more than a score of whiskey-casks.

After ten minutes with the rifle butt there was nothing to show for the cache but broken barrels and a trough of wet sand where the liquor had run down the bed of the dry gully.

It was time, Morse thought, to play his own small part in the entertainment.

"After you, gentlemen," Beresford said, stepping aside to let them take the trail up.

Morse too moved back to let Barney pass. The eyes of the two men met for a fraction of a second. Tom's lips framed silently one word. In that time a message was given and received.

The young man followed Barney, the constable at his heels. Morse stumbled, slipped to all fours, and slid back. He flung out his arms to steady himself and careened back against the constable. His flying hands caught at the scarlet coat. His bent head and shoulders thrust Beresford back and down.

Barney started to run.

The officer struggled to hold his footing against the awkward incubus, to throw the man off so that he could pursue Barney. His efforts were vain. Morse, evidently trying to regain his equilibrium, plunged wildly at him and sent him ploughing into the willows. The Montanan landed heavily on top, pinned him down, and smothered him.

The scarlet coat was a center of barrel hoops, bushes, staves, and wildly jerking arms and legs.

Morse made heroic efforts to untangle himself from the clutter. Once or twice he extricated himself almost, only to lose his balance on the slippery bushes and come skating down again on the officer just as he was trying to rise.

It was a scene for a moving-picture comedy, if the screen had been a feature of that day.

When at last the two men emerged from the gulch, Barney was nowhere to be seen. With him had vanished the mount of Beresford.

The constable laughed nonchalantly. He had just lost a prisoner, which was against the unwritten law of the Force, but he had gained another in his place. It would not be long till he had Barney too.

"Pretty work," he said appreciatively. "You couldn't have done it better if you'd done it on purpose, could you?"

"Done what?" asked Morse, with bland naïveté.

"Made a pillow and a bed of me, skated on me, bowled me over like a tenpin."

"I ce'tainly was awkward. Couldn't get my footin' at all, seemed like. Why, where's Barney?" Apparently the trader had just made a discovery.

"Ask of the winds, 'Oh, where?'" Beresford dusted off his

coat, his trousers, and his cap. When he had removed the evidence of the battle of the gulch, he set his cap at the proper angle and cocked an inquiring eye at the other. "I suppose you know you're under arrest."

"Why, no! Am I? What for? Which of the statues, laws, and ordinances of Queen Vic have I been bustin' without knowin' of them?"

"For aiding and abetting the escape of a prisoner."

"Did I do all that? And when did I do it?"

"While you were doing that war-dance on what was left of my manhandled geography."

"Can you arrest a fellow for slippin'?"

"Depends on how badly he slips. I'm going to take a chance on arresting you, anyhow."

"Gonna take away my six-shooter and handcuff me?"

"I'll take your revolver. If necessary, I'll put on the cuffs."

Morse looked at him, not without admiration. The man in the scarlet jacket wasted nothing. There was about him no superfluity of build, of gesture, of voice. Beneath the close-fitting uniform the muscles rippled and played when he moved. His shoulders and arms were those of a college oarsman. Lean-flanked and clean-limbed, he was in the hey-day of a splendid youth. It showed in the steady eyes set wide in the tanned face, in the carriage of the close-cropped, curly head, in the spring of the step. The Montanan recognized in him a kinship of dynamic force.

"Just what would I be doing?" the whiskey-runner asked, smiling.

Beresford met his smile. "I fancy I'll find that out pretty soon. Your revolver, please." He held out his hand, palm up.

"Let's get this straight. We're man to man. What'll you do if I find I've got no time to go to Fort Macleod with you?"

"Take you with me."

"Dead or alive?"

"No, alive."

"And if I won't go?" asked Morse.

"Oh, you'll go." The officer's bearing radiated a quiet, imperturbable confidence. His hand was still extended. "*If* you please."

"No hurry. Do you know what you're up against? When I draw this gun I can put a bullet through your head and ride away?"

"Yes."

"Unless, of course, you plug me first."

"Can't do that. Against the regulations."

"Much obliged for that information. You've got only a dead man's chance then—if I show fight."

"Better not. Game hardly worth the candle. My pals would run you down," the constable advised coolly.

"You still intend to arrest me?"

"Oh, yes."

As Morse looked at him, patient as an animal of prey, steady, fearless, an undramatic Anglo-Saxon who meant to go through with the day's work, he began to understand the power that was to make the North-West Mounted Police such a force in the land. The only way he could prevent this man from arresting him was to kill the constable; and if he killed him, other jaunty red-coated youths would come to kill or be killed. It came to him that he was up against a new order which would wipe Bully West and his kind from the land.

He handed his revolver to Beresford. "I'll ride with you."

"Good. Have to borrow your horse till we reach Whoop-Up. You won't mind walking?"

"Not at all. Some folks think that's what legs were made for," answered Morse, grinning.

As he strode across the prairie beside the horse, Morse was still puzzling over the situation. He perceived that the strength of the officer's position was wholly a moral one. A lawbreaker was confronted with an ugly alternative. The only way to escape arrest was to commit murder. Most men would not go that far, and of those who would the great majority would be deterred because eventually punishment was sure. The slightest hesitation, the least apparent doubt, a flicker of fear on the officer's face, would be fatal to success. He won because he serenely expected to win, and because there was back of him a silent, impalpable force as irresistible as the movement of a glacier.

Beresford must have known that the men who lived at Whoop-Up were unfriendly to the North-West Mounted. Some of them had been put out of business. Their property had been destroyed and confiscated. Fines had been imposed on them. The current whisper was that the whiskey-smugglers would retaliate against the constables in person whenever there was a chance to do so with impunity. Some day a debonair wearer of the scarlet coat would ride out gayly from one of the forts and a riderless horse would return at dusk. There were outlaws who would ask nothing better than a chance to dry-gulch one of these inquisitive riders of the plains.

But Beresford rode into the stockade and swung from the saddle with smiling confidence. He nodded here and there casually to dark, sullen men who watched his movements with implacably hostile eyes.

His words were addressed to Reddy Madden. "Can you let me have a horse for a few days and charge it to the Force? I've lost mine."

Some one sniggered offensively. Barney had evidently reached Whoop-Up and was in hiding.

"Your horse came in a while ago, constable," Madden said civilly. "It's in the coral back of the store."

"Did it come in without a rider?" Beresford asked.

The question was unnecessary. The horse would have gone to Fort Macleod and not have come to Whoop-Up unless a rider had guided it here. But sometimes one found out things from unwilling witnesses if one asked questions.

"Didn't notice. I was in the store myself."

"Thought perhaps you hadn't noticed," the officer said. "None of the other gentlemen noticed either, did you?"

The "other gentlemen" held a dogged, sulky silence.

A girl cantered through the gate of the stockade and up to the store. At sight of Morse her eyes passed swiftly to Beresford. His answered smilingly what she had asked. It was all over in a flash, but it told the man from Montana who the informer was that had betrayed to the police the place of the whiskey cache.

To the best of her limited chance, Jessie McRae was paying an installment on the debt she owed Bully West and Tom Morse.

CHAPTER VIII

At Sweet Water Creek

BEFORE a fire of buffalo chips Constable Beresford and his prisoner smoked the pipe of peace. Morse sat on his heels, legs crossed, after the manner of the camper. The officer lounged at full length, an elbow dug into the sand as a support for his head. The Montanan was on parole, so that for the moment at least their relations were forgotten.

"After the buffalo—what?" asked the American. "The end

43

of the Indian—is that what it means? And desolation on the plains. Nobody left but the Hudson's Bay Company trappers, d'you reckon?"

The Canadian answered in one word. "Cattle."

"Some, maybe," Morse assented. "But, holy Moses, think of the millions it would take to stock this country."

"Bet you the country's stocked inside of five years of the time the buffalo are cleared out. Look at what the big Texas drives are doing in Colorado and Wyoming and Montana. Get over the idea that this land up here is a desert. That's a fool notion our school geographies are responsible for. Great American Desert? Great American fiddlesticks! It's a man's country, if you like; but I've yet to see the beat of it."

Morse had ceased to pay attention. His head was tilted, and he was listening.

"Some one ridin' this way," he said presently. "Hear the hoofs click on the shale. Who is it? I wonder. An' what do they want? When folks' intentions hasn't been declared it's a good notion to hold a hand you can raise on."

Without haste and without delay Beresford got to his feet. "We'll step back into the shadow," he announced.

"Looks reasonable to me," agreed the smuggler.

They waited in the semi-darkness back of the campfire.

Some one shouted. "Hello, the camp!" At the sound of that clear, bell-like voice Morse lifted his head to listen better.

The constable answered the call.

Two riders came into the light. One was a girl, the other a slim, straight young Indian in deerskin shirt and trousers. The girl swung from the saddle and came forward to the camp-fire. The companion of her ride shadowed her.

Beresford and his prisoner advanced from the darkness.

"Bully West's after you. He's sworn to kill you," the girl called to the constable.

"How do you know?"

"Onistah heard him." She indicated with a wave of her hand the lithe-limbed youth beside her. "Onistah was passing the stable—behind it, back of the corral. This West was gathering a mob to follow you—said he was going to hang you for destroying his whiskey."

"He is, eh?" Beresford's salient jaw set. His light blue eyes gleamed hard and chill. He would see about that.

"They'll be here soon. This West was sure you'd camp here at Sweet Water Creek, close to the ford." A note of excitement pulsed in the girl's voice. "We heard 'em once behind us on the road. You'd better hurry."

The constable swung toward the Montanan. His eyes bored

into those of the prisoner. Would this man keep his parole or not? He would find out pretty soon.

"Saddle up, Morse. I'll pack my kit. We'll hit the trail."

"Listen." Jessie stood a moment, head lifted. "What's that?"

Onistah moved a step forward, so that for a moment the firelight flickered over the copper-colored face. Tom Morse made a discovery. This man was the Blackfoot he had rescued from the Crees.

"Horses," the Indian said, and held up the fingers of both hands to indicate the numbers. "Coming up creek. Here soon."

"We'll move back to the big rocks and I'll make a stand there," the officer told the whiskey-runner. "Slap the saddles on without cinching. We've got no time to lose." His voice lost its curtness as he turned to the girl. "Miss McRae, I'll not forget this. Very likely you've saved my life. Now you and Onistah had better slip away quietly. You mustn't be seen here."

"Why mustn't I?" she asked quickly. "I don't care who sees me."

She looked at Morse as she spoke, head up, with that little touch of scornful defiance in the quivering nostrils that seemed to express a spirit free and unafraid. The sense of superiority is generally not a lovely manifestation in any human being, but there are moments when it tells of something fine, a disdain of actions low and mean.

Morse strode away to the place where the horses were picketed. He could hear voices farther down the creek, caught once a snatch of words.

"... must be somewhere near, I tell you."

Noiselessly he slipped on the saddles, pulled the picket-pins, and moved toward the big rocks.

The place was a landmark. The erosion of the ages had played strange tricks with the sandstone. The rocks rose like huge red toadstools or like prehistoric animals of vast size. One of them was known as the Three Bears, another as the Elephant.

Among these boulders Morse found the party he had just left. The officer was still trying to persuade Jessie McRae to attempt escape. She refused, stubbornly.

"There are three of us here. Onistah is a good shot. So am I. For that matter, if anybody is going to escape, it had better be you," she said.

"Too late now," Morse said. "See, they've found the camp-fire."

Nine or ten riders had come out of the darkness and were

approaching the camping-ground. West was in the lead. Morse recognized Barney and Brad Stearns. Two of the others were half-breeds, one an Indian trailer of the Piegan tribe.

"He must 'a' heard us comin' and pulled out," Barney said.

"Then he's back in the red rocks," boomed West triumphantly.

"Soon find out." Brad Stearns turned the head of his horse toward the rocks and shouted. "Hello, Tom! You there?"

No answer came from the rocks.

"Don't prove a thing," West broke out impatiently. "This fellow's got Tom buffaloed. Didn't he make him smash the barrels? Didn't he take away his six-gun from him and bring him along like he hadn't any mind of his own? Tom's yellow. Got a streak a foot wide."

"Nothin' of the kind," denied Stearns, indignation in his voice. "I done brought up that boy by hand—learned him all he knows about ridin' and ropin'. He'll do to take along."

"Hmp! He always fooled you, Brad. Different here. I'm aimin' to give him the wallopin' of his life when I meet up with him. And that'll be soon, if he's up there in the rocks. I'm goin' a-shootin'." Bully West drew his revolver and rode forward.

The constable had disposed of his forces so that behind the cover of the sandstone boulders they commanded the approach. He had tried to persuade Jessie that this was not her fight, but a question from her had silenced him.

"If that Bully West finds me here, after he's killed you, d' you think I can get him to let me go because it wasn't my fight?"

She had asked it with flashing eyes, in which for an instant he had seen the savagery of fear leap out. Beresford was troubled. The girl was right enough. If West went the length of murder, he would be an outlaw. Sleeping Dawn would not be safe with him after she had ridden out to warn his enemy that he was coming. The fellow was a primeval brute. His reputation had run over the whole border country of Rupert's Land.

Now he appealed to Morse. "If they get me, will you try to save Miss McRae? This fellow West is a devil, I hear."

The officer caught a gleam of hot red eyes. "I'll 'tend to that. We'll mix first, him 'n' me. Question now is, do I get a gun?"

"What for?"

"Didn't you hear him make his brags about what he was gonna do to me? If there's shootin' I'm in on it, ain't I?"

"No. You're a prisoner. I can't arm you unless your life is in danger."

West pulled up his horse about sixty yards from the rocks. He shouted a profane order. The purport of it was that Beresford had better come out with his hands up if he didn't want to be dragged out by a rope around his neck. The man's speech crackled with oaths and obscenity.

The constable stepped into the open a few yards. "What do you want?" he asked.

"You." The whiskey-runner screamed it in a sudden gust of passion. "Think you can make a fool of Bully West? Think you can bust up our cargo an' get away with it? I'll show you where you head in at."

"Don't make any mistake, West," advised the officer, his voice cold as the splash of ice-water. "Three of us are here, all with rifles, all dead shots. If you attack us, some of you are going to get killed."

"That's a lie. You're alone—except for Tom Morse, an' he ain't fool enough to fight to go to jail. I've got you where I want you." West swung from the saddle and came straddling forward. In the uncertain light he looked more like some misbegotten ogre than a human being.

"That's far enough," warned Beresford, not a trace of excitement in manner or speech. His hands hung by his sides. He gave no sign of knowing that he had a revolver strapped to his hip ready for action.

The liquor smuggler stopped to pour out abuse. He was working himself up to a passion that would justify murder. The weapon in his hand swept wildly back and forth. Presently it would focus down to a deadly concentration in which all motion would cease.

The torrent of vilification died on the man's lips. He stared past the constable with bulging eyes. From the rocks three figures had come. Two of them carried rifles. All three of them he recognized. His astonishment paralyzed the scurrilous tongue. What was McRae's girl doing at the camp of the officer?

It was characteristic of him that he suspected the worst of her. Either Tom Morse or this red-coat had beaten him to his prey. Jealousy and outraged vanity flared up in him so that discretion vanished.

The barrel of his revolver came down and began to spit flame.

Beresford gave orders. "Back to the rocks." He retreated, backward, firing as he moved.

The companions of West surged forward. Shots, shouts, the shifting blur of moving figures, filled the night. Under cover of the darkness the defenders reached again the big rocks.

The constable counted noses. "Everybody all right?" he asked. Then, abruptly, he snapped out: "Who was responsible for that crazy business of you coming out into the open?"

"Me," said the girl. "I wanted that West to know you weren't alone."

"Didn't you know better than to let her do it?" the officer demanded of Morse.

"He couldn't help it. He tried to keep me back. What right has he to interfere with me?" she wanted to know, stiffening.

"You'll do as I say now," the constable said crisply. "Get back of that rock there, Miss McRae, and stay there. Don't move from cover unless I tell you to."

Her dark, stormy eyes challenged his, but she moved sullenly to obey. Rebel though she was, the code of the frontier claimed and held her respect. She had learned of life that there were times when her will must be subordinated for the general good.

CHAPTER IX

Tom Makes A Collection

THE attackers drew back and gathered together for consultation. West's anger had stirred their own smoldering resentment at the police, had dominated them, and had brought them on a journey of vengeance. But they had not come out with any intention of storming a defended fortress. The enthusiasm of the small mob ebbed.

"I reckon we done bit off more'n we can chaw," Harvey Gosse murmured, rubbing his bristly chin. "I ain't what you might call noways anxious to have them fellows spill lead into me."

"Ten of us here. One man, an Injun, an' a breed girl over there. You lookin' for better odds, Harv?" jeered the leader of the party.

"I never heard that a feller was any less dead because an Injun or a girl shot him," the lank smuggler retorted.

"Be reasonable, Bully," urged Barney with his ingratiating whine. "We come out to fix the red-coat. We figured he was alone except for Tom, an' o' course Tom's with us. But this here's a different proposition. Too many witnesses ag'in' us. I reckon you ain't tellin' us it's safe to shoot up Angus McRae's daughter even if she is a métis."

"Forget her," the big whiskey-runner snarled. "She won't be a witness against us."

"Why won't she?"

"Hell's hinges! Do I have to tell you all my plans? I'm sayin' she won't. That goes." He flung out a gesture of scarcely restrained rage. He was not one who could reason away opposition with any patience. It was his temperament to override it.

Brad Stearns rubbed his bald head. He always did when he was working out a mental problem. West's declaration could mean only one of two things. Either the girl would not be alive to give witness or she would be silent because she had thrown in her lot with the big trader.

The old-timer knew West's vanity and his weakness for women. From Tom Morse he had heard of his offer to McRae for the girl. Now he had no doubt what the man intended.

But what of her? What of the girl he had seen at her father's camp, the heart's desire of the rugged old Scotchman? In the lightness of her step, in the lift of her head, in speech and gesture and expression of face, she was of the white race, an inheritor of its civilization and of its traditions. Only her dusky color and a certain wild shyness seemed born of the native blood in her. She was proud, passionate, high-spirited. Would she tamely accept Bully West for her master and go to his tent as his squaw? Brad didn't believe it. She would fight—fight desperately, with barbaric savagery.

Her fight would avail her nothing. If driven to it, West would take her with him into the fastnesses of the Lone Lands. They would disappear from the sight of men for months. He would travel swiftly with her to the great river. Every sweep of his canoe paddle would carry them deeper into that virgin North where they could live on what his rifle and rod won for the pot. A little salt, pemmican, and flour would be all the supplies he needed to take with them.

Brad had no intention of being a cat's-paw for him. The older man had come along to save Tom Morse from prison and for no other reason. He did not intend to be swept into indiscriminate crime.

"Don't go with me, Bully," Stearns said. "Count me out. Right here's where I head for Whoop-Up."

He turned his horse's head and rode into the darkness.

West looked after him, cursing. "We're better off without the white-livered coyote," he said at last.

"Brad ain't so fur off at that. I'd like blame well to be moseyin' to Whoop-Up my own self," Gosse said uneasily."

"You'll stay right here an' go through with this job, Harv," West told him flatly. "All you boys'll do just that. If any of you's got a different notion we'll settle that here an' now. How about it?" He straddled up and down in front of his men, menacing them with knotted fists and sulky eyes.

Nobody cared to argue the matter with him. He showed his broken teeth in a sour grin.

"Tha's settled, then," he went on. "It's my say-so. My orders go—if there's no objections."

His outthrust head, set low on the hunched shoulders, moved from right to left threateningly as his gaze passed from one to another. If there were any objections they were not mentioned aloud.

"Now we know where we're at," he continued. "It'll be thisaway. Most of us will scatter out an' fire at the rocks from the front here; the others'll sneak round an' come up from behind—get right into the rocks before this bully-puss fellow knows it. If you get a chance, plug him in the back, but don't hurt the Injun girl. Y' understand? I want her alive an' not wounded. If she gets shot up, some one's liable to get his head knocked off."

But it did not, after all, turn out quite the way West had planned it. He left out of account one factor—a man among the rocks who had been denied a weapon and any part in the fighting.

The feint from the front was animated enough. The attackers scattered and from behind clumps of brush grass and bushes poured in a fire that kept the defenders busy. Barney, with the half-breeds and the Indian at heel, made a wide circle and crept up to the red sandstone outcroppings. He did not relish the job any more than those behind him did, but he was a creature of West and usually did as he was told after a bit of grumbling. It was not safe for him to refuse.

To Tom Morse, used to Bully West and his ways, the frontal attack did not seem quite genuine. It was desultory and ineffective. Why? What trick did Bully have up his sleeve? Tom put himself in his place to see what he would do.

And instantly he knew. The real attack would come from the rear. With the firing of the first shot back there, Bully

West would charge. Taken on both sides the garrison would fall easy victims.

The constable and Onistah were busy answering the fire of the smugglers. Sleeping Dawn was crouched down behind two rocks, the barrel of her rifle gleaming through a slit of open space between them. She was compromising between the orders given her and the anxiety in her to fight back Bully West. As much as she could she kept under cover, while at the same time firing into the darkness whenever she thought she saw a movement.

Morse slipped rearward on a tour of investigation. The ground here fell away rather sharply, so that one coming from behind would have to climb over a boulder field rising to the big rocks. It took Tom only a casual examination to see that a surprise would have to be launched by way of a sort of rough natural stairway.

A flat shoulder of sandstone dominated the stairway from above. Upon this Morse crouched, every sense alert to detect the presence of any one stealing up the pass. He waited, eager and yet patient. What he was going to attempt had its risk, but the danger whipped the blood in his veins to a still excitement.

Occasionally, at intervals, the rifles cracked. Except for that no other sound came to him. He could keep no count of time. It seemed to him that hours slipped away. In reality it could have been only a few minutes.

Below, from the foot of the winding stairway, there was a sound, such a one as might come from the grinding of loose rubble beneath the sole of a boot. Presently the man on the ledge heard it again, this time more distinctly. Some one was crawling up the rocks.

Tom peered into the darkness intently. He could see nothing except the flat rocks disappearing vaguely in the gloom. Nor could he hear again the crunch of a footstep on disintegrated sandstone. His nerves grew taut. Could he have made a mistake? Was there another way up from behind?

Then, at the turn of the stairway, a few feet below him, a figure rose in silhouette. It appeared with extraordinary caution, first a head, then the barrel of a rifle, finally a crouched body followed by bowed legs. On hands and knees it crept forward, hitching the weapon along beside it. Exactly opposite Morse, under the very shadow of the sloping ledge on which he lay, the figure rose and straightened.

The man stood there for a second, making up his mind to

move on. He was one of the half-breeds West had brought with him. Almost into his ear came a stern whisper.

"Hands up! I've got you covered. Don't move. Don't say a word."

Two arms shot skyward. In the fingers of one hand a rifle was clenched.

Morse leaned forward and caught hold of it. "I'll take this," he said. The brown fingers relaxed. "Skirt round the edge of the rock there. Lie face down in that hollow. Got a six-shooter."

He had. Morse took it from him.

"If you move or speak one word, I'll pump lead into you," the Montanan cautioned.

The half-breed looked into his chill eyes and decided to take no chances. He lay down on his face with hands stretched out exactly as ordered.

His captor returned to the shoulder of rock above the trail. Presently another head projected itself out of the darkness. A man crept up, and like the first stopped to take stock of his surroundings.

Against the back of his neck something cold pressed.

"Stick up your hands, Barney," a voice ordered.

The little man let out a yelp. "Mother o' Moses, don't shoot."

"How many more of you?" asked Morse sharply.

"One more."

The man behind the rifle collected his weapons and put Barney alongside his companion. Within five minutes he had added a third man to the collection.

With a sardonic grin he drove them before him to Beresford.

"I'm a prisoner an' not in this show, you was careful to explain to me, Mr. Constable, but I busted the rules an' regulations to collect a few specimens of my own," he drawled by way of explanation.

Beresford's eyes gleamed. The debonair impudence of the procedure appealed mightily to him. He did not know how this young fellow had done it, but he must have acted with cool nerve and superb daring.

"Where were they? And how did you get 'em without a six-shooter?"

"They was driftin' up the pass to say 'How-d' you-do?' from the back stairway. I borrowed a gun from one o' them. I asked 'em to come along with me and they reckoned they would."

The booming of a rifle echoed in the rocks to the left.

From out of them Jessie McRae came flying, something akin to terror in her face.

"I've shot that West. He tried to run in on me and—and—I shot him." Her voice broke into an hysterical sob.

"Thought I told you to keep out of this," the constable said. "I seem to have a lot of valuable volunteer help. What with you and friend Morse here—" He broke off, touched at her distress. "Never mind about that, Miss McRae. He had it coming to him. I'll go out and size up the damage to him, if his friends have had enough—and chances are they have."

They had. Gosse advanced waving a red bandanna handkerchief as a flag of truce.

"We got a plenty," he said frankly. "West's down, an' another of the boys got winged. No use us goin' on with this darned foolishness. We're ready to call it off if you'll turn Morse loose."

Beresford had walked out to meet him. He answered, curtly. "No."

The long, lank whiskey-runner rubbed his chin bristles awkwardly. "We 'lowed maybe—"

"I keep my prisoners, both Morse and Barney."

"Barney!" repeated Gosse, surprised.

"Yes, we've got him and two others. I don't want them. I'll turn 'em over to you. But not Morse and Barney. They're going to the post with me for whiskey-running."

Gosse went back to the camp-fire, where the Whoop-Up men had carried their wounded leader. Except West, they were all glad to drop the battle. The big smuggler, lying on the ground with a bullet in his thigh, cursed them for a group of chicken-hearted quitters. His anger could not shake their decision. They knew when they had had enough.

The armistice concluded, Beresford and Morse walked over to the camp-fire to find out how badly West was hurt.

"Sorry I had to hit you, but you would have it, you know," the constable told him grimly.

The man snapped his teeth at him like a wolf in a trap. "You didn't hit me, you liar. It was that li'l' hell-cat of McRae. You tell her for me I'll get her right for this, sure as my name's Bully West."

There was something horribly menacing in his rage. In the jumping light of the flames the face was that of a demon, a countenance twisted and tortured by the impotent lust to destroy.

Morse spoke, looking steadily at him in his quiet way. "I'm servin' notice, West, that you're to let that girl alone."

There was a sound in the big whiskey-runner's throat like

that of an infuriated wild animal. He glared at Morse, a torrent of abuse struggling for utterance. All that he could say was, "You damned traitor."

The eyes of the younger man did not waver. "It goes. I'll see you're shot like a wolf if you harm her."

The wounded smuggler's fury outleaped prudence. In a surge of momentary insanity he saw red. The barrel of his revolver rose swiftly. A bullet sang past Morse's ear. Before he could fire again, Harvey Gosse had flung himself on the man and wrested the weapon from his hand.

Hard-eyed and motionless, Morse looked down at the madman without saying a word. It was Beresford who said ironically, "Talking about those who keep faith."

"You hadn't oughta of done that, Bully," Gosse expostulated. "We'd done agreed this feud was off for to-night."

"Get your horses and clear out of here," the constable ordered. "If this man's able to fight he's able to travel. You can make camp farther down the creek."

A few minutes later the clatter of horse-hoofs died away. Beresford was alone with his prisoners and his guests.

Those who were still among the big rocks came forward to the camp-fire. Jessie arrived before the others. She had crept to the camp on the heels of Beresford and Morse, driven by her great anxiety to find out how badly West was hurt.

From the shadows of a buffalo wallow she had seen and heard what had taken place.

One glance of troubled curiosity she flashed at Morse. What sort of man was this quiet, brown-faced American who smuggled whiskey in to ruin the tribes, who could ruthlessly hold a girl to a bargain that included horse-whipping for her, who for some reason of his own fought beside the man taking him to imprisonment, and who had flung defiance at the terrible Bully West on her behalf? She hated him. She always would. But with her dislike of him ran another feeling now, born of the knowledge of new angles in him.

He was hard as nails, but he would do to ride the river with.

CHAPTER X

A Camp-Fire Tale

ANOTHER surprise was waiting for Jessie. As soon as Onistah came into the circle of light, he walked straight to the whiskey-smuggler.

"You save my life from Crees. Thanks," he said in English. Onistah offered his hand.

The white man took it. He was embarrassed. "Oh, well, I kinda took a hand."

The Indian was not through."Onistah never forget. He pay some day."

Tom waved this aside. "How's the leg? Seems to be all right now."

Swiftly Jessie turned to the Indian and asked him a question in the native tongue. He answered. They exchanged another sentence or two.

The girl spoke to Morse. "Onistah is my brother. I too thank you," she said stiffly.

"Your brother! He's not Angus McRae's son, is he?"

"No. And I'm not his daughter—really. I'll tell you about that," she said with a touch of the defensive defiance that always came into her manner when the subject of her birth was referred to.

She did, later, over the camp-fire.

It is fortunate that desire and opportunity do not always march together. The constable and Morse had both been dead men if Bully West could have killed with a wish. Sleeping Dawn would have been on the road to an existence worse than death. Instead, they sat in front of the coals of buffalo chips while the big smuggler and his companions rode away from an ignominious field of battle.

When the constable and his prisoner had first struck camp, there had been two of them. Now there were six. For in addition to Jessie McRae, the Blackfoot, and Barney, another had come out of the night and hailed them with a "Hello, the camp!" This last self-invited guest was Brad Stearns, who

55

had not ridden to Whoop-Up as he had announced, but had watched events from a distance on the chance that he might be of help to Tom Morse.

Jessie agreed with Beresford that she must stay in camp till morning. There was nothing else for her to do. She could not very well ride the night out with Onistah on the road back to the fort. But she stayed with great reluctance.

Her modesty was in arms. Never before had she, a girl alone, been forced to make camp with five men as companions, all but one of them almost strangers to her. The experience was one that shocked her sense of fitness.

She was troubled and distressed, and she showed it. Her impulsiveness had swept her into an adventure that might have been tragic, that still held potentialities of disaster. For she could not forget the look on West's face when he had sworn to get even with her. This man was a terrible enemy, because of his boldness, his evil mind, and his lack of restraining conscience.

Yet even now she could not blame herself for what she had done. The constable's life was at stake. It had been necessary to move swiftly and decisively.

Sitting before the fire, Sleeping Dawn began to tell her story. She told it to Beresford as an apology for having ridden forty miles with Onistah to save his life. It was, if he chose so to accept it, an explanation of how she came to do so unwomanly a thing.

"Onistah's mother is my mother," she said. "When I was a baby my own mother died. Stokimatis is her sister. I do not know who my father was, but I have heard he was an American. Stokimatis took me to her tepee and I lived there with her and Onistah till I was five or six. Then Angus McRae saw me one day. He liked me, so he bought me for three yards of tobacco, a looking-glass, and five wolf pelts."

It may perhaps have been by chance that the girl's eyes met those of Morse. The blood burned beneath the tan of her dusky cheeks, but her proud eyes did not flinch while she told the damning facts about her parentage and life. She was of the métis, the child of an unknown father. So far as she knew her mother had never been married. She had been bought and sold like a Negro slave in the South. Let any one that wanted to despise her make the most of all this.

So far as any expression went Tom Morse looked hard as pig iron. He did not want to blunder, so he said nothing. But the girl would have been amazed if she could have read his thoughts. She seemed to him a rare flower that has blossomed in a foul swamp.

"If Angus McRae took you for his daughter, it was because he loved you," Beresford said gently.

"Yes." The mobile face was suddenly tender with emotion. "What can any father do more than he has done for me? I learned to read and write at his knee. He taught me the old songs of Scotland that he's so fond of. He tried to make me good and true. Afterward he sent me to Winnipeg to school for two years."

"Good for Angus McRae," the young soldier said.

She smiled, a little wistfully. "He wants me to be Scotch, but of course I can't be that even though I sing 'Should auld acquaintance' to him. I'm what I am."

Ever since she had learned to think for herself, she had struggled against the sense of racial inferiority. Even in the Lone Lands men of education had crossed her path. There was Father Giguère, tall and austere and filled with the wisdom of years, a scholar who had left his dear France to serve on the outposts of civilization. And there was the old priest's devoted friend Philip Muir, of whom the story ran that he was heir to a vast estate across the seas. Others she had seen at Winnipeg. And now this scarlet-coated soldier Beresford.

Instinctively she recognized the difference between them and the trappers and traders who frequented the North woods. In her bed at night she had more than once wept herself to sleep because life had built an impassable barrier between what she was and what she wanted to be.

"To the Scot nobody is quite like a Scot," Beresford admitted with a smile. "When he wants to make you one, Mr. McRae pays you a great compliment."

The girl flashed a look of gratitude at him and went on with her story. "Whenever we are near Stokimatis, I go to see her. She has always been very fond of me. It wasn't really for money she sold me, but because she knew Angus McRae could bring me up better than she could. I was with her to-day when Onistah came in and told us what this West was going to do. There wasn't time for me to reach Father. I couldn't trust anybody at Whoop-Up, and I was afraid if Onistah came along, you wouldn't believe him. You know how people are about—about Indians. So I saddled a horse and rode with him."

"That was fine of you. I'll never forget it, Miss McRae," the young soldier said quietly, his eyes for an instant full on hers. "I don't think I've ever met another girl who would have had the good sense and the courage to do it."

Her eyes fell from his. She felt a queer delightful thrill

run through her blood. He still respected her, was even grateful to her for what she had done. No experience in the ways of men and maids warned her that there was another cause for the quickened pulse. Youth had looked into the eyes of youth and made the world-old call of sex to sex.

In a little pocket opening from the draw. Morse arranged blankets for the girl's bed. He left Beresford to explain to her that she could sleep there alone without fear, since a guard would keep watch against any possible surprise attack.

When the soldier did tell her this, Jessie smiled back her reassurance. "I'm not afraid—not the least littlest bit," she said buoyantly. "I'll sleep right away."

But she did not. Jessie was awake to the finger-tips, her veins apulse with the flow of rushing rivers of life. Her chaotic thoughts centered about two men. One had followed crooked trails for his own profit. There was something in him hard and unyielding as flint. He would go to his chosen end, whatever that might be, over and through any obstacles that might rise. But to-night, on her behalf, he had thrown down the gauntlet to Bully West, the most dreaded desperado on the border. Why had he done it? Was he sorry because he had forced her father to horsewhip her? Or was his warning merely the snarl of one wolf at another?

The other man was of a different stamp. He had brought with him from the world whence he had come a debonair friendliness, an ease of manner, a smile very boyish and charming. In his jaunty forage cap and scarlet jacket he was one to catch and hold the eye by reason of his engaging personality. He too had fought her batttle. She had heard him, in that casually careless way of his, try to take the blame of having wounded West. Her happy thoughts went running out to him gratefully.

Not the least cause of her gratitude was that there had not been the remotest hint in his manner that there was any difference between her and any white girl he might meet.

CHAPTER XI
C. N. Morse Turns Over A Leaf

THE North-West Mounted Police had authority not only to arrest, but to try and to sentence prisoners. The soldierly inspector who sat in judgment on Morse at Fort Macleod heard the evidence and stroked an iron-gray mustache reflectively. As he understood it, his business was to stop whiskey-running rather than to send men to jail. Beresford's report on this young man was in his favor. The inspector adventured into psychology.

"Studied the Indians any—the effect of alcohol on them?" he asked Morse.

"Some," the prisoner answered.

"Don't you think it bad for them?"

"Yes, sir."

"Perhaps you've been here longer than I. Isn't this whiskey-smuggling bad business all round?"

"Not for the smuggler. Speakin' as an outsider, I reckon he does it because he makes money," Morse answered impersonally.

"For the country, I mean. For the trapper, for the needs, for the Indians."

"No doubt about that."

"You're a nephew of C. N. Morse, aren't you?"

"Yes, sir."

"Wish you'd take him a message from me. Tell him that it's bad business for a big trading firm like his to be smuggling whiskey." The officer raised a hand to stop the young man's protest. "Yes, I know you're going to tell me that we haven't proved he's been smuggling. We'll pass that point. Carry him my message. Just say it's bad business. You can tell him if you want to that we're here to put an end to it and we're going to do it. But stress the fact that it isn't good business. Understand?"

"Yes."

"Very well, sir." A glint of a smile showed in the inspector's eyes. "I'll give you a Scotch verdict, young man. Not guilty, but don't do it again. You're discharged."

"Barney, too?"

"Hmp! He's a horse of another color. Think we'll send him over the plains."

"Why make two bites of a cherry, sir? He can't be guilty if I'm not," the released prisoner said.

"Did I say you weren't?" Inspector MacLean countered.

"Not worth the powder, is he, sir?" Tom insinuated nonchalantly. "Rather a fathead, Barney is. If he's guilty, it's not as a principal. You'd much better send me up."

The officer laughed behind the hand that stroked the mustache. "Do you want to be judge and jury as well as prisoner, my lad?"

"Thought perhaps my uncle would understand the spirit of your message better if Barney went along with me, Inspector." The brown eyes were open and guileless.

MacLean studied the Montanan deliberately. He began to recognize unusual qualities in this youth.

"Can't say I care for your friend Barney. He's a bad egg, or I miss my guess."

"Not much taken with him myself. Thought if I'd get him to travel south with me it might save you some trouble."

"It might," the Inspector agreed. "It's his first offense so far as I know." Under bristling eyebrows he shot a swift look at this self-assured youngster. He had noticed that men matured at an early age on the frontier. The school of emergency developed them fast. But Morse struck him as more competent even than the other boyish plainsmen he had met. "Will you be responsible for him?"

The Montanan came to scratch reluctantly. He had no desire to be bear leader for such a doubtful specimen as Barney.

"Yes," he said, after a pause.

"Keep him in the States, will you?"

"Yes."

"Take him along, then. Wish you luck of him."

As soon as he reached Fort Benton, Tom reported to his uncle. He told the story of the whiskey cargo and its fate, together with his own adventures subsequent to that time.

The head of the trading firm was a long, loose-jointed Yankee who had drifted West in his youth. Since then he had acquired gray hairs and large business interests. At Inspector MacLean's mess.ge he grinned.

"Thinks it's bad business, does he?"

"Told me to tell you so," Tom answered.

"Didn't say why, I guess."

60

"No."

The old New Englander fished from a hip pocket a plug of tobacco, cut off a liberal chew, and stowed this in his cheek. Then, lounging back in the chair, he cocked a shrewd eye at his nephew.

"Wonder what he meant."

Tom volunteered no opinion. He recognized his uncle's canny habit of fishing in other people's minds for confirmation of what was in his own.

"Got any idee what he was drivin' at?" the old pioneer went on.

"Sorta."

C. N. Morse chuckled. "Got a notion myself. Let's hear yours."

"The trade with the North-West Mounted is gonna be big for a while. The Force needs all kinds of supplies. It'll have to deal through some firm in Benton as a clearin' house. He's servin' notice that unless C. N. Morse & Company mends its ways, it can't do business with the N.W.M.P."

"That all?" asked the head of the firm.

"That's only half of it. The other half is that no firm of whiskey-runners will be allowed to trade across the line."

C. N. gave another little chirrup of mirth. "Keep your brains whittled up, don't you? Any advice you'd like to give?"

Tom was not to be drawn. "None, sir."

"No comments, son? Passin' it up to Uncle Newt, eh?"

"You're the head of the firm. I'm hired to do as I'm told."

"You figure on obeyin' orders and lettin' it go at that?"

"Not quite." The young fellow's square chin jutted out. "For instance, I'm not gonna smuggle liquor through any more. I had my eyes opened this trip. You haven't been on the ground like I have. If you want a plain word for it, Uncle Newt—"

"Speak right out in meetin', Tom. Shouldn't wonder but what I can stand it." The transplanted Yankee slanted at his nephew a quizzical smile. "I been hearin' more or less plain language for quite a spell, son."

Tom gave it to him straight from the shoulder, quietly but without apology. "Sellin' whiskey to the tribes results in wholesale murder, sir."

"Strong talk, boy," his uncle drawled.

"Not too strong. You know I don't mean anything personal, Uncle Newt. To understand this thing you've got to go up there an' see it. The plains tribes up there go crazy over firewater an' start killin' each other. It's a crime to let 'em have it."

61

Young Morse began to tell stories of instances that had come under his own observation, of others that he had heard from reliable sources. Presently he found himself embarked on the tale of his adventures with Sleeping Dawn.

The fur-trader heard him patiently. The dusty wrinkled boots of the merchant rested on the desk. His chair was tilted back in such a way that the weight of his body was distributed between the back of his neck, the lower end of the spine, and his heels. He looked a picture of sleepy, indolent ease, but Tom knew he was not missing the least detail.

A shadow darkened the doorway of the office. Behind it straddled a huge, ungainly figure.

"'Lo, West! How're tricks?" C. N. Morse asked in his lazy way. He did not rise from the chair or offer to shake hands, but that might be because it was not his custom to exert himself.

West stopped in his stride, choking with wrath. He had caught sight of Tom and was glaring at him. "You're here, eh? Sneaked home to try to square yourself with the old man, did ya?" The trail foreman turned to the uncle. "I wanta tell you he double-crossed you for fair, C. N. He's got a heluva nerve to come back here after playin' in with the police the way he done up there."

"I've heard something about that," the fur-trader admitted cautiously. "You told me Tom an' you didn't exactly gee."

"He'll never drive another bull-team for me again." West tacked to his pronouncement a curdling oath.

"We'll call that settled, then. You're through bull-whackin', Tom." There was a little twitch of whimsical mirth at the corners of the old man's mouth.

"Now you're shoutin', C. N. Threw me down from start to finish, he did. First off, when the breed girl busted the casks, he took her home 'stead of bringin' her to me. Then at old McRae's camp when I was defendin' myself, he jumped me too. My notion is from the way he acted that he let on to the red-coat where the cache was. Finally when I rode out to rescue him, he sided in with the other fellow. Hadn't been for him I'd never 'a' had this slug in my leg." The big smuggler spoke with extraordinary vehemence, spicing his speech liberally with sulphurous language.

The grizzled Yankee accepted the foreman's attitude with a wave of the hand that dismissed any counter-argument. But there was an ironic gleam in his eye.

"'Nough said, West. If you're that sot on it, the boy quits the company pay-roll as an employee right now. I won't have him annoyin' you another hour. He becomes a member of the firm to-day."

The big bully's jaw sagged. He stared at his lean employer as though a small bomb had exploded at his feet and numbed his brains. But he was no more surprised than Tom, whose wooden face was expressionless.

"Goddlemighty! Ain't I jus' been tellin' you how he wrecked the whole show—how he sold out to that bunch of spies the Canadian Gov'ment has done sent up there?" exploded West.

"Oh, I don't guess he did that," Morse, Senior, said lightly. "We got to remember that times are changin', West. Law's comin' into the country an' we old-timers oughta meet it half-way with the glad hand. You can't buck the Union Jack any more than you could Uncle Sam. I figure I've sent my last shipment of liquor across the line."

"Scared, are you?" sneered the trail boss.

"Maybe I am. Reckon I'm too old to play the smuggler's game. And I've got a hankerin' for respectability—want the firm to stand well with the new settlers. Legitimate business from now on. That's our motto, boys."

"What church you been j'inin', C. N.?"

"Well, maybe it'll come to that too. Think I'd make a good deacon?" the merchant asked amiably, untwining his legs and rising to stretch.

West slammed a big fist on the table so that the inkwell and the pens jumped. "All I got to say is that this new Sunday-school outfit you aim to run won't have no use for a he-man. I'm quittin' you right now."

The foreman made the threat as a bluff. He was the most surprised man in Montana when his employer called it quietly, speaking still in the slow, nasal voice of perfect good-nature.

"Maybe you're right, West. That's for you to say, of course. You know your own business best. Figure out your time an' I'll have Benson write you a check. Hope you find a good job."

The sense of baffled anger in West foamed up. His head dropped down and forward threateningly.

"You do, eh? Lemme tell you this, C. N. I don't ask no odds of you or any other guy. Jes' because you're the head of a big outfit you can't run on me. I won't stand for it a minute."

"Of course not. I'd know better'n to try that with you. No hard feelings even if you quit us." It was a characteristic of

63

the New Englander that while he was a forceful figure in this man's country, he rarely quarreled with any one.

"That so? Well, you listen here. I been layin' off that new pardner of yours because he's yore kin. Not any more. Different now. He's liable to have a heluva time an' don't you forget it for a minute."

The fur-trader chewed his cud imperturbably. When he spoke it was still without a trace of acrimony.

"Guess you'll think better of that maybe, West. Guess you're a little hot under the collar, ain't you? Don't hardly pay to hold grudges, does it? There was Rhinegoldt now. Kept nursin' his wrongs an' finally landed in the pen. Bad medicine, looks like to me."

West was no imbecile. He understood the threat underneath the suave words of the storekeeper. Rhinegoldt had gone to the penitentiary because C. N. Morse had willed it so. The inference was that another lawbreaker might go for the same reason. The trail boss knew that this was no idle threat. Morse could put him behind the bars any time he chose. The evidence was in his hands.

The bully glared at him. "You try that, C. N. Jus' try it once. There'll be a sudden death in the Morse family if you do. Mebbe two. Me, I'd gun you both for a copper cent. Don't fool yourself a minute."

"Kinda foolish talk, West. Don't buy you anything. Guess you better go home an' cool off, hadn't you? I'll have your time made up to-day, unless you want your check right now."

The broken teeth of the desperado clicked as his jaw clamped. He looked from the smiling, steady-eyed trader to the brown-faced youth who watched the scene with such cool, alert attention. He fought with a wild, furious impulse in himself to go through with his threat, to clean up and head out into the wilds. But some saving sense of prudence held his hand. C. N. Morse was too big game for him.

"To hell with the check," he snarled, and swinging on his heel jingled out of the office.

The nephew spoke first. "You got rid of him on purpose."

"Looked that way to you, did it?" the uncle asked in his usual indirect way.

"Why?"

"Guess you'd say it was because he won't fit into the new policy of the firm. Guess you'd say he'd always be gettin' us into trouble with his overbearin' and crooked ways."

"That's true. He would."

"Maybe it would be a good idee to watch him mighty close.

64

They say he's a bad hombre. Might be unlucky for any one he got the drop on."

Tom knew he was being warnéd. "I'll look out for him," he promised.

The older man changed the subject smilingly. "Here's where C. N. Morse & Company turns over a leaf, son. No more business gambles. Legitimate trade only. That the idee you're figurin' on makin' me live up to?"

"Suits me if it does you," Tom answered cheerfully. "But where do I come in? What's my job in the firm? You'll notice I haven't said 'Thanks' yet."

"You?" C. N. gave him a sly, dry smile. "Oh, all you have to do is to handle our business north of the line—buy, sell, trade, build up friendly relations with the Indians and trappers, keep friendly with the police, and a few little things like that."

Tom grinned.

"Won't have a thing to do, will I?"

CHAPTER XII

Tom Ducks Trouble

To Tom Morse, sitting within the railed space that served for an office in the company store at Faraway, came a light-stepping youth in trim boots, scarlet jacket, and forage cap set at a jaunty angle.

"'Lo, Uncle Sam," he said, saluting gayly.

"'Lo, Johnny Canuck. Where you been for a year and heaven knows how many months?"

"Up Peace River, after Pierre Poulette, fellow who killed Buckskin Jerry."

Tom took in Beresford's lean body, a gauntness of the boyish face, hollows under the eyes that had not been there when first they had met. There had come to him whispers of the long trek into the frozen Lone Lands made by the officer and his Indian guide. He could guess the dark and dismal winter spent by the two alone, without books, without the comforts of life, far from any other human being. It must have been

65

an experience to try the soul. But it had not shaken the Canadian's blithe joy in living.

"Get him?" the Montanan asked.

The answer he could guess. The North-West Mounted always brought back those they were sent for. Already the Force was building up the tradition that made them for a generation rulers of half a continent.

"Got him." Thus briefly the red-coat dismissed an experience that had taken toll of his vitality greater than five years of civilized existence. "Been back a week. Inspector Crouch sent me here to have a look-see."

"At what? He ain't suspectin' any one at Faraway of stretchin', bendin', or bustin' the laws."

Tom cocked a merry eye at his visitor. Rumor had it that Faraway was a cesspool of iniquity. It was far from the border. When sheriffs of Montana became too active, there was usually an influx of population at the post, of rough, hard-eyed men who crossed the line and pushed north to safety.

"Seems to be. You're not by any chance lookin' for trouble?"

"Duckin' it," answered Tom promptly.

The officer smiled genially. "It's knocking at your door." His knuckles rapped on the desk.

"If I ever bumped into a Santa Claus of joy—"

"Oh, thanks!" Beresford murmured.

"—you certainly ain't him. Onload your grief."

"The theme of my discourse is aborigines, their dispositions, animadversions, and propensities," explained the constable. "According to the latest scientific hypotheses, the metempsychosis—"

Tom threw up his hands. "Help! Help! I never studied geology none. Don't know this hypotenuse you're pow-wowin' about any more 'n my paint hawss does. Come again in one syllables."

"Noticed any trouble among the Crees lately—that is, any more than usual?"

The junior partner of C. N. Morse & Company considered. "Why, yes, seems to me I have—heap much swagger and noise, plenty rag-chewin' and tomahawk swingin'."

"Why?"

"Whiskey, likely."

"Where do they get it?"

Tom looked at the soldier quizzically. "Your guess is good as mine," he drawled.

"I'm guessing West and Whaley."

Morse made no comment. Bully West had thrown in his

66

fortune with Dug Whaley, a gambler who had drifted from one mining camp to another and been washed by the tide of circumstance into the Northwest. Ostensibly they supplied blankets, guns, food, and other necessities to the tribes, but there was a strong suspicion that they made their profit in whiskey smuggled across the plains.

"But to guess it and to prove it are different propositions. How am I going to hang it on them? I can't make a bally fool of myself by prodding around in their bales and boxes. If I didn't find anything—and it'd be a long shot against me —West and his gang would stick their tongues in their cheeks and N.W.M.P. stock would shoot down. No, I've got to make sure, jump 'em, and tie 'em up by finding the goods on the wagons."

"Fat chance," speculated Tom.

"That's where you come in."

"Oh, I come in there, do I? I begin to hear Old Man Trouble knockin' at my door like you promised. Break it kinda easy. Am I to go up an' ask Bully West where he keeps his fire-water cached? Or what?"

"Yes. Only don't mention to him that you're asking. Your firm and his trade back and forth, don't they?"

"Forth, but not back. When they've got to have some goods—if it's neck or nothing with them—they buy from us. We don't buy from them. You couldn't exactly call us neighborly."

Beresford explained. "West's just freighted in a cargo of goods. I can guarantee that if he brought any liquor with him —and I've good reason to think he did—it hasn't been unloaded yet. To-morrow the wagons will scatter. I can't follow all of 'em. If I cinch Mr. West, it's got to be to-night."

"I see. You want me to give you my blessin'. I'll come through with a fine big large one. Go to it, constable. Hogtie West with proof. Soak him good. Send him up for 'steen years. You got my sympathy an' approval, one for the grief you're liable to bump into, the other for your good intentions."

The officer's grin had a touch of the proverbial Cheshire cat's malice. "Glad you approve. But you keep that sympathy for yourself. I'm asking you to pull the chestnut out of the fire for me. You'd better look out or you'll burn your paw."

"Just remember I ain't promisin' a thing. I'm a respectable business man now, and, as I said, duckin' trouble."

"Find out for me in which wagon the liquor is. That's all I ask."

"How can I find out? I'm no mind reader."

"Drift over casually and offer to buy goods. Poke around a bit. Keep cases on 'em. Notice the wagons they steer you away from."

Tom thought it over and shook his head. "No, I don't reckon I will."

"Any particular reason?"

"Don't look to me hardly like playin' the game. I'm ferninst West every turn of the road. He's crooked as a dog's hind laig. But it wouldn't be right square for me to spy on him. Different with you. That's what you're paid for. You're out to run him down any way you can. He knows that. It's a game of hide an' go seek between you an' him. Best man wins."

The red-coat assented at once. "Right you are. I'll get some one else." He rose to go. "See you later maybe."

Tom nodded. "Sorry I can't oblige, but you see how it is."

"Quite. I oughtn't to have asked you."

Beresford strode briskly out of the store.

Through the window Morse saw him a moment later in whispered conversation with Onistah. They were standing back of an outlying shed, in such a position that they could not be seen from the road.

CHAPTER XIII

The Constable Bores Through Difficulties

THE early Northern dusk was falling when Beresford dropped into the store again. Except for two halfbreeds and the clerk dickering at the far end of the building over half a dozen silver fox furs Morse had the place to himself.

Yet the officer took the precaution to lower his voice. "I want an auger and a wooden plug the same size. Get 'em to me without anybody knowing it."

The manager of the C. N. Morse & Company Northern Stores presently shoved across the counter to him a gunnysack with a feed of oats. "Want it charged to the Force, I reckon?"

"Yes."

"Say, constable, I wancha to look at these moccasins I'm

orderin' for the Inspector. Is this what he wants? Or isn't it?"

Tom led the way into his office. He handed the shoe to Beresford. "What's doin'?" he asked swiftly, between sentences.

The soldier inspected the footwear. "About right, I'd say. Thought you'd find what you were looking for. A fellow usually does when he goes at it real earnest."

The eyes in the brown face were twinkling merrily.

"Findin' the goods is one thing. Gettin' 'em's quite another," Tom suggested.

The voice of one of the trappers rose in protest. "By gar, it iss what you call dirt cheap. I make you a present. V'la!"

"Got to bore through difficulties," Beresford said. "Then you're liable to bump into disappointment. But you can't ever tell till you try."

His friend began to catch the drift of the officer's purpose. He was looking for a liquor shipment, *and he had bought an auger to bore through difficulties.*

Tom's eyes glowed. "Come over to the storeroom an' take a look at my stock. Want you to see I'm gonna have these moccasins made from good material."

They kept step across the corral, gay, light-hearted sons of the frontier, both hard as nails, packed muscles rippling like those of forest panthers. Their years added would not total more than twoscore and five, but life had taken hold of them young and trained them to its purposes, had shot them through and through with hardihood and endurance and the cool prevision that forestalls disaster.

"I'm in on this," the Montanan said.

"Meaning?"

"That I buy chips, take a hand, sit in, deal cards."

The level gaze of the police officer studied him speculatively. "Now why this change of heart?"

"You get me wrong. I'm with you to a finish in puttin' West and Whaley out of business. They're a hell-raisin' outfit, an' this country'll be well rid of 'em. Only thing is I wanta play my cards above the table. I couldn't spy on these men. Leastways, it didn't look quite square to me. But this is a bronc of another color. Lead me to that trouble you was promisin' a while ago."

Beresford led him to it, by way of a rain-washed gully, up which they trod their devious path slowly and without noise. From the gully they snaked through the dry grass to a small ditch that had been built to drain the camping-ground during spring freshets. This wound into the midst of the wagon train encampment.

The plainsmen crept along the dry ditch with laborious care. They advanced no single inch without first taking care to move aside any twig the snapping of which might betray them.

From the beginning of the adventure until its climax no word was spoken. Beresford led, the trader followed at his heels.

The voices of men drifted to them from a camp-fire in the shelter of the wagons. There were, Tom guessed, about four of them. Their words came clear through the velvet night. They talked the casual elemental topics common to their kind.

There was a moonlit open space to be crossed. The constable took it swiftly with long strides, reached a wagon, and dodged under it. His companion held to the cover of the ditch. He was not needed closer.

The officer lay flat on his back, set the point of the auger to the woodwork of the bed, and began to turn. Circles and half-circles of shavings flaked out and fell upon him. He worked steadily. Presently the resistance of the wood ceased. The bit had eaten its way through.

Beresford withdrew the tool and tried again, this time a few inches from the hole he had made. The pressure lessened as before, but in a second or two the steel took a fresh hold. The handle moved slowly and steadily.

A few drops of moisture dripped down, then a small stream. The constable held his hand under this and tasted the flow. It was rum.

Swiftly he withdrew the bit, fitted the plug into the hole, and pushed it home.

He crawled from under the wagon, skirted along the far side of it, ran to the next white-topped vehicle, and plumped out upon the campers with a short, sharp word of command.

"Up with your hands! Quick!"

For a moment the surprised quartette were too amazed to obey.

"What in Halifax—?"

"Shove 'em up!" came the crisp, peremptory order.

Eight hands wavered skyward.

"Is this a hold-up—or what?" one of the teamsters wanted to know sulkily.

"Call it whatever you like. You with the fur cap hitch up the mules to the second wagon. Don't make a mistake and try for a getaway. You'll be a dead smuggler."

The man hesitated. Was this red-coat alone?

Tom strolled out of the ditch, a sawed-off shotgun under his arm. "I judge you bored through your difficulties, constable," he said cheerfully.

"Through the bed of the wagon and the end of a rum keg. Stir your stumps, gentlemen of the whiskey-running brigade. We're on the way to Fort Edmonton if it suits you."

If it did not suit them, they made no audible protest of disagreement. Growls were their only comment when, under direction of Beresford, the Montanan stripped them of their weapons and kept guard on the fur-capped man—his name appeared to be Lemoine—while the latter brought the mules to the wagon pointed out by the officer.

"Hook 'em," ordered Morse curtly.

The French-Indian trapper hitched the team to the wagon. Presently it moved beyond the circle of firelight into the darkness. Morse sat beside the driver, the short-barreled weapon across his knees. Three men walked behind the wagon. A fourth, in the uniform of the North-West Mounted, brought up the rear on horseback.

CHAPTER XIV

Scarlet-Coats In Action

WHEN Bully West discovered that such part of the cargo of wet goods as was in wagon number two had disappeared and along with it the four mule-skinners, his mind jumped to an instant conclusion. That it happened to be the wrong one was natural enough to his sulky, suspicious mind.

"Goddlemighty, they've double-crossed us," he swore to his partner, with an explosion of accompanying profanity. "Figure on cleanin' up on the goods an' cuttin' back to the States. That's what they aim to do. Before I can head 'em off. Me, I'll show 'em they can't play monkey tricks on Bully West."

This explanation did not satisfy Whaley. The straight black line of the brows above the cold eyes met in frowning thought.

"I've got a hunch you're barkin' up the wrong tree," he lisped with a shrug of shoulders.

Voice and gesture were surprising in that they were expressions of this personality totally unexpected. Both were almost womanlike in their delicacy. They suggested the purr and soft padding of a cat, an odd contradiction to the white, bloodless face with the inky brows. The eyes of "Poker" Whaley could throw fear into the most reckless bull-whacker on the border. They held fascinating and sinister possibilities of evil.

"Soon see. We'll hit the trail right away after them," Bully replied.

Whaley's thin lip curled. He looked at West as though he read to the bottom of that shallow mind and meant to make the most of his knowledge.

"Yes," he murmured, as though to himself. "Some one ought to stay with the rest of the outfit, but I reckon I'd better go along. Likely you couldn't handle all of 'em if they showed fight."

West's answer was a roar of outraged vanity. "Me! Not round up them tame sheep. I'll drive 'em back with their tongues hangin' out. Understand?"

At break of day he was in the saddle. An experienced trailer, West found no difficulty in following the wagon tracks. No attempt had been made to cover the flight. The whiskey-runner could trace at a road gait the narrow tracks along the winding road.

The country through which he traveled was the borderland between the plains and the great forests that rolled in unbroken stretch to the frozen North. Sometimes he rode over undulating prairie. Again he moved through strips of woodland or skirted beautiful lakes from the reedy edges of which ducks or geese rose whirring at his approach. A pair of coyotes took one long look at him and skulked into a ravine. Once a great moose started from a thicket of willows and galloped over a hill.

West heeded none of this. No joy touched him as he breasted summits and looked down on wide sweeps of forest and rippling water. The tracks of the wheel rims engaged entirely his sulky, lowering gaze. If the brutish face reflected his thoughts, they must have been far from pleasant ones.

The sun flooded the landscape, climbed the sky vault, slid toward the horizon. Dusk found him at the edge of a wooded lake.

He looked across and gave a subdued whoop of triumph. From the timber on the opposite shore came a tenuous smoke skein. A man came to the water with a bucket, filled it, and disappeared in the woods. Bully West knew he had caught up with those he was tracking.

The smuggler circled the lower end of the lake and rode through the timber toward the smoke. At a safe distance he dismounted, tied the horse to a young pine, and carefully examined his rifle. Very cautiously he stalked the camp, moving toward it with the skill and the stealth of a Sarcee scout.

Camp had been pitched in a small open space surrounded by bushes. Through the thicket, on the south side, he picked a way, pushing away each sapling and weed noiselessly to make room for the passage of his huge body. For such a bulk of a figure he moved lightly. Twice he stopped by reason of the crackle of a snapping twig, but no sign of alarm came from his prey.

They sat hunched—the four of them—before a blazing log fire, squatting on their heels in the comfortable fashion of the outdoors man the world over. Their talk was fragmentary. None gave any sign of alertness toward any possible approaching danger.

No longer wary, West broke through the last of the bushes and straddled into the open.

"Well, boys, hope you got some grub left for yore boss," he jeered, triumph riding voice and manner heavily.

He waited for the startled dismay he expected. None came. The drama of the moment did not meet his expectation. The teamsters looked at him, sullenly, without visible fear or amazement. None of them rose or spoke.

Sultry anger began to burn in West's eyes. "Thought you'd slip one over on the old man, eh? Thought you could put over a raw steal an' get away with it. Well, lemme tell you where you get off at. I'm gonna whale every last one of you to a frazzle. With a big club. An' I'm gonna drive you back to Faraway like a bunch of whipped curs. Understand?"

Still they said nothing. It began to penetrate the thick skull of the trader that there was something unnatural about their crouched silence. Why didn't they try to explain? Or make a break for a getaway?

He could think of nothing better to say, after a volley of curses, than to repeat his threat. "A thunderin' good wallopin', first off. Then we hit the trail together, you-all an' me."

From out of the bushes behind him a voice came. "That last's a good prophecy, Mr. West. It'll be just as you say."

The big fellow wheeled, the rifle jumping to his shoulder. Instantly he knew he had been tricked, led into a trap. They

73

must have heard him coming, whoever they were, and left his own men for bait.

From the other side two streaks of scarlet launched themselves at him. West turned to meet them. A third flash of red dived for his knees. He went down as though hit by a battering ram.

But not to stay down. The huge gorilla-shaped figure struggled to its feet, fighting desperately to throw off the three redcoats long enough to drag out a revolver. He was like a bear surrounded by leaping dogs. No sooner had he buffeted one away than the others were dragging him down. Try as he would, he could not get set. The attackers always staggered him before he could quite free himself for action. They swarmed all over him, fought close to avoid his sweeping lunges, hauled him to his knees by sheer weight of the pack.

Lemoine flung one swift look around and saw that his captors were very busy. Now if ever was the time to take a hand in the mêlée. Swiftly he rose. He spoke a hurried word in French.

"One moment, s'il vous plaît." From the bushes another man had emerged, one not in uniform. Lemoine had forgotten him. "Not your fight. Better keep out," he advised, and pointed the suggestion with a short-barreled shotgun.

The trapper looked at him. "Is it that this iss your fight, Mistair Morse?" he demanded.

"Fair enough. I'll keep out too."

The soldiers had West down by this time. They were struggling to handcuff him. He fought furiously, his great arms and legs threshing about like flails. Not till he had worn himself out could they pinion him.

Beresford rose at last, the job done. His coat was ripped almost from one shoulder. "My word, he's a whale of an animal," he panted. "If I hadn't chanced to meet you boys he'd have eaten me alive."

The big smuggler struggled for breath. When at last he found words, it was for furious and horrible curses.

Not till hours later did he get as far as a plain question. "What does this mean? Where are you taking me, you damned spies?" he roared.

Beresford politely gave him information. "To the penitentiary, I hope, Mr. West, for breaking Her Majesty's revenue laws."

CHAPTER XV
Kissing Day

ALL week Jessie and her foster-mother Matapi-Koma had been busy cooking and baking for the great occasion. Fergus had brought in a sack full of cottontails and two skunks. To these his father had added the smoked hindquarters of a young buffalo, half a barrel of dried fish, and fifty pounds of pemmican. For Angus liked to dispense hospitality in feudal fashion.

Ever since Jessie had opened her eyes at the sound of Matapi-Koma's "Koos koos kwa" (Wake up!), in the predawn darkness of the wintry Northern morn, she had heard the crunch of snow beneath the webs of the footmen and the runners of the sleds. For both full-blood Crees and half-breeds were pouring into Faraway to take part in the festivities of Ooche-me-gou-kesigow (Kissing Day).

The traders at the post and their families would join in the revels. With the exception of Morse, they had all taken Indian wives, in the loose marriage of the country, and for both business and family reasons they maintained a close relationship with the natives. Most of their children used the mother tongue, though they could make shift to express themselves in English. In this respect as in others the younger McRaes were superior. They talked English well. They could read and write. Their father had instilled in them a reverence for the Scriptures and some knowledge of both the Old and New Testaments. It was his habit to hold family prayers every evening. Usually half a dozen guests were present at these services in addition to his immediate household.

With the Indians came their dogs, wolfish creatures, prick-eared and sharp-muzzled, with straight, bristling hair. It was twenty below zero, but the gaunt animals neither sought nor were given shelter. They roamed about in front of the fort stockade, snapping at each other or galloping off on rabbit hunts through the timber.

The custom was that on this day the braves of the tribe

kissed every woman they met in token of friendship and good-will. To fail of saluting one, young or old, was a breach of good manners. Since daybreak they had been marching in to Angus McRae's house and gravely kissing his wife and daughter.

Jessie did not like it. She was a fastidious young person. But she could not escape without mortally offending the solemn-eyed warriors who offered this evidence of their esteem. As much as possible she contrived to be busy upstairs, but at least a dozen times she was fairly cornered and made the best of it.

At dinner she and the other women of the fort waited on their guests and watched prodigious quantities of food disappear rapidly. When the meal was ended, the dancing began. The Crees shuffled around in a circle, hopping from one foot to the other in time to the beating of a skin drum. The half-breeds and whites danced the jigs and reels the former had brought with them from the Red River country. They took the floor in couples. The men did double-shuffles and cut pigeon wings, moving faster and faster as the fiddler quickened the tune till they gave up at last exhausted. Their partners performed as vigorously, the moccasined feet twinkling in and out so fast that the beads flashed.

Because it was the largest building in the place, the dance was held in the C. N. Morse & Company store. From behind the counter Jessie applauded the performers. She did not care to take part herself. The years she had spent at school had given her a certain dignity.

A flash of scarlet caught her eye. Two troopers of the Mounted Police had come into the room and one of them was taking off his fur overcoat. The trim, lean-flanked figure and close-cropped, curly head she recognized at once with quickened pulse. When Winthrop Beresford came into her neighborhood, Jessie McRae's cheek always flew a flag of greeting.

A squaw came up to the young soldier and offered innocently her face for a kiss.

Beresford knew the tribal custom. It was his business to help establish friendly relations between the Mounted and the natives. He kissed the wrinkled cheek gallantly. A second dusky lady shuffled forward, and after her a third. The constable did his duty.

His roving eye caught Jessie's, and found an imp of mischief dancing there. She was enjoying the predicament in which he found himself. Out of the tail of that same eye he

76

discovered that two more flat-footed squaws were headed in his direction.

He moved briskly across the floor to the counter, vaulted it, and stood beside Jessie. She was still laughing at him.

"You're afraid," she challenged. "You ran away."

A little devil of adventurous mirth was blown to flame in him. "I saw another lady, lonely and unkissed. The Force answers every call of distress."

Her chin tilted ever so little as she answered swiftly.

> "He who will not when he may,
> When he will he shall have nay."

Before she had more than time to guess that he would really dare, the officer leaned forward and kissed the girl's dusky cheek.

The color flamed into it. Jessie flung a quick, startled look at him.

"Kissing Day, Sleeping Dawn," he said, smiling.

Instantly she followed his lead. "Sleeping Dawn hopes that the Great Spirit will give to the soldier of the Great Mother across the seas many happy kissing days in his life."

"And to you. Will you dance with me?"

"Not to-day, thank you. I don't jig in public."

"I was speaking to Miss McRae and not to Sleeping Dawn, and I was asking her to waltz with me."

She accepted him as a partner and they took the floor. The other dancers by tacit consent stepped back to watch this new step, so rhythmic, light, and graceful. It shocked a little their sense of fitness that the man's arm should enfold the maiden, but they were full of lively curiosity to see how the dance was done.

A novel excitement pulsed through the girl's veins. It was not the kiss alone, though that had something to do with the exhilaration that flooded her. Formally his kiss had meant only a recognition of the day. Actually it had held for both of them a more personal significance, the swift outreach of youth to youth. But the dance was an escape. She had learned at Winnipeg the waltz of the white race. No other girl at Faraway knew the step. She chose to think that the constable had asked her because this stressed the predominance of her father's blood in her. It was a symbol to all present that the ways of the Anglo-Saxon were her ways.

She had the light, straight figure, the sense of rhythm, the instinctively instant response of the born waltzer. As she glided over the floor in the arms of Beresford, the girl knew pure happiness. Not till he was leading her back to the counter did she wake from the spell the music and motion had woven over her.

A pair of cold eyes in a white, bloodless face watched her beneath thin black brows. A shock ran through her, as though she had been drenched with icy water. She shivered. There was a sinister menace in that steady, level gaze. More than once she had felt it. Deep in her heart she knew, from the world-old experience of her sex, that the man desired her, that he was biding his time with the patience and the ruthlessness of a panther. "Poker" Whaley had in him a power of dangerous evil notable in a country where bad men were not scarce.

The officer whispered news to Jessie. "Bully West broke jail two weeks ago. He killed a guard. We're here looking for him."

"He hasn't been here. At least I haven't heard it," she answered hurriedly.

For Whaley, in his slow, feline fashion, was moving toward them.

Bluntly the gambler claimed his right. "Ooche-me-gou-kesigow," he said.

The girl shook her head. "Are you a Cree, Mr. Whaley?"

For that he had an answer. "Is Beresford?"

"Mr. Beresford is a stranger. He didn't know the custom —that it doesn't apply to me except with Indians. I was taken by surprise."

Whaley was a man of parts. He had been educated for a priest, but had kicked over the traces. There was in him too much of the Lucifer for the narrow trail the father of a parish must follow.

He bowed. "Then I must content myself with a dance."

Jessie hesitated. It was known that he was a libertine. The devotion of his young Cree wife was repaid with sneers and the whiplash. But he was an ill man to make an enemy of. For her family's sake rather than her own she yielded reluctantly.

Though a heavy-set man, he was an excellent waltzer. He moved evenly and powerfully. But in the girl's heart resentment flamed. She knew he was holding her too close to him, taking advantage of her modesty in a way she could not escape without public protest.

"I'm faint," she told him after they had danced a few minutes.

"Oh, you'll be all right," he said, still swinging her to the music.

78

She stopped. "No, I've had enough." Jessie had caught sight of her brother Fergus at the other end of the room. She joined him. Tom Morse was standing by his side.

Whaley nodded indifferently toward the men and smiled at Jessie, but that cold lip smile showed neither warmth nor friendliness. "We'll dance again—many times," he said.

The girl's eyes flashed. "We'll have to ask Mrs. Whaley about that. I don't see her here to-night. I hope she's quite well."

It was impossible to tell from the chill, expressionless face of the squaw-man whether her barb had stung or not. "She's where she belongs, at home in the kitchen. It's her business to be well. I reckon she is. I don't ask her."

"You're not a demonstrative husband, then?"

"Husband!" He shrugged his shoulders insolently. "Oh, well! What's in a name?"

She knew the convenient code of his kind. They took to themselves Indian wives, with or without some form of marriage ceremony, and flung them aside when they grew tired of the tie or found it galling. There was another kind of squaw-man, the type represented by her father. He had joined his life to that of Matapi-Koma for better or worse until such time as death should separate them.

In Jessie's bosom a generous indignation burned. There was a reason why just now Whaley should give his wife much care and affection. She turned her shoulder and began to talk with Fergus and Tom Morse, definitely excluding the gambler from the conversation.

He was not one to be embarrassed by a snub. He held his ground, narrowed eyes watching her with the vigilant patience of the panther—he sometimes made her think of. Presently he forced a reëntry.

"What's this I hear about Bully West escaping from jail?"

Fergus answered. "Two-three weeks ago. Killed a guard, they say. He was headin' west an' north last word they had of him."

All of them were thinking the same thing, that the man would reach Faraway if he could, lie hidden till he had rustled an outfit, then strike out with a dog team deeper into the Lone Lands.

"Here's wishin' him luck," his partner said coolly.

"All the luck he deserves," amended Morse quietly.

"You can't keep a good man down," Whaley boasted, looking straight at the other Indian trader. "I wouldn't wonder but what he'll pay a few debts when he gets here."

Tom smiled and offered another suggestion. "If he gets here and has time. He'll have to hurry."

His gaze shifted across the room to Beresford, alert, gay, indomitable, and as implacable as fate.

CHAPTER XVI
A Business Deal

IT was thirty below zero. The packed snow crunched under the feet of Morse as he moved down what served Faraway for a main street. The clock in the store registered mid-afternoon, but within a few minutes the sub-Arctic sun would set, night would fall, and aurora lights would glow in the west.

Four false suns were visible around the true one, the whole forming a cross of five orbs. Each of these swam in perpendicular segments of a circle of prismatic colors. Even as the young man looked, the lowest of the cluster lights plunged out of sight. By the time he had reached the McRae house, darkness hung over the white and frozen land.

Jessie opened the door to his knock and led him into the living-room of the family, where also the trapper's household ate and Fergus slept. It was a rough enough place, with its mud-chinked log walls and its floor of whipsawed lumber. But directly opposite the door was a log-piled ~~~ ~~ that radiated comfort and cheerfulness. Buffalo robes served as rugs and upon the walls had been hung furs of silver fox, timber wolves, mink, and beaver. On a shelf was a small library of not more than twenty-five books, but they were ones that only a lover of good reading would have chosen. Shakespeare and Burns held honored places there. Scott's poems and three or four of his novels were in the collection. In worn leather bindings were "Tristram Shandy," and Smollett's "Complete History of England." Bunyan's "Pilgrim's Progress" shouldered Butler's "Hudibras" and Baxter's "The Saint's Everlasting Rest." Into this choice company one frivolous modern novel had stolen its way. "Nicholas Nickleby" had been brought from Winnipeg by Jessie when she returned from school. The girl had read them all from cover to cover, most of them many times. Angus too knew them all, with the exception of the upstart "storybook" written by a London newspaper man of whom he had never before heard.

"I'm alone," Jessie explained. "Father and Fergus have gone out to the traps. They'll not be back till to-morow. Mother's with Mrs. Whaley."

Tom knew that the trader's wife was not well. She was expecting to be confined in a few weeks.

He was embarrassed at being alone with the girl inside the walls of a house. His relations with Angus McRae reached civility, but not cordiality. The stern old Scotchman had never invited him to drop in and call. He resented the fact that through the instrumentality of Morse he had been forced to horsewhip the lass he loved, and the trader knew he was not forgiven his share in the episode and probably never would be. Now Tom had come only because a matter of business had to be settled one way or the other at once.

"Blandoine is leavin' for Whoop-Up in the mornin'. I came to see your father about those robes. If we buy, it'll have to be now. I can send 'em down with Blandoine," he explained.

She nodded, briskly. "Father said you could have them at your price if you'll pay what he asked for those not split. They're good hides—cows and young bulls.[1]

"It's a deal," the fur-trader said promptly. "Glad to get 'em, though I'm payin' all I can afford for the split ones."

"I'll get the key to the storehouse," Jessie said.

She walked out of the room with the springy, feather-footed step that distinguished her among all the women that he knew. In a few moments she was back. Instead of giving him the key, she put it down on the table near his hand.

Beneath the tan the dark blood beat into his face. He knew she had done this in order not to run the risk of touching him.

For a long moment his gaze gripped and held her. Between them passed speech without words. His eyes asked if he were outside the pale completely, if he could never wipe out the memory of that first cruel meeting. Hers answered proudly that, half-breed though she was, he was to her only a

---

[1] A split robe was one cut down the middle and sewn together with sinews. The ones skinned from the animal in a single piece were much more valuable, but the native women usually prepared the hides the other way because of the weight in handling. One of the reasons the Indians gave the missionaries in favor of polygamy was that one wife could not dress a buffalo robe without assistance. The braves themselves did not condescend to menial labor of this kind. (W. M. R.)

wolfer, of less interest than Black, the leader of her father's dog train.

He picked up the key and left, wild thoughts whirling through his mind. He loved her. Of what use was it trying longer to disguise it from himself. Of the inferior blood she might be, yet his whole being went out to her in deep desire. He wanted her for his mate. He craved her in every fiber of his clean, passionate manhood, as he had never before longed for a woman in his life. And she hated him—hated him with all the blazing scorn of a young proud soul whose fine body had endured degradation on his account. He was a leper, to be classed with Bully West.

Nor did he blame her. How could she feel otherwise and hold her self-respect? The irony of it brought a bitter smile to his lips. If she only knew it, the years would avenge her a hundredfold. For he had cut himself off from even the chance of the joy that might have been his.

In the sky an aurora flashed with scintillating splendor. The heavens were aglow with ever-changing bars and columns of colored fire.

Morse did not know it. Not till he had passed a dozen steps beyond a man in heavy furs did his mind register recognition of him as Whaley. He did not even wonder what business was taking the gambler toward Angus McRae's house.

Business obtruded its claims. He arranged with Blandoine to take the robes out with him and walked back to the McRae storehouse. It adjoined the large log cabin where the Scotchman and his family lived.

Blandoine and he went over the robes carefully in order that there should be no mistake as to which ones the trainmaster took. This done, Morse locked the door and handed the key to his companion.

To him there was borne the sound of voices—one low and deep, the other swift and high. He caught no words, but he became aware that a queer excitement tingled through his veins. At the roots of his hair there was an odd, prickling sensation. He could give himself no reason, but some instinct of danger rang in him like a bell. The low bass and the light high treble—they reached him alternately, cutting into each other, over-riding each other, clashing in agitated dissent.

Then—a shrill scream for help!

Morse could never afterward remember opening the door of the log house. It seemed to him that he burst through it like a battering-ram, took the kitchen in two strides, and hurled himself against the sturdy home-made door which led into the living-room.

82

This checked him, for some one had slid into its socket the bar used as a bolt. He looked around the kitchen and found in one swift glance what he wanted. It was a large back log for the fireplace.

With this held at full length under his arm he crashed forward. The wood splintered. He charged again, incited by a second call for succor. This time his attack dashed the bolt and socket from their place. Morse stumbled into the room like a drunken man.

CHAPTER XVII
A Board Creaks

AFTER Morse had closed the door, Jessie listened until the crisp crunch of his footsteps had died away. She subdued an impulse to call him back and put into words her quarrel against him.

From the table she picked up a gun-cover of moose leather she was making and moved to the fireplace. Automatically her fingers fitted into place a fringe of red cloth. (This had been cut from an old petticoat, but the source of the decoration would remain a secret, not on any account to be made known to him who was to receive the gift.) Usually her hands were busy ones, but now they fell away from the work listlessly.

The pine logs crackled, lighting one end of the room and filling the air with aromatic pungency. As she gazed into the red coals her mind was active.

She knew that her scorn of the fur-trader was a fraud. Into her hatred of him she threw an energy always primitive and sometimes savage. But he held her entire respect. It was not pleasant to admit this. Her mind clung to the shadowy excuse that he had been a wolfer, although the Indians looked on him now as a good friend and a trader who would not take advantage of them. Angus McRae himself had said there was no better citizen in the Northland.

No, she could not hold Tom Morse in contempt as she would have liked. But she could cherish her animosity and feed it on memories that scorched her as the whiplash had her smooth and tender flesh. She would never forgive him—never. Not if he humbled himself in the dust.

Toward Angus McRae she held no grudge whatever. He had done only his duty as he saw it. The circumstances had forced his hand, for her word had pledged him to punishment. But this man who had walked into her life so roughly, mastered her by physical force, dragged her to the ignominy of the whip, and afterward had dared to do her a service—when she woke at night and thought of him she still burned with shame and anger. He had been both author and witness of her humiliation.

The girl's reverie stirred reflection of other men, for already she had suitors in plenty. Upon one of them her musing lingered. He had brought to her gifts of the friendly smile, of comradeship, of youth's debonair give-and-take. She did not try to analyze her feeling for Winthrop Beresford. It was enough to know that he had brought into her existence the sparkle of joy.

For life had stalked before her with an altogether too tragic mien. In this somber land men did not laugh much. Their smiles held a background of gravity. Icy winter reigned two thirds of the year and summer was a brief hot blaze following no spring. Nature demanded of those who lived here that they struggle to find subsistence. In that conflict human beings forgot that they had been brought into the world to enjoy it with careless rapture.

Somewhere in the house a board creaked. Jessie heard it inattentively, for in the bitter cold woodwork was always snapping and cracking.

Beresford had offered her a new philosophy of life. She did not quite accept it, yet it fascinated. He believed that the duty of happiness was laid on people as certainly as the duty of honesty. She remembered that once he had said . . .

There had come to her no sound, but Jessie knew that some one had opened the door and was standing on the threshold watching her. She turned her head. Her self-invited guest was Whaley.

Jessie rose. "What do you want?"

She was startled at the man's silent entry, ready to be alarmed if necessary, but not yet afraid. It was as though her thoughts waited for the cue he would presently give. Some instinct for safety made her cautious. She did not tell the free trader that her father and Fergus were away from home.

He looked at her, appraisingly, from head to foot, in such a way that she felt his gaze had stripped her.

"You know what I want. You know what I'm going to get
. . . some day," he purred in his slow, feline way.

She pushed from her mind a growing apprehension.

"Father and Fergus—if you want them—"

"Have I said I wanted them?" he asked. "They're out in
the woods trappin'. I'm not lookin' for them. The two of us'll
be company for each other."

"Go," she said, anger flaring at his insolence. "Go. You've
no business here."

"I'm not here for business, but for pleasure, my dear."

The cold, fishy eyes in his white face gloated. Suddenly she
wanted to scream and pushed back the desire scornfully. If she
did, nobody would hear her. This had to be fought out one to
one.

"Why didn't you knock?" she demanded.

"We'll say I did and that you didn't hear me," he answered
suavely. "What's it matter among friends anyhow?"

"What do you want?" By sheer will power she kept her
voice low.

"Your mother's over at the house. I dropped in to say
she'll probably stay all night."

"Is your wife worse?"

He lifted the black brows that contrasted so sharply with
the pallor of the face. "Really you get ahead of me, my dear.
I don't recall ever getting married."

"That's a hateful thing to say," she flamed, and bit her lower
lip with small white teeth to keep from telling the squaw-man
what she thought of him. The Cree girl he had taken to wife
was going down into the Valley of the Shadow to bear him a
child while he callously repudiated her.

He opened his fur coat and came to the fireplace. "I can
say nicer things—to the right girl," he said, and looked mean-
ingly at her.

"I'll have to go get Susie Lemoine to stay with me," Jessie
said hurriedly. "I didn't know Mother wasn't coming home."

She made a move toward a fur lying across the back of a
chair.

He laid a hand upon her arm. "What's your rush? What are
you dodgin' for, girl? I'm good as Susie to keep the goblins
from gettin' you."

"Don't touch me." Her eyes sparked fire.

"You're mighty high-heeled for a nitchie. I reckon you
forget you're Sleeping Dawn, daughter of a Blackfoot squaw."

"I'm Jessie McRae, daughter of Angus, and if you insult
me, you'll have to settle with him."

He gave a short snort of laughter. "Wake up, girl. What's

the use of foolin' yourself? You're a breed. McRae's tried to forget it and so have you. But all the time you know damn well you're half Injun."

Jessie looked at him with angry contempt, then wheeled for the door.

Whaley had anticipated that and was there before her. His narrowed, covetous eyes held her while one hand behind his back slid the bolt into place.

"Let me out!" she cried.

"Be reasonable. I'm not aimin' to hurt you."

"Stand aside and let me through."

He managed another insinuating laugh. "Have some sense. Quit ridin' that high horse and listen while I talk to you."

But she was frightened by this time as much as she was incensed. A drum of dread was beating in her panicky heart. She saw in his eyes what she had never before seen on a face that looked into hers—though she was to note it often in the dreadful days that followed—the ruthless appetite of a wild beast crouching for its kill.

"Let me go! Let me go!" Her voice was shrilly out of control. "Unbar the door, I tell you!"

"I'm a big man in this country. Before I'm through I'll be head chief among the trappers for hundreds of miles. I'm offerin' you the chance of a lifetime. Throw in with me and you'll ride in your coach at Winnipeg some day." Voice and words were soft and smooth, but back of them Jessie felt the panther couched for its spring.

She could only repeat her demand, in a cry that reached its ictus in a sob.

"If you're dreamin' about that red-coat spy—hopin' he'll marry you after he's played fast and loose with you—why, forget such foolishness. I know his kind. When he's had his fling, he'll go back to his own people and settle down. He's lookin' for a woman, not a wife."

"That's a lie!" she flung out, rage for the moment in ascendent. "Open that door or I'll—"

Swiftly his hand shot forward and caught her wrist. "What'll you do?" he asked, and triumph rode in his eyes.

She screamed. One of his hands clamped down over her mouth, the other went round her waist and drew the slim body to him. She fought, straining from him, throwing back her head in another lifted shriek for help.

As well she might have matched her strength with a buffalo bull. He was still under forty, heavy-set, bones packed with heavy muscles. It seemed to her that all the power of her vital youth vanished and left only limp and flaccid weakness. He snatched her close and kissed the dusky eyes, the soft cheeks, the colorful lips . . .

She became aware that he was holding her from him, listening. There was a crash of wood.

Again her call for help rang out.

Whaley flung her from him. He crouched, every nerve and muscle tense, lips drawn back in a snarl. She saw that in his hand there was a revolver.

Against the door a heavy weight was hurled. The wood burst into splinters as the bolt shot from the socket. Drunkenly a man plunged across the threshold, staggering from the impact of the shock.

CHAPTER XVIII

A Gun Roars

THE two men glared at each other, silently, their faces distorted to gargoyles in the leaping and uncertain light. Wary, vigilant, tense, they faced each other as might jungle tigers waiting for the best moment to attack.

There was a chance for the situation to adjust itself without bloodshed. Whaley could not afford to kill and Morse had no desire to force his hand.

Jessie's fear outran her judgment. She saw the menace of the revolver trained on her rescuer and thought the gambler was about to fire. She leaped for the weapon, and so precipitated what she dreaded.

The gun roared. A bullet flew past Morse and buried itself in a log. Next instant, clinging with both hands to Whaley's wrist, Jessie found herself being tossed to and fro as the man struggled to free his arm. Flung at a tangent against the wall, she fell at the foot of the couch where Fergus slept.

Again the blaze and roar of the revolver filled the room. Morse plunged head down at his enemy, still carrying the log he had used as a battering-ram. It caught the gambler at that point of the stomach known as the solar plexus. Whaley went down and out of consciousness like an ox that has been pole-axed.

Tom picked up the revolver and dropped it into the pocket of his fur coat. He stooped to make sure that his foe was beyond the power of doing damage. Then he lifted Jessie from the corner where she lay huddled.

"Hurt?" he asked.

The girl shuddered. "No. Is he—is he killed?"

"Wind knocked out of him. Nothing more."

"He didn't hit you?"

There was the ghost of a smile in his eyes. "No, I hit him."

"He was horrid. I—I—" Again a little shiver ran through her body. She felt very weak at the knees and caught for a moment at the lapel of his coat to steady herself. Neither of them was conscious of the fact that she was in his arms, clinging to him while she won back self-control.

"It's all right now. Don't worry. Lucky I came back to show Blandoine which furs to take."

"If you hadn't—" She drew a ragged breath that was half a sob.

Morse loved her the more for the strain of feminine hysteria that made her for the moment a soft and tender child to be comforted. He had known her competent, savage, disdainful, one in whom vital and passionate life flowed quick. He had never before seen the weakness in her reaching out to strength. That by sheer luck it was *his* power to which she clung filled him with deep delight.

He began to discount his joy lest she do it instead. His arm fell away from her waist.

"I 'most wrecked the house," he said with a humorous glance at the door. "I don't always bring one o' the walls with me when I come into a room."

"He bolted the door," she explained rather needlessly. "He wouldn't let me out."

"I heard you call," he answered, without much more point.

She glanced at the man lying on the floor. "You don't think he might be—" She stopped, unwilling to use the word.

Tom knelt beside him and felt his heart.

"It's beating," he said. And added quickly, "His eyes are open."

It was true. The cold, fishy eyes had flickered open and were taking stock of the situation. The gambler instantly chose his line of defense. He spoke, presently.

"What in the devil was bitin' you, Morse? Just because I was jokin' the girl, you come rampagin' in and knock me galley west with a big club. I'll not stand for that. Soon as I'm fit to handle myself, you and I'll have a settlement."

"Get up and get out," ordered the younger man.

"When I get good and ready. Don't try to run on me, young fellow. Some other fools have found that dangerous."

Whaley sat up, groaned, and pressed his hands upon the abdomen at the point where he had been struck.

The reddish-brown glint in the eyes of Morse advertised the cold rage of the Montanan. He caught the gambler by the collar and pulled him to his feet.

"Get out, you yellow wolf!" he repeated in a low, savage voice.

The white-faced trader was still wobbly on his feet. He felt both sore and sick at the pit of his stomach, in no mood for any further altercation with this hard-hitting athlete. But he would not go without saving his face.

"I don't know what business you've got to order me out —unless—" His gaze included the girl for a moment, and the insult of his leer was unmistakable.

Morse caught him by the scruff of the neck, ran him out of the room, and flung him down the steps into the road. The gambler tripped on the long buffalo coat he was wearing and rolled over in the snow. Slowly he got to his feet and locked eyes with the other.

Rage almost choked his words. "You'll be sorry for this one o' these days, Morse. I'll get you right. Nobody has ever put one over on Poker Whaley and nobody ever will. Don't forget that."

Tom Morse wasted no words. He stood silently on the steps, a splendid, supple figure of menacing power, and watched his foe pass down the road. There was in him a cruel and passionate desire to take the gambler and break him with his hands, to beat him till he crawled away a weak and wounded creature fit for a hospital. He clamped his teeth hard and fought down the impulse.

Presently he turned and walked slowly back into the house. His face was still set and his hands clenched. He knew that if Whaley had hurt Jessie, he would have killed him with his naked fingers.

"You can't stay here. Where do you want me to take you?" he asked, and his cold hardness reminded her of the Tom Morse who had led her to the whip one other night.

She did not know that inside he was a caldron of emotion and that it was only by freezing himself he could keep down the volcanic eruption.

"I'll go to Susie Lemoine's," she said in a small, obedient voice.

With his hands in his pockets he stood and let her find a fur coat and slip into it. He had a sense of frustration. He wanted to let go of himself and tell all that was in his torrid heart. Instead, he encased himself in ice and drove her farther from him.

They walked down the road side by side, neither of them speaking. She too was a victim of chaotic feeling. It would be long before she could forget how he had broken through the door and saved her.

But she could not find the words to tell him so. They parted at the door of Lemoine's cabin with a chill "Goodnight" that left them both unhappy and dissatisfied.

CHAPTER XIX

"D'You Wonder She Hates Me?"

To Morse came Angus McRae with the right hand of friendship the day after the battle in the log house.

Eyes blue as Highland lochs fastened to those of the fur-trader. "Lad, I canna tell ye what's in my heart. 'The Lord bless thee, and keep thee. The Lord make his face shine upon thee, and be gracious unto thee. The Lord lift up his countenance upon thee, and give thee peace.'"

Tom, embarrassed, made light of the affair. "Lucky I was Johnnie-on-the-Spot."

The old Scot shook his head. "No luck sent ye back to hear the skreigh o' the lass, but the whisper of the guid Father withoot whose permission not even a sparrow falls to the ground. He chose you as the instrument. I'll never be forgettin' what you did for my dawtie, Tom Morse. Jess will have thankit you, but I add mine to hers."

In point of fact Jessie had not thanked him in set words. She had been in too great an agitation of spirit to think of it. But Morse did not say so.

"Oh, that's all right. Any one would have done it. Mighty glad I was near enough. Hope she doesn't feel any worse for the shock."

"Not a bit. I'm here to ask ye to let bygones be bygones. I've nursed a grudge, but, man, it's clean washed oot o' my heart. Here's my hand, if you'll tak it."

Tom did, gladly. He discovered at the same moment that the sun was striking sparks of light from a thousand snow crystals. It was a good world, if one only looked for the evidence of it.

"The latchstring is always oot for you at the hame of Angus McRae. Will you no' drap in for a crack the nicht?" asked the trapper.

"Not to-night. Sometime. I'll see." Tom found himself in the position of one who finds open to him a long-desired pleasure and is too shy to avail himself of it immediately. "Have you seen Whaley yet to-day?" he asked, to turn the subject.

The hunter's lip grew straight and grim. "I have not. He's no' at the store. The clerk says a messenger called for him early this mornin' and he left the clachan at once. Will he be hidin' oot, do you think?"

Tom shook his head. "Not Whaley. He'll bluff it through. The fellow's not yellow. Probably he'll laugh it off and say he was only stealin' a kiss an' that Miss Jessie was silly to make a fuss about it."

"We'll let it go at that—after I've told him publicly what I think o' him."

Where Whaley had been nobody in Faraway knew. When he returned at sunset, he went direct to the store and took off his snowshoes. He was knocking the packed and frozen slush from them at the moment Angus McRae confronted him.

The trader laughed, from the lips, just as Tom had prophesied he would do. "I reckon I owe you an apology, McRae," he said. "That li'l' wild-cat of yours lost her head when I jollied her and Morse broke the door down like the jackass he is."

The dressing-down that Angus McRae gave Whaley is still remembered by one or two old-timers in the Northwest. In crisp, biting words he freed his mind without once lapsing into profanity. He finished with a warning. "Tak tent you never speak to the lass again, or you an' me'll come to grips."

The storekeeper heard him out, a sneering smile on his white face. Inside, he raged with furious anger, but he did not let his feelings come to the surface. He was a man who had the patience to wait for his vengeance. The longer it was delayed, the heavier would it be. A characteristic of his cold, callous temperament was that he took fire slowly, but, once lit, his hate endured like peat coals in a grate. A vain man, his dignity was precious to him. He writhed at the defeat Morse had put upon him, at his failure with Jessie, at the scornful public rebuke of her father. Upon all three of these some day he would work a sweet revenge. Like all gamblers, he followed hunches. Soon, one of these told him, his chance would come. When it did he would make all three of them sweat blood.

Beresford met Tom Morse later in the day. He cocked a whimsical eye at the fur-trader.

"I hear McRae's going to sue you for damages to his house," he said.

"Where did you hear all that?" asked his friend, apparently busy inspecting a half-dozen beaver furs.

"And Whaley, for damages to his internal machinery. Don't you know you can't catapult through a man's tummy with a young pine tree and not injure his physical geography?" the constable reproached.

"When you're through spoofin' me, as you subjects of the Queen call it," suggested Tom.

"Why, then, I'll tell you to keep an eye on Whaley. He doesn't love you a whole lot for what you did, and he's liable to do you up first chance he gets."

"I'm not lookin' for trouble, but if Whaley wants a fight—"

"He doesn't—not your kind of a fight. His idea will be to have you foul before he strikes. Walk with an eye in the back of your head. Sleep with it open. Don't sit at windows after lamps are lit—not without curtains all down. Play all your cards close." The red-coat spoke casually, slapping his boot with a small riding-switch. He was smiling. None the less Tom knew he was in dead earnest.

"Sounds like good advice. I'll take it," the trader said easily. "Anything more on your chest?"

"Why, yes. Where did Whaley go to-day? What called him out of town on a hurry-up trip of a few hours?"

"Don't know. Do you?"

"No, but I'm a good guesser."

"Meanin'?"

"Bully West. Holed up somewhere out in the woods. A fellow came in this morning and got Whaley, who snowshoed back with him at once."

Tom nodded agreement. "Maybeso. Whaley was away five or six hours. That means he probably traveled from eight to ten miles out."

"Question is, in what direction? Nobody saw him go or come—at least, so as to know that he didn't circle round the town and come in from the other side."

"He'll go again, with supplies for West. Watch him."

"I'll do just that."

"He might send some one with them."

"Yes, he might do that," admitted Beresford. "I'll keep an eye on the store and see what goes out. We want West. He's a cowardly murderer—killed the man who trusted him—shot him in the back. This country will be well rid of him when he's hanged for what he did to poor Tim Kelly."

"He's a rotten bad lot, but he's dangerous. Never forget that," warned the fur-buyer. "If he ever gets the drop on you for a moment, you're gone."

"Of course we may be barking up the wrong tree," the officer reflected aloud. "Maybe West isn't within five hundred miles of here. Maybe he headed off another way. But I don't think it. He had to get back to where he was known so as to get an outfit. That meant either this country or Montana. And the word is that he was seen coming this way both at Slide Out and crossing Old Man's River after he made his get-away."

"He's likely figurin' on losin' himself in the North woods."

"My notion, too. Say, Tom, I have an invitation from a young lady for you and me. I'm to bring you to supper, Jessie McRae says. To-night. Venison and sheep pemmican —and real plum pudding, son. You're to smoke the pipe of peace with Angus and warm yourself in the smiles of Miss Jessie and Matapi-Koma. How's the programme suit you?"

Tom flushed. "I don't reckon I'll go," he said after a moment's deliberation.

His friend clapped an affectionate hand on his shoulder. "Cards down, old fellow. Spill the story of this deadly feud between you and Jessie and I'll give you an outside opinion on it."

The Montanan looked at him bleakly. "Haven't you heard? If you haven't, you're the only man in this country that hasn't."

"You mean—about the whipping?" Beresford asked gently.

"That's all," Morse answered bitterly. "Nothing a-tall. I merely had her horsewhipped. You wouldn't think any girl would object to that, would you?"

"I'd like to hear the right of it. How did it happen?"

"The devil was in me, I reckon. We were runnin' across the line that consignment of whiskey you found and destroyed near Whoop-Up. She came on our camp one night, crept up, and smashed some barrels. I caught her. She fought like a wild-cat." Morse pulled up the sleeve of his coat and showed a long, ragged scar on the arm. "Gave me that as a li'l' souvenir to remember her by. You see, she was afraid I'd take her back to camp. So she fought. You know West. I wouldn't have taken her to him."

"What did you do?"

"After I got her down, we came to terms. I was to take her to McRae's camp and she was to be horsewhipped by him. My arm was hurtin' like sin, and I was thinkin' her only a wild young Injun."

"So you took her home?"

"And McRae flogged her. You know him. He's Scotch—and thorough. It was a sickening business. When he got through, he was white as snow. I felt like a murderer. D'you wonder she hates me?"

Beresford's smile was winning. "Is it because she hates you that she wants you to come to supper to-night?"

"It's because she's in debt to me—or thinks she is, for of course she isn't—and wants to pay it and get rid of it as soon as she can. I tell you, Win, she couldn't bear to touch my hand when she gave me the key to the storehouse the other night—laid it down on the table for me to pick up. It has actually become physical with her. She'd shudder if I touched her. I'm not going to supper there. Why should I take advantage of a hold I have on her generosity? No, I'll not go."

And from that position Beresford could not move him.

After supper the constable found a chance to see Jessie alone. She was working over the last touches of the gun-case.

"When it's finished who gets it?" he asked, sitting down gracefully on the arm of a big chair.

She flashed a teasing glance at him. "Who do you think deserves it?"

"I deserve it," he assured her at once. "But it isn't the deserving always who get the rewards in this world. Very likely you'll give it to some chap like Tom Morse."

"Who wouldn't come to supper when we asked him." She lifted steady, inquiring eyes. "What was the real reason he didn't come?"

"Said he couldn't get away from the store because—"

"Yes, I heard that. I'm asking for the real reason, Win."

He gave it. "Tom thinks you hate him and he won't force himself on your generosity."

"Oh!" She seemed to be considering that.

"Do you?"

"Do I what?"

"Hate him."

She felt a flush burning beneath the dusky brown of her cheeks. "If you knew what he'd done to me—"

"Perhaps I do," he said, very gently.

94

Her dark eyes studied him intently. "He told you?"

"No, one hears gossip. He hates himself because of it. Tom's white, Jessie."

"And I'm Indian. Of course that does make a difference. If he'd had a white girl whipped, you couldn't defend him," she flamed.

"You know I didn't mean that, little pal." His sunny smile was disarming. "What I mean is that he's sorry for what he did. Why not give him a chance to be friends?"

"Well, we gave him a chance to-night, didn't we? And he chose not to take it. What do you want me to do—go and thank him kindly for having me whipped?"

Beresford gave up with a shrug. He knew when he had said enough. Some day the seed he had dropped might germinate.

"Wouldn't it be a good idea to work a W. B. on that case?" he asked with friendly impudence. "Then if I lost it, whoever found it could return it."

"I don't give presents to people who lose them," she parried.

Her dancing eyes were very bright as they met his. She loved the trim lines of his clean beautiful youth and the soul expressed by them.

Matapi-Koma waddled into the room and the Mounted Policeman transferred his attention to her. She weighed two hundred twelve pounds, but was not sensitive on the subject. Beresford claimed anxiously that she was growing thin.

The Indian woman merely smiled on him benignantly. She liked him, as all women did. And she hoped that he would stay in the country and marry Sleeping Dawn.

CHAPTER XX

Onistah Reads Sign

McRae fitted Jessie's snowshoes.

"You'll be hame before the dark, lass," he said, a little anxiously.

"Yes, Father."

The hunter turned to Onistah. "She's in your care, lad. Gin the weather changes, or threatens to, let the traps go and strike for the toon. You're no' to tak chances."

"Back assam weputch (very early)," promised the Blackfoot.

He was proud of the trust confided to him. To him McRae was a great man. Among many of the trappers and the free traders the old Scot's word was law. They came to him with their disputes for settlement and abided by his decisions. For Angus was not only the patriarch of the clan, if such a loose confederation of followers could be called a clan; he was esteemed for his goodness and practical common sense.

Onistah's heart swelled with an emotion that was more than vanity. His heart filled with gladness that Jessie should choose him as guide and companion to snowshoe with her out into the white forests where her traps were set. For the young Indian loved her dumbly, without any hope of reward, in much the same way that some of her rough soldiers must have loved Joan of Arc. Jessie was a mistress whose least whim he felt it a duty to obey. He had worshiped her ever since he had seen her, a little eager warm-hearted child, playing in his mother's wigwam. She was as much beyond his reach as the North Star. Yet her swift tender smile was for him just as it was for Fergus.

They shuffled out of the village into the forest that crept up to the settlement on all sides. Soon they were deep in its shadows, pushing along the edge of a muskeg which they skirted carefully in order not to be hampered by its treacherous boggy footing.

Jessie wore a caribou-skin capote with the fur on as a protection against the cold wind. Her moccasins were of smoked moose-skin decorated with the flower-pattern bead embroidery so much in use among the French half-breeds of the North. The socks inside them were of duffle and the leggings of strouds, both materials manufactured for the Hudson's Bay Company for its trappers.

The day was comparatively warm, but the snow was not slushy nor very deep. None the less she was glad when they reached the trapping ground and Onistah called a halt for dinner. She was tired, from the weight of the snow on her shoes, and her feet were blistered by reason of the lacings which cut into the duffle and the tender flesh inside.

Onistah built a fire of poplar, which presently crackled like a battle front and shot red-hot coals at them in an irregular fusillade. Upon this they made tea, heated pemmican and bannocks, and thawed a jar of preserves Jessie had made the previous summer of service berries and wild raspberries. Before it they dried their moccasins, socks, and leggings.

Afterward they separated to make a round of the traps, agreeing to meet an hour and a half later at the place of their dinner camp.

The Blackfoot found one of the small traps torn to pieces, probably by a bear, for he saw its tracks in the snow. He rebuilt the snare and baited it with parts of a rabbit he had shot. In one trap he discovered a skunk and in another a timber wolf. When he came in sight of the rendezvous, he was late.

Jessie was not there. He waited half an hour in growing anxiety before he went to meet her. Night would fall soon. He must find her while it was still light enough to follow her tracks. The disasters that might have fallen upon her crowded his mind. A bear might have attacked her. She might be lost or tangled in the swampy muskeg. Perhaps she had accidentally shot herself.

As swiftly as he could he snowshoed through the forest, following the plain trail she had left. It carried him to a trap from which she had taken prey, for it was newly baited and the snow was sprinkled with blood. Before he reached the second gin, the excitement in him quickened. Some one in snowshoes had cut her path and had deflected to pursue. Onistah knew that the one following was a white man. The points of the shoes toed out. Crees toed in, just the same on webs as in moccasins.

His imagination was active. What white man had any business in these woods? Why should he leave that business to overtake Jessie McRae? Onistah did not quite know why he was worried, but involuntarily he quickened his pace.

Less than a quarter of a mile farther on, he read another chapter of the story written in the trampled snow. There had been a struggle. His mistress had been overpowered. He could see where she had been flung into a white bank and dragged out of it. She had tried to run and had got hardly a dozen yards before recapture. From that point the tracks moved forward in a straight line, those of the smaller webs blotted out by the ones made by the larger. The man was driving the girl before him.

Who was he? Where was he taking her? For what purpose? Onistah could not guess. He knew that McRae had made enemies, as any forceful character on the frontier must. The Scotchman had kicked out lazy ne'er-do-wells from his camp. As a free trader he had matched himself against the Hudson's Bay Company. But of those at war with him few would stoop to revenge themselves on his daughter. The Blackfoot had not heard of the recent trouble between Whaley and the McRaes, nor had the word reached him that Bully West was free again. Wherefore he was puzzled at what the signs on the snow told him.

Yet he knew he had read them correctly. The final proof of it to him was that Jessie broke trail and not the man. If he were a friend he would lead the way. He was at her heels because he wanted to make sure that she did not try to escape or to attack him.

The tracks led down into the muskeg. It was spitting snow, but he had no difficulty in seeing where the trail led from hummock to hummock in the miry earth. The going here was difficult, for the thick moss was full of short, stiff brush that caught the webbed shoes and tripped the traveler. It was hard to find level footing. The mounds were uneven, and more than once Onistah plunged knee-deep from one into the swamp.

He crossed the muskeg and climbed an ascent into the woods, swinging sharply to the right. There was no uncertainty as to the direction of the tracks in the snow. If they veered for a few yards, it was only to miss a tree or to circle down timber. Whoever he might be, the man who had taken Jessie prisoner knew exactly where he was going.

The Blackfoot knew by the impressions of the webs that he was a large, heavy man. Once or twice he saw stains of tobacco juice on the snow. The broken bits of a whiskey-bottle flung against a tree did not tend to reassure him.

He saw smoke. It came from a tangle of undergrowth in a depression of the forest. Very cautiously, with the patience of his race, he circled round the cabin through the timber and crept up to it on hands and knees. Every foot of the way he took advantage of such cover as was to be had.

The window was a small, single-paned affair built in the end opposite the door. Onistah edged close to it and listened. He heard the drone of voices, one heavy and snarling, another low and persuasive.

His heart jumped at the sound of a third voice, a high-pitched treble. He would have known it among a thousand. It had called to him in the swirl of many a wind-swept storm. He had heard it on the long traverse, in the stillness of the lone night, at lakeside camps built far from any other human being. His imagination had heard it on the summer breeze as he paddled across a sun-drenched lake in his birch-bark canoe.

The Blackfoot raised his head till he could look through the window.

Jessie McRae sat on a stool facing him. Two men were in the room. One strode heavily up and down while the other watched him warily.

CHAPTER XXI

On The Frontier Of Despair

THE compulsion of life had denied Jessie the niceness given girls by the complexities of modern civilization. She had been brought up close to raw stark nature. The habits of animals were familiar to her and the vices of the biped man.

A traveler in the sub-Arctic is forced by the deadly cold of the North into a near intimacy of living with his fellows. Jessie had more than once taken a long sled journey with her father. On one occasion she had slept in a filthy Indian wigwam with a dozen natives all breathing the same foul, unventilated air. Again she had huddled up against the dogs, with her father and two French half-breeds, to keep in her the spark of life a blizzard's breath was trying to blow out.

On such a trip some of the common decencies of existence are dropped. The extreme low temperature makes it impossible for one to wash either face or hands without the skin chapping and breaking. Food at which one would revolt under other circumstances is devoured eagerly.

Jessie was the kind of girl such a life had made her, with modifications in the direction of fineness induced by McRae's sturdy character, her schooling at Winnipeg, and the higher plane of the family standard. As might have been expected, she had courage, energy, and that quality of decisive action bred by primitive conditions.

But she had retained, too, a cleanness of spirit hardly to be looked for in such a primeval daughter of Eve. Her imagination and her reading had saved the girl's sweet modesty. A certain detachment made it possible for her to ignore the squalor of the actual and see it only as a surface triviality, to let her mind dwell in inner concepts of goodness and beauty while bestiality crossed the path she trod.

So when she found in one of the gins a lynx savage with

the pain of bruised flesh and broken bone snapped by the jaws of the trap, the girl did what needed to be done swiftly and with a minimum of reluctance.

She was close to the second trap when the sound of webs slithering along the snow brought her up short. Her first thought was that Onistah had changed his mind and followed her, but as soon as the snowshoer came out of the thick timber, she saw that he was not an Indian.

He was a huge man, and he bulked larger by reason of the heavy furs that enveloped him. His rate of travel was rapid enough, but there was about the gait an awkward slouch that reminded her of a grizzly. Some sullenness of temperament seemed to find expression in the fellow's movements.

The hood of his fur was drawn well forward over the face. He wore blue glasses, as a protection against snow-blindness apparently. Jessie smiled, judging him a tenderfoot; for except in March and April there is small danger of the sun glare which destroys sight. Yet he hardly looked like a newcomer to the North. For one thing he used the web shoes as an expert does. Before he stopped beside her, she was prepared to revise a too hasty opinion.

Jessie recoiled at the last moment, even before she recognized him. It was too late to take precautions now. He caught her by the wrist and tore off his glasses, at the same time shaking back the hood.

"Glad to death to meet up with you, missie," he grinned evilly through broken, tobacco-stained teeth.

The blood drenched out of her heart. She looked at the man, silent and despairing. His presence here could mean to her nothing less than disaster. The girl's white lips tried to frame words they could not utter.

"Took by surprise, ain't you?" he jeered. "But plumb pleased to see old Bully West again, eh? It's a damn long lane that ain't got a crook in it somewheres. An' here we are at the turn together, jus' you 'n' me, comfy, like I done promised it would be when I last seen you."

She writhed in a swift, abortive attempt to break his hold.

He threw back his head in a roar of laughter, then with a twist of his fingers brought his captive to her knees.

Sharp teeth flashed in a gleam of white. He gave a roar of pain and tore away his hand. She had bit him savagely in the wrist, as she had once done with another man on a memorable occasion.

"Goddlemighty!" he bellowed. "You damn li'l hellcat!"

She was on her feet and away instantly. But one of the snowshoes had come off in the struggle. At each step she took the left foot plunged through the white crust and impeded progress.

In a dozen strides he had reached her. A great arm swung round and buffeted the runner on the side of the head. The blow lifted the girl from her feet and flung her into a drift two yards away.

She looked up, dazed from the shock. The man was standing over her, a huge, threatening, ill-shaped Colossus.

"Get up!" he ordered harshly, and seized her by the shoulder.

She found herself on her feet, either because she had risen or because he had jerked her up. A ringing in the head and a nausea made for dizziness.

"I'll learn you!" he exploded with curses. "Try that again an' I'll beat yore head off. You're Bully West's woman, un'erstand? When I say 'Come!' step lively. When I say 'Go!' get a move on you."

"I'll not." Despite her fear she faced him with spirit. "My friends are near. They'll come and settle with you for this."

He put a check on his temper. Very likely what she said was true. It was not reasonable to suppose that she was alone in the forest many miles from Faraway. She had come, of course, to look at the traps, but some one must have accompanied her. Who? And how many? The skulking caution of his wild-beast nature asserted itself. He had better play safe. Time enough to tame the girl when he had her deep in the Lone Lands far from any other human being except himself. Just now the first need was to put many miles between them and the inevitable pursuit.

"Come," he said. "We'll go."

She started back for the snowshoe that had been torn off. Beside it lay her rifle. If she could get hold of it again—

The great hulk moved beside her, his thumb and fingers round the back of her neck. Before they reached the weapon, he twisted her aside so cruelly that a flame of pain ran down her spine. She cried out.

He laughed as he stooped for the gun and the web. "Don' play none o' yore monkey tricks on Bully West. He knew it all 'fore you was born."

The pressure of his grip swung Jessie to the left. He gave her a push that sent her reeling and flung at her the snowshoe.

"Hump yoreself now."

She knelt and adjusted the web. She would have fought if there had been the least chance of success. But there was none. Nor could she run away. The fellow was a callous, black-hearted ruffian. He would shoot her down rather than see her

101

escape. If she became stubborn and refused to move, he would cheerfully torture her until she screamed with agony. There was nothing he would like better. No, for the present she must take orders.

"Hit the trail, missie. Down past that big tree," he snapped.

"Where are you taking me?"

"Don't ask me questions. Do like I tell you."

The girl took one look at his heavy, brutal face and did as she was told. Onistah would find her. When she did not show up at the rendezvous, he would follow her trail and discover that something was amiss. Good old Onistah never had failed her. He was true as tried steel and in all the North woods there was no better tracker.

There would be a fight. If West saw him first, he would shoot the Blackfoot at sight. She did not need to guess that. He would do it for two reasons. The first was the general one that he did not want any of her friends to know where he was. The more specific one was that he already had a grudge against the young Indian that he would be glad to pay once for all.

Jessie's one hope was that Onistah would hasten to the rescue. Yet she dreaded the moment of his coming. He was a gentle soul, one of Father Giguère's converts. It was altogether likely that he would walk into the camp of the escaped convict openly and become a victim of the murderer's guile. Onistah did not lack courage. He would fight if he had to do so. Indeed, she knew that he would go through fire to save her. But bravery was not enough. She could almost have wished that her foster-brother was as full of devilish treachery as the huge ape-man slouching at her heels. Then the chances of the battle would be more even.

The desperado drove her down into the muskeg, directing the girl's course with a flow of obscene and ribald profanity.

It is doubtful if she heard him. As her lithe, supple limbs carried her from one moss hump to another, she was busy with the problem of escape. She must get away soon. Every hour increased the danger. The sun would sink shortly. If she were still this ruffian's prisoner when the long Arctic night fell, she would suffer the tortures of the damned. She faced the fact squarely, though her cheeks blanched at the prospect and the heart inside her withered.

From the sloping side of a hummock her foot slipped and she slid into the icy bog to her knees. Within a few minutes duffles and leggings were frozen and she was suffering at each step.

Out of the muskeg they came into the woods. A flake of

snow fell on Jessie's cheek and chilled her blood. For she knew that if it came on to snow before Onistah took the trail or even before he reached the place to which West was taking her, the chances of a rescue would be very much diminished. A storm would wipe out the tracks they had made.

"Swing back o' the rock and into the brush," West growled. Then, as she took the narrow trail through the brush that had grown up among half a dozen small down trees, he barked a question: "Whadjasay yore Injun name was?"

"My name is Jessie McRae," she answered with a flash of angry pride. "You know who I am—the daughter of Angus McRae. And if you do me any harm, he'll hunt you down and kill you like a wolf."

He caught her by the arm and whirled the girl round. His big yellow canines snapped like tusks and he snarled at her through clenched jaws. "Did you hear yore master's voice? I said, what was yore squaw name?"

She almost shrieked from the pain of his fingers' savage clutch into her flesh. The courage died out of her arteries.

"Sleeping Dawn they called me."

"Too long," he pronounced. "I'll call you Dawn." The sight of her terror of him, the foretaste of the triumph he was to enjoy, restored him for a moment to a brutal good-humor. "An' when I yell 'Dawn' at you o' mornin's, it'll be for you to hump yoreself an' git up to build the fires and rustle breakfast. I'll treat you fine if you behave, but if you git sulky, you'll taste the dog-whip. I'm boss. You'll have a heluva time if you don't come runnin' when I snap my fingers. Un'erstand?"

She broke down in a wailing appeal to whatever good there was in him. "Let me go back to Father! I know you've broke prison. If you're good to me, he'll help you escape. You know he has friends everywhere. They'll hide you from the redcoats. He'll give you an outfit to get away—money—anything you want. Oh, let me go, and—and—"

He grinned, and the sight of his evil mirth told her she had failed.

"Didn't I tell you I'd git you right some day? Didn't I promise Angus McRae I'd pay him back aplenty for kickin' me outa his hide camp? Ain't you the li'l' hell-cat that busted my whiskey-kegs, that ran to the red-coat spy an' told him where the cache was, that shot me up when I set out to dry-gulch him, as you might say? Where do you figure you got a license to expect Bully West to listen to Sunday-school pap about being good to you? You're my squaw, an' lucky at that you got a real two-fisted man. Hell's hinges! What's eatin' you?"

"Never!" she cried. "It's true what I told you once. I'd rather die. Oh, if you've got a spark of manhood in you, don't make me kill myself. I'm just a girl. If I ever did you wrong, I'm sorry. I'll make it right. My father—"

"Listen." His raucous voice cut through her entreaties. "I've heard more'n plenty about McRae. All I want o' him is to get a bead on him once with a rifle. Get me? Now this other talk—about killin' yoreself—nothin' to it a-tall. Go to it if tha's how you feel. Yore huntin'-knife's right there in yore belt." He reached forward and plucked it from its sheath, then handed it to her blade first, stepping back a pace at once to make sure she did not use it on him. "You got yore chance now. Kill away. I'll stand right here an' see nobody interferes with you."

She shifted the knife and gripped the handle. A tumult seethed in her brain. She saw nothing but that evil, grinning face, hideous and menacing. For a moment murder boiled up in her, red-hot and sinister. If she could kill him now as he stood jeering at her—drive the blade into that thick bull neck. . . .

The madness passed. She could not do it even if it were within her power. The urge to kill was not strong enough. It was not overwhelming. And in the next thought she knew, too, that she could not kill herself either. The blind need to live, the animal impulse of self-preservation, at whatever cost, whatever shame, was as yet more powerful than the horror of the fate impending.

She flung the knife down into the snow in a fury of disgust and self-contempt.

His head went back in a characteristic roar of revolting mirth. He had won. Bully West knew how to conquer 'em, no matter how wild they were.

With feet dragging, head drooped, and spirits at the zero hour, Jessie moved down a ravine into sight of a cabin. Smoke rose from the chimney languidly.

"Home," announced West.

To the girl, at the edge of desperation, that log house appeared as the grave of her youth. All the pride and glory and joy that had made life so vital a thing were to be buried here. When next she came out into the sunlight she would be a broken creature—the property of this horrible caricature of a man.

Her captor opened the door and pushed the girl inside.

She stood on the threshold, eyes dilating, heart suddenly athrob with hope.

A man sitting on a stool before the open fire turned his head to see who had come in.

CHAPTER XXII

"My Damn Pretty Li'l' High-Steppin' Squaw"

THE man on the stool was Whaley.

One glance at the girl and one at West's triumphant gargoyle grin was enough. He understood the situation better than words could tell it.

To Jessie, at this critical moment of her life, even Whaley seemed a God-send. She pushed across the room awkwardly, not waiting to free herself of the webs packed with snow. In the dusky eyes there was a cry for help.

"Save me from him!" she cried simply, as a child might have done. "You will, won't you?"

The black eyebrows in the cold, white face drew to a line. The gambler's gaze, expressionless as a blank wall, met hers steadily.

"Why don't you send for your friend Morse?" he asked. "He's in that business. I ain't."

It was as though he had struck her in the face. The eyes that clung to his were horror-filled. Did there really live men so heartless that they would not lift a hand to snatch a child from a ferocious wolf?

West's laughter barked out, rapacious and savage. "She's mine, jus' like I said she'd be. My damn pretty li'l' high-steppin' squaw."

His partner looked at him bleakly. "Oh, she's yours, is she?"

"You bet yore boots. I'll show her—make her eat outa my hand," boasted the convict.

"Will you show McRae too—and all his friends, as well as the North-West Mounted? Will you make 'em all eat out of your hands?"

"Whadjamean?"

"Why, I had a notion you were loaded up with trouble and didn't need to hunt more," sneered the gambler. "I had a notion the red-coats were on your heels to take you across the plains to hang you."

"I'll learn 'em about that," the huge fugitive bragged. "They say I'm a killer. Let it ride. I'll sure enough let 'em see they're good guessers."

Whaley shrugged his shoulders and looked at him with cold contempt. "You've got a bare chance for a getaway if you travel light and fast. I'd want long odds to back it," he said coolly.

"That's a heluva thing to tell a friend," West snarled.

"It's the truth. Take it or leave it. But if you try to bull this through your own way and don't let me run it, you're done for."

"How done for?"

The gambler did not answer. He turned to Jessie. "Unless you want your feet to freeze, you'd better get those duffles off."

The girl took off her mits and tried to unfasten the leggings after she had kicked the snowshoes from her feet. But her stiff fingers could not loosen the knots.

The free trader stooped and did it for her while West watched him sulkily. Jessie unwound the cloth and removed moccasins and duffles. She sat barefooted before the fire, but not too close.

"If they're frozen I'll get snow," Whaley offered.

"They're not frozen, thank you," she answered.

"Whadjamean done for?" repeated West.

His partner's derisive, scornful eye rested on him. "Use your brains, man. The Mounted are after you hot and heavy. You know their record. They get the man they go after. Take this fellow Beresford, the one that jugged you."

The big ruffian shook a furious fist in the air. "Curse him!" he shouted, and added a dozen crackling oaths.

"Curse him and welcome," Whaley replied. "But don't fool yourself about him. He's a go-getter. Didn't he go up Peace River after Pierre Poulette? Didn't he drag him back with cuffs on 'most a year later? That's what you've got against you, three hundred red-coats like him."

"You tryin' to scare me?" demanded West sullenly.

"I'm trying to hammer some common sense into your head. Your chance for a safe getaway rests on one thing. You've got to have friends in the Lone Lands who'll hide you till you can slip out of the country. Can you do that if the trappers

—friends of McRae, nearly all of 'em—carry the word of what you did to this girl?"

"I'm gonna take her with me." West stuck doggedly to his idea. He knew what he wanted. His life was forfeit, anyhow. He might as well go through to a finish.

From where she sat before the great fire Jessie's whisper reached Whaley. "Don't let him, please." It was an ineffective little wail straight from the heart.

Whaley went on, as though he had not heard. "It's your deal, not mine. I'm just telling you. Take this girl along, and your life's not worth a plugged nickel."

"Hell's hinges! In two days she'll be crazy about me. Tha's how I am with women."

"In two days she'll hate the ground you walk on, if she hasn't killed herself or you by that time."

Waves of acute pain were pricking into Jessie's legs from the pink toes to the calves. She was massaging them to restore circulation and had to set her teeth to keep from crying.

But her subconscious mind was wholly on what passed between the men. She knew that Whaley was trying to reëstablish over the other the mental dominance he had always held. It was a frail enough tenure, no doubt, likely to be upset at any moment by vanity, suspicion, or heady gusts of passion. In it, such as it was, lay a hope. Watching the gambler's cold, impassive face, the stony look in the poker eyes, she judged him tenacious and strong-willed. For reasons of his own he was fighting her battle. He had no intention of letting West take her with him.

Why? What was the motive in the back of his mind? She acquitted the man of benevolence. If his wishes chanced to march with hers, it was because of no altruism. He held a bitter grudge against Angus McRae and incidentally against her for the humiliation of his defeat at the hands of Morse. To satisfy this he had only to walk out of the house and leave her to an ugly fate. Why did he not do this? Was he playing a deep game of his own in which she was merely a pawn?

She turned the steaming duffles over on the mud hearth to dry the other side. She drew back the moccasins and the leggings that the heat might not scorch them. The sharp pain waves still beat into her feet and up her limbs. To change her position she drew up a stool and sat on it. This she had pushed back to a corner of the fireplace.

For Bully West was straddling up and down the room, a pent volcano ready to explode. He knew Whaley's advice was good. It would be suicide to encumber himself with this girl

107

in his flight. But he had never disciplined his desires. He wanted her. He meant to take her. Passion, the lust for revenge, the bully streak in him that gloated at the sight of some one young and fine trembling before him: all these were factors contributing to the same end. By gar, he would have what he had set his mind on, no matter what Whaley said.

Jessie knew the fellow was dangerous as a wounded buffalo bull in a corral. He would have his way if he had to smash and trample down any one that opposed him. Her eyes moved to Whaley's black-browed, bloodless face. How far would the gambler go in opposition to the other?

As her glance shifted back to West, it was arrested at the window. The girl's heart lost a beat, then sang a pæan of joy. For the copper-colored face of Onistah was framed in the pane.

CHAPTER XXIII

A Foretaste Of Hell

JESSIE's eyes flew to West and to Whaley. As yet neither of them had seen the Blackfoot. She raised a hand and pretended to brush back a lock of hair.

The Indian recognized it as a signal that she had seen him. His head disappeared.

Thoughts in the girl's mind raced. If Winthrop Beresford or Tom Morse had been outside instead of Onistah, she would not have attempted to give directions. Either of them would have been more competent than she to work out the problem. But the Blackfoot lacked initiative. He would do faithfully whatever he was told to do, but any independent action attempted by him was likely to be indecisive. She could not conceive of Onistah holding his own against two such men as these except by slaughtering them from the window before they knew he was there. He had not in him sufficient dominating ego.

Whaley was an unknown quantity. It was impossible to foresee how he would accept the intrusion of Onistah. Since he was playing his own game, the chances are that he would resent it. In West's case there could be no doubt. If it was necessary to his plans, he would not hesitate an instant to kill the Indian.

Reluctantly, she made up her mind to send him back to Faraway for help. He would travel fast. Within five hours at the outside he ought to be back with her father or Beresford. Surely, with Whaley on her side, she ought to be safe till then.

She caught sight of Onistah again, his eyes level with the window-sill. He was waiting for instructions.

Jessie gave them to him straight and plain. She spoke to Whaley, but for the Blackfoot's ear.

"Bring my father here. At once. I want him. Won't you, please?"

Whaley's blank poker stare focused on her. "The last word I had from Angus McRae was to keep out of your affairs. I can take a hint without waiting for a church to fall on me. Get some one else to take your messages."

"If you're going back to town I thought—perhaps—you'd tell him how much I need him," she pleaded. "Then he'd come —right away."

Onistah's head vanished. He knew what he had to do and no doubt was already on the trail. Outside it was dark. She could hear the swirling of the wind and the beat of sleet against the window-pane. A storm was rising. She prayed it might not be a blizzard. Weather permitting, her father should be here by eight or nine o'clock.

West, straddling past, snarled at her. "Get Angus McRae outa yore head. Him an' you's come to the partin' o' the ways. You're travelin' with me now. Un'erstand?"

His partner, sneering coldly, offered a suggestion. "If you expect to travel far you'd better get your webs to hitting snow. This girl wasn't out looking at the traps all by herself. Her trail leads straight here. Her friends are probably headed this way right now."

"Tha's right." West stopped in his stride. His slow brain stalled. "What d'you reckon I better do? If there's only one or two we might—"

"No," vetoed Whaley. "Nothing like that. Your play is to get out. And keep getting out when they crowd you. No killing."

"Goddlemighty, I'm a wolf, not a rabbit. If they crowd me, I'll sure pump lead," the desperado growled. Then, "D'you mean light out to-night?"

"To-night."

"Where'll I go?"

"Porcupine Creek, I'd say. There's an old cabin there Jac-

109

ques Perritot used to live in. The snow'll blot out our tracks."

"You goin' too?"

"I'll see you that far," Whaley answered briefly.

"Better bring down the dogs from the coulée, then."

The gambler looked at him with the cool insolence that characterized him. "When did I hire out as your flunkey, West?"

The outlaw's head was thrust forward and down. He glared at his partner, who met this manifestation of anger with hard eyes into which no expression crept. West was not insane enough to alienate his last ally. He drew back sullenly.

"All right. I'll go, since you're so particular." As his heavy body swung round awkwardly, the man's eyes fell on Jessie. She had lifted one small foot and was starting to pull on one of the duffle stockings. He stood a moment, gloating over the beautifully shaped ankle and lower limb, then slouched forward and snatched her up from the stool into his arms.

His savage, desirous eyes had given her an instant's warning. She was half up before his arms, massive as young trees, dragged her into his embrace.

"But before I go I'll have a kiss from my squaw," he roared. "Just to show her that Bully West has branded her and claims ownership."

She fought, fiercely, desperately, pushing against his rough bearded face and big barrel chest with all the force in her lithe young body. She was as a child to him. His triumphant laughter pealed as he crushed her warm soft trunk against his own and buried her in his opened coat. With an ungentle hand he forced round the averted head till the fear-filled eyes met his.

"Kiss yore man," he ordered.

The girl said nothing. She still struggled to escape, using every ounce of strength she possessed.

The fury of her resistance amused him. He laughed again, throwing back the heavy bristling jaw in a roar of mirth.

"Yore man—yore master," he amended.

He smothered her with his foul kisses, ravished her lips, her eyes, the soft hot cheeks, the oval of the chin, and the lovely curve of the throat. She was physically nauseated when he flung her from him against the wall and strode from the room with another horrible whoop of exultation.

She clung to the wall, panting, eyes closed. A shocking sense of degradation flooded her soul. She felt as though she were drowning in it, fathoms deep.

Her lids fluttered open and she saw the gambler. He was

still sitting on the stool. A mocking, cynical smile was in the eyes that met Jessie's.

"And Tom Morse—where, oh, where is he?" the man jeered.

A chill shook her. Dry sobs welled up in her throat. She was lost. For the first time she knew the cold clutch of despair at her heart. Whaley did not intend to lift a hand for her. He had sat there and let West work his will.

"Angus McRae gave me instructions aplenty," he explained maliciously. "I was to keep my hands off you. I was to mind my own business. When you see him again—if you ever do—will you tell him I did exactly as he said?"

She did not answer. What was there to say? In the cabin was no sound except that of her dry, sobbing breath.

Whaley rose and came across the room. He had thrown aside the gambler's mask of impassivity. His eyes were shining strangely.

"I'm going—now—out into the storm. What about you? If you're here when West comes back, you know what it means. Make your choice. Will you go with me or stay with him?"

"You're going home?"

"Yes." His smile was enigmatic. It carried neither warmth nor conviction.

The man had played his cards well. He had let West give her a foretaste of the hell in store for her. Anything rather than that, she thought. And surely Whaley would take her home. He was no outlaw, but a responsible citizen who must go back to Faraway to live. He had to face her father and Winthrop Beresford of the Mounted—and Tom Morse. He would not harm her. He dared not.

But she took one vain precaution. "You promise to take me to my father. You'll not—be like him." A lift of the head indicated the man who had just gone out.

"He's a fool. I'm not. That's the difference." He shrugged his shoulders. "Make your own choice. If you'd rather stay here—"

But she had made it. She was getting hurriedly into her furs and was putting on her mittens. Already she had adjusted the snowshoes.

"We'd better hurry," she urged. "He might come back."

"It'll be bad luck for him if he does," the gambler said coolly. "You ready?"

She nodded that she was.

In another moment they were out of the warm room and into the storm. The wind was coming in whistling gusts, carrying with it a fine sleet that whipped the face and stung the eyeballs. Before she had been out in the storm five minutes, Jessie had lost all sense of direction.

Whaley was an expert woodsman. He plunged into the forest, without hesitation, so surely that she felt he must know where he was going. The girl followed at his heels, head down against the blast.

Before this day she had not for months taken a long trip on webs. Leg muscles, called into use without training, were sore and stiff. In the darkness the soft snow piled up on the shoes. Each step became a drag. The lacings and straps lacerated her tender flesh till she knew her duffles were soaked with blood. More than once she dropped back so far that she lost sight of Whaley. Each time he came back with words of encouragement and good cheer.

"Not far now," he would promise. "Across a little bog and then camp. Keep coming."

Once he found her sitting on the snow, her back to a tree.

"You'd better go on alone. I'm done," she told him drearily.

He was not angry at her. Nor did he bully or browbeat.

"Tough sledding," he said gently. "But we're 'most there. Got to keep going. Can't quit now."

He helped Jessie to her feet and led the way down into a spongy morass. The brush slapped her face. It caught in the meshes of her shoes and flung her down. The miry earth, oozing over the edges of the frames, clogged her feet and clung to them like pitch.

Whaley did his best to help, but when at last she crept up to the higher ground beyond the bog every muscle ached with fatigue.

They were almost upon it before she saw a log cabin looming out of the darkness.

She sank on the floor exhausted. Whaley disappeared into the storm again. Sleepily she wondered where he was going. She must have dozed, for when her eyes next reported to the brain, there was a brisk fire of birch bark burning and her companion was dragging broken bits of dead and down timber into the house.

"Looks like she's getting her back up for a blizzard. Better have plenty of fuel in," he explained.

"Where are we?" she asked drowsily.

"Cabin on Bull Creek," he answered. "Better get off your footwear."

While she did this her mind woke to activity. Why had he brought her here? They had no food. How would they live if a blizzard blew up and snowed them in? And even if they had supplies, how could she live alone for days with this man in a cabin eight by ten?

As though he guessed what was in her mind, he answered plausibly enough one of the questions.

"No chance to reach Faraway. Too stormy. It was neck or nothing. Had to take what we could get."

"What'll we do if—if there's a blizzard?" she asked timidly.

"Sit tight."

"Without food?"

"If it lasts too long, I'll have to wait for a lull and make a try for Faraway. No use worrying. We can't help what's coming. Got to face the music."

Her eyes swept the empty cabin. No bed. No table. One home-made three-legged stool. A battered kettle. It was an uninviting prospect, even if she had not had to face possible starvation while she was caged with a stranger who might any minute develop wolfish hunger for her as he had done only forty-eight hours before.

He did not look at her steadily. His gaze was in the red glow of the fire a good deal. She talked, and he answered in monosyllables. When he looked at her, his eyes glowed with the hot red light reflected from the fire. Live coals seemed to burn in them.

In spite of the heat a little shiver ran down her spine.

Silence became too significant. She was afraid of it. So she talked, persistently, at times a little hysterically. Her memory was good. If she liked a piece of poetry, she could learn it by reading it over a few times. So, in her desperation, she "spoke pieces" to this man whose face was a gray mask, just as the girls had done at her school in Winnipeg.

Often, at night camps, she had recited for her father. If she had no dramatic talent, at least she had a sweet, clear voice, an earnestness that never ranted, and some native or acquired skill in handling inflections.

"Do you like Shakespeare?" she asked. "My father's very fond of him. I know parts of several of the plays. 'Henry V' now. That's good. There's a bit where he's talking to his soldiers before they fight the French. Would you like that?"

"Go on," he said gruffly, sultry eyes on the fire.

With a good deal of spirit she flung out the gallant lines. He began to watch her, vivid, eager, so pathetically anxious to entertain him with her small stock of wares.

"But, if it be a sin to covet honor,
I am the most offending soul alive."

113

There was about her a quality very fine and taking. He caught it first in those two lines, and again when her full young voice swelled to English Harry's prophecy.

> "And Crispin Crispian shall ne'er go by,
> From this day to the ending of the world,
> But we in it shall be remembered.
> We few, we happy few, we band of brothers:
> For he to-day that sheds his blood with me
> Shall be my brother; be he ne'er so vile,
> This day shall gentle his condition:
> And gentlemen in England now abed
> Shall think themselves accurs'd they were not here,
> And hold their manhoods cheap whiles any speaks
> That fought with us upon Saint Crispin's day."

As he watched her, old memories stirred in him. He had come from a good family in the Western Reserve, where he had rough-and-tumbled up through the grades into High School. After a year here he had gone to a Catholic School, Sacred Heart College, and had studied for the priesthood. He recalled his mother, a gentle, white-haired old lady, with fond pride in him; his father, who had been the soul of honor. By some queer chance she had lit on the very lines that he had learned from the old school reader and recited before an audience the last day prior to vacation.

He woke from his reveries to discover that she was giving him Tennyson, that fragment from "Guinevere" when Arthur tells her of the dream her guilt has tarnished. And as she spoke there stirred in him the long-forgotten aspirations of his youth.

> ". . . for indeed I knew
> Of no more subtle master under heaven
> Than is the maiden passion for a maid,
> Not only to keep down the base in man,
> But teach high thought and amiable words
> And courtliness, and the desire of fame,
> And love of truth, and all that makes a man."

His eyes were no longer impassive. There was in them, for the moment at least, a hunted, haggard look. He saw himself as he was, in a blaze of light that burned down to his very soul.

And he saw her too transformed—not a half-breed, the fair prey of any man's passion, but a clean, proud, high-spirited white girl who lived in the spirit as well as the flesh.

"You're tired. Better lie down and sleep," he told her, very gently.

Jessie looked at him, and she knew she was safe. She might sleep without fear. This man would not harm her any more than Beresford or Morse would have done. Some chemical change had occurred in his thoughts that protected her. She did not know what it was, but her pæan of prayer went up to heaven in a little rush of thanksgiving.

She did not voice her gratitude to him. But the look she gave him was more expressive than words.

Out of the storm a voice raucous and profane came to them faintly.

"Ah, crapaud Wulf, pren' garde. Yeu-oh! (To the right!) Git down to it, Fox. Sacré demon! Cha! Cha! (To the left!)"

Then the crack of a whip and a volley of oaths.

The two in the cabin looked at each other. One was white to the lips. The other smiled grimly. It was the gambler who spoke their common thought.

"Bully West, by all that's holy!"

CHAPTER XXIV

West Makes A Decision

CAME to those in the cabin a string of oaths, the crack of a whip lashing out savagely, and the yelps of dogs from a crouching, cowering team.

Whaley slipped a revolver from his belt to the right-hand pocket of his fur coat.

The door burst open. A man stood on the threshold, a huge figure crusted with snow, beard and eyebrows ice-matted. He looked like the storm king who had ridden the gale out of the north. This on the outside, at a first glance only. For the black scowl he flung at his partner was so deadly that it seemed to come red-hot from a furnace of hate and evil passion.

"Run to earth!" he roared. "Thought you'd hole up, you damned fox, where I wouldn't find you. Thought you'd give Bully West the slip, you 'n' that li'l' hell-cat. Talk about

115

Porcupine Creek, eh? Tried to send me mushin' over there while you 'n' her——"

What the fellow said sent a hot wave creeping over the girl's face to the roots of her hair. The gambler did not speak, but his eyes, filmed and wary, never lifted from the other's bloated face.

"Figured I'd forget the ol' whiskey cache, eh? Figured you could gimme the double-cross an' git away with it? Hell's hinges, Bully West's no fool! He's forgot more'n you ever knew."

The man swaggered forward, the lash of the whip trailing across the puncheon floor. Triumph rode in his voice and straddled in his gait. He stood with his back to the fireplace absorbing heat, hands behind him and feet set wide. His eyes gloated over the victims he had trapped. Presently he would settle with both of them.

"Not a word to say for yoreselves, either one o' you," he jeered. "Good enough. I'll do what talkin' 's needed, then I'll strip the hide off'n both o' you." With a flirt of the arm he sent the lash of the dog-whip snaking out toward Jessie.

She shrank back against the wall, needlessly. It was a threat, not an attack; a promise of what was to come.

"Let her alone." They were the first words Whaley had spoken. In his soft, purring voice they carried out the suggestion of his crouched tenseness. If West was the grizzly bear, the other was the forest panther, more feline, but just as dangerous.

The convict looked at him, eyes narrowed, head thrust forward and down. "What's that?"

"I said to let her alone."

West's face heliographed amazement. "Meanin'—?"

"Meaning exactly what I say. You'll not touch her."

It was a moment before this flat defiance reached the brain of the big man through the penumbra of his mental fog. When it did, he strode across the room with the roar of a wild animal and snatched the girl to him. He would show whether any one could come between him and his woman.

In three long steps Whaley padded across the floor. Something cold and round pressed against the back of the outlaw's tough red neck.

"Drop that whip."

The order came in a low-voiced imperative. West hesitated. This man—his partner—would surely never shoot him about such a trifle. Still—

"What's eatin' you?" he growled. "Put up that gun. You ain't fool enough to shoot."

116

"Think that hard enough and you'll never live to know better. Hands off the girl."

The slow brain of West functioned. He had been taken wholly by surprise, but as his cunning mind worked the situation out, he saw how much it would be to Whaley's profit to get rid of him. The gambler would get the girl and the reward for West's destruction. He would inherit his share of their joint business and would reinstate himself as a good citizen with the Mounted and with McRae's friends.

Surlily the desperado yielded. "All right, if you're so set on it."

"Drop the whip."

The fingers of West opened and the handle fell to the floor. Deftly the other removed a revolver from its place under the outlaw's left armpit.

West glared at him. That moment the fugitive made up his mind that he would kill Whaley at the first good opportunity. A tide of poisonous hatred raced through his veins. Its expression but not its virulence was temporarily checked by wholesome fear. He must be careful that the gambler did not get him first.

His voice took on a whine intended for good fellowship. "I reckon I was too pre-emtory. O' course I was sore the way you two left me holdin' the sack. Any one would 'a' been now, wouldn't they? But no use friends fallin' out. We got to make the best of things."

Whaley's chill face did not warm. He knew the man with whom he was dealing. When he began to butter his phrases, it was time to look out for him. He would forget that his partner had brought him from Faraway a dog-team with which to escape, that he was supplying him with funds to carry him through the winter. He would remember only that he had balked and humiliated him.

"Better get into the house the stuff from the sled," the gambler said. "And we'll rustle wood. No telling how long this storm'll last."

"Tha's right," agreed West. "When I saw them sun dogs to-day I figured we was in for a blizzard. Too bad you didn't outfit me for a longer trip."

A gale was blowing from the north, carrying on its whistling breath a fine hard sleet that cut the eyeballs like powdered glass. The men fought their way to the sled and wrestled with the knots of the frozen ropes that bound the load. The lumps of ice that had gathered round these had to be knocked off with hammers before they could be freed. When they staggered into the house with their packs, both men were half-frozen. Their hands were so stiff that the fingers were jointless.

They stopped only long enough to limber up the muscles. Whaley handed to Jessie the revolver he had taken from West.

"Keep this," he said. His look was significant. It told her that in the hunt for wood he might be blinded by the blizzard and lost. If he failed to return and West came back alone, she would know what to do with it.

Into the storm the two plunged a second time. They carried ropes and an axe. Since West had arrived, the gale had greatly increased. The wind now was booming in deep, sullen roars and the temperature had fallen twenty degrees already. The sled dogs were nowhere to be seen or heard. They had burrowed down into the snow where the house would shelter them from the hurricane as much as possible.

The men reached the edge of the creek. They struggled in the frozen drifts with such small dead trees as they could find. In the darkness Whaley used the axe as best he could at imminent risk to his legs. Though they worked only a few feet apart, they had to shout to make their voices carry.

"We better be movin' back," West called through his open palms. "We got all we can haul."

They roped the wood and dragged it over the snow in the direction they knew the house to be. Presently they found the sled and from it deflected toward the house.

Jessie had hot tea waiting for them. They kicked off their webs and piled the salvaged wood into the other end of the cabin, after which they hunkered down before the fire to drink tea and eat pemmican and bannocks.

They had with them about fifty pounds of frozen fish for the dogs and provisions enough to last the three of them four or five meals. Whaley had brought West supplies enough to carry him only to Lookout, where he was to stock for a long traverse into the wilds.

As the hours passed there grew up between the gambler and the girl a tacit partnership of mutual defense. No word was spoken of it, but each knew that the sulky brute in the chimney corner was dangerous. He would be held by no scruples of conscience, no laws of friendship or decency. If the chance came he would strike.

The storm raged and howled. It flung itself at the cabin with what seemed a ravenous and implacable fury. The shriek of it was now like the skirling of a thousand bagpipes, again like the wailing of numberless lost souls.

Inside, West snored heavily, his ill-shaped head drooping on the big barrel chest of the man. Jessie slept while Whaley kept guard. Later she would watch in her turn.

There were moments when the gale died down, but only to roar again with a frenzy of increased violence.

The gray day broke and found the blizzard at its height.

CHAPTER XXV

For The Wee Lamb Lost

BERESFORD, in front of the C. N. Morse & Company trading-post, watched his horse paw at the snow in search of grass underneath. It was a sign that the animal was prairie-bred. On the plains near the border grass cures as it stands, retaining its nutriment as hay. The native pony pushes the snow aside with its forefoot and finds its feed. But in the timber country of the North grass grows long and coarse. When its sap dries out, it rots.

The officer was thinking that he had better put both horse and cariole up for the winter. It was time now for dogs and sled. Even in summer this was not a country for horses. There were so many lakes that a birch-bark canoe covered the miles faster.

Darkness was sweeping down over the land, and with it the first flakes of a coming storm. Beresford had expected this, for earlier in the day he had seen two bright mock suns in the sky. The Indians had told him that these sun dogs were warnings of severe cold and probably a blizzard.

Out of the edge of the forest a man on snowshoes came. He was moving fast. Beresford, watching him idly, noticed that he toed in. Therefore he was probably a Cree trapper. But the Crees were usually indolent travelers. They did not cover ground as this man was doing.

The man was an Indian. The soldier presently certified his first guess as to that. But not until the native was almost at the store did he recognize him as Onistah.

The Blackfoot wasted no time in leading up to what he had to say. "Sleeping Dawn she prisoner of Bully West and Whaley. She say bring her father. She tell me bring him quick."

Beresford's body lost its easy grace instantly and became rigid. His voice rang with sharp authority.

"Where is she?"

"She at Jasper's cabin on Cache Creek. She frightened."

As though the mention of Sleeping Dawn's name had reached him by some process of telepathy, Tom Morse had come out and stood in the door of the store. The trooper wheeled to him.

"Get me a dog-team, Tom. That fellow West has got Jessie McRae with him on Cache Creek. We've got to move quick."

The storekeeper felt as though the bottom had dropped out of his heart. He glanced up at the lowering night. "Storm brewing. We'll get started right away." Without a moment's delay he disappeared inside the store to make his preparations.

Onistah carried the news to McRae.

The blood washed out of the ruddy-whiskered face of the Scot, but his sole comment was a Scriptural phrase of faith. "I have been young, and now am old; yet have I not seen the righteous forsaken . . ."

It was less than half an hour later that four men and a dog-train moved up the main street of Faraway and disappeared in the forest. Morse broke trail and McRae drove the tandem. Onistah, who had already traveled many miles, brought up the rear. The trooper exchanged places with Morse after an hour's travel.

They were taking a short-cut and it led them through dead and down timber that delayed the party. Tom was a good axeman, and more than once he had to chop away obstructing logs. At other times by main strength the men lifted or dragged the sled over bad places.

The swirling storm made it difficult to know where they were going or to choose the best way. They floundered through deep snow and heavy underbrush, faces bleeding from the whip of willow switches suddenly released and feet so torn by the straps of the snowshoes that the trail showed stains of blood which had soaked from the moccasins.

Onistah, already weary, began to lag. They dared not wait for him. There was, they felt, not a moment to be lost. McRae's clean-shaven upper lip was a straight, grim surface. He voiced no fears, no doubts, but the others knew from their own anxiety how much he must be suffering.

The gale increased. It drove in bitter blasts of fine stinging sleet. When for a few hundred yards they drew out of the thick forest into an open grove, it lashed them so furiously they could scarcely move in the teeth of it.

The dogs were whimpering at their task. More than once they stopped, exhausted by the wind against which they were battling. Their eyes turned dumbly to McRae for instructions.

He could only drive them back to the trail Morse was breaking.

The train was one of the best in the North. The leader was a large St. Bernard, weighing about one hundred sixty pounds, intelligent, faithful, and full of courage. He stood thirty-four inches high at his fore shoulder. Not once did Cuffy falter. Even when the others quit, he was ready to put his weight to the load.

Through the howling of the wind Beresford shouted into the ear of Morse. "Can't be far now. Question is can we find Jasper's in this blizzard."

Morse shook his head. It did not seem likely. Far and near were words which had no meaning. A white, shrieking monster seemed to be hemming them in. Their world diminished to the space their outstretched arms could reach. The only guide they had was Cache Creek, along the bank of which they were traveling. Jasper's deserted cabin lay back from it a few hundred yards, but Tom had not any data to tell him when he ought to leave the creek.

Cuffy solved the problem for him. The St. Bernard stopped, refused the trail Beresford and Morse were beating down in the deep snow. He raised his head, seemed to scent a haven, whined, and tried to plunge to the left.

McRae came forward and shouted to his friends. "We'll gi'e Cuffy his head. He'll maybe ken mair than we do the nicht."

The trail-breakers turned from the creek, occasionally stopping to make sure Cuffy was satisfied. Through heavy brush they forced a way into a coulée. The St. Bernard led them plump against the wall of a cabin.

There was a light inside, the fitful, leaping glow of fire flames. The men stumbled through drifts to the door, McRae in the lead. The Scotchman found the latch and flung open the door. The other two followed him inside.

The room was empty.

At first they could not believe their eyes. It was not reasonable to suppose that any sane human beings would have left a comfortable house to face such a storm. But this was just what they must have done. The state of the fire, which was dying down to hot coals, told them it had not been replenished for hours. West and Whaley clearly had decided they were not safe here and had set out for another hiding-place.

The men looked at each other in blank silence. The same thought was in the mind of all. For the present they must give up the pursuit. It would not be possible to try to carry on any farther in such a blizzard. Yet the younger men waited for McRae to come to his decision. If he called on them to do more, they would make a try with him.

121

"We'll stay here," Angus said quietly. "Build up the fire, lads, and we'll cast back for Onistah."

Neither of the others spoke. They knew it must have cost the Scotchman a pang to give up even for the night. He had done it only because he recognized that he had no right to sacrifice all their lives in vain.

The dogs took the back trail reluctantly. The sled had been unloaded and was lighter. Moreover, they followed a trail already broken except where the sweep of the wind had filled it up. McRae cheered them to their work.

"Up wi' ye, Koona! Guid dog. Cha, cha! You'll be doin' gran' work, Cuffy. Marché!"

Morse stumbled over Onistah where he lay in the trail. The Blackfoot was still conscious, though he was drowsing into that sleep which is fatal to Arctic travelers caught in a blizzard. He had crawled on hands and feet through the snow after his knees failed him. It must have been only a few minutes after he completely collapsed that they found him.

He was given a gulp or two of whiskey and put on the sled. Again the dogs buckled to the pull. A quarter of an hour later the party reached the cabin.

Onistah was given first aid. Feet and face were rubbed with snow to restore circulation and to prevent frost-bite. He had been rescued in time to save him from any permanent ill effects.

In the back of all their minds lay a haunting fear. What had become of Jessie? There was a chance that the blizzard had caught the party before it reached its destination. Neither West nor Whaley was an inexperienced musher. They knew the difficulties of sub-Arctic travel and how to cope with them. But the storm had blown up with unusual swiftness.

Even if the party had reached safety, the girl's troubles were not ended. With the coming of darkness her peril would increase. As long as Whaley was with West there was hope. The gambler was cold-blooded as a fish, but he had the saving sense of sanity. If he meant to return to Faraway—and there was no reason why he should not—he dared not let any harm befall the girl. But West was a ruffian unmitigated. His ruthless passion might drive him to any evil.

In front of the fire they discussed probabilities. Where had the two free traders taken the girl? Not far, in the face of such a storm. They canvassed places likely to serve as retreats for West.

Once McRae, speaking out of his tortured heart, made an indirect reference to what all of them were thinking. He was looking somberly into the fire as he spoke.

"Yea, the darkness hideth not from Thee, but the night shineth as the day: the darkness and the light are both alike to Thee."

He found in his religion a stay and comfort. If he knew that under cover of darkness evil men do evil deeds, he could reassure himself with the promise that the hairs of his daughter's head were numbered and that she was under divine protection.

From a pocket next his shirt he drew a small package in oilskin. It was a Bible he had carried many years. By the light of the leaping flames he read a chapter from the New Testament and the twenty-third Psalm, after which the storm-bound men knelt while he prayed that God would guard and keep safe "the wee lamb lost in the tempest far frae the fold."

Morse and Beresford were tough as hickory withes. None in the North woods had more iron in the blood than they. Emergencies had tested them time and again. But neither of them was ashamed to kneel with the big rugged Scotchman while he poured his heart out in a petition for his lass. The security of the girl whom all four loved each in his own way was out of the hands of her friends. To know that McRae had found a sure rock upon which to lean brought the younger men too some measure of peace.

CHAPTER XXVI

A Rescue

THE gray day wore itself away into the deeper darkness of early dusk. Like a wild beast attacking its prey, the hurricane still leaped with deep and sullen roars at the little cabin on Bull Creek. It beat upon it in wild, swirling gusts. It flung blasts of wind, laden with snow and sleet, against the log walls and piled drifts round them almost to the eaves.

Long since Whaley had been forced to take the dogs into the cabin to save them from freezing to death. It was impossible for any of the three human beings to venture out for more than a few minutes at a time. Even then they had to keep close to the walls in order not to lose contact with the house.

When feeding-time came the dogs made pandemonium. They were half-famished, as teams in the Lone Lands usually are, and the smell of the frozen fish thawing before the fire set them frantic. West and Whaley protected Jessie while she turned the fish. This was not easy. The plunging animals almost rushed the men off their feet. They had to be beaten back cruelly with the whip-stocks, for they were wild as wolves and only the sharpest pain would restrain them.

The half-thawed fish were flung to them in turn. There was a snarl, a snap of the jaws, a gulp, and the fish was gone. Over one or two that fell in the pack the train worried and fought, with sharp yelps and growls, until the last fragment had been torn to pieces and disappeared.

Afterward the storm-bound trio drank tea and ate pemmican, still fighting back the pack. West laid open the nose of one in an ugly cut with the iron-bound end of his whip-butt. Perhaps he was not wholly to blame. Many of the dog-trains of the North are taught to understand nothing but the sting of the whip and will respond only to brutal treatment.

The second night was a repetition of the first. The three were divided into two camps. Whaley or Jessie McRae watched West every minute. There was a look in his eye they distrusted, a sulky malice back of which seemed to smoke banked fires of murderous desire. He lay on the floor and slept a good deal in short cat-naps. Apparently his dreams were not pleasant. He would growl incoherently through set teeth and clench great hairy fists in spasms of rage. Out of these he wakened with a start to glare around suspiciously at the others. It was clear the thought was in the back of his mind that they might destroy him while he was asleep.

Throughout the third day the storm continued unabated. Whaley and West discussed the situation. Except for a few pounds of fish, their provisions were gone. If the blizzard did not moderate, they would soon face starvation.

During the night the wind died down. Day broke clear, a faint and wintry sun in the sky.

To West the other man made a proposal. "Have to get out and hunt food. We'll find caribou in some of the coulées along the creek. What say?"

The convict looked at him with sly cunning. "How about this girl? Think I'm gonna leave her to mush out an' put the police on my trail? No, sir. I'll take her snowshoes with me."

Whaley shrugged his shoulders. "She couldn't find her way home if she had shoes. But please yourself about that."

124

West's shifty gaze slid over him. The proposal of a hunt suited him. He must have a supply of food to carry him to Lookout. Whaley was a good shot and an expert trailer. If there were caribou or moose in the vicinity, he was likely to make a kill. In any event there would be hundreds of white rabbits scurrying through the woods. He decided craftily to make use of the gambler, and after he was through with him—

The men took with them part of the tea and enough fish to feed the dogs once. They expected to find game sufficient to supply themselves and stock up for a few days. Whaley insisted on leaving Jessie her rifle, in order that she might shoot a rabbit or two if any ventured near the cabin. She had three frozen fish and a handful of tea.

Before they started Whaley drew Jessie aside. "Can't say how long we'll be gone. Maybe two days—or three. You'll have to make out with what you've got till we get back." He hesitated a moment, then his cold, hard eyes held fast to hers. "Maybe only one of us will come back. Keep your eyes open. If there's only one of us—and it's West—don't let him get into the house. Shoot him down. Take his snowshoes and the team. Follow the creek down about five miles, then strike southwest till you come to Clear Lake. You know your way home from there."

Her dark eyes dilated. "Do you think he means to—to—?"

The man nodded. "He's afraid of me—thinks I mean to set the police on his trail. If he can he'll get rid of me. But not yet—not till we've got a couple of caribou. I'll be watching him all the time."

"How can you watch him while you're hunting?"

He lifted his shoulders in a shrug. It was quite true that West could shoot him in the back during the hunt. But Whaley knew the man pretty well. He would make sure of meat before he struck. After the sled was loaded, Whaley did not intend to turn his back on the fellow.

Jessie had not been brought up in the North woods for nothing. She had seen her brother Fergus make many a rabbit snare. Now she contrived to fashion one out of some old strips of skin she found in the cabin. After she had bent down a young sapling and fastened it to a fallen log, she busied herself making a second one.

Without snowshoes she did not find it possible to travel far, but she managed to shoot a fox that adventured near the hut in the hope of finding something to fill its lean and empty paunch.

Before leaving, Whaley had brought into the house a supply

of wood, but Jessie added to this during the day by hauling birch poles from the edge of the creek.

Darkness fell early. The girl built up a roaring fire and piled the wood up against the door so that nobody could get in without waking her. The rifle lay close at hand. She slept long and soundly. When she shook the drowsiness from her eyes, the sun was shining through the window.

She breakfasted on stew made from a hind-quarter of fox. After she had visited her snares and reset one that had been sprung, she gathered balsam boughs for a bed and carried them to the house to dry before the fire. Whaley had left her a small hatchet, and with this she began to shape a snowshoe from a piece of the puncheon floor. All day she worked at this, and by night had a rough sort of wood ski that might serve at need. With red-hot coals, during the long evening, she burned holes in it through which to put the straps. The skin of the fox, cut into long strips, would do for thongs. It would be a crude, primitive device, but she thought that at a pinch she might travel a few miles on it. To-morrow she would make a mate for it, she decided.

Except for the bed of balsam boughs, her arrangements for the night were just as they had been the first day. Again she built up a big fire, piled the wood in front of the door, and put the rifle within reach. Again she was asleep almost at once, within a minute of the time when she nestled down to find a soft spot in the springy mattress she had made.

Jessie worked hard on the second ski. By noon she had it pretty well shaped. Unfortunately a small split in the wood developed into a larger one. She was forced to throw it aside and begin on another piece.

A hundred times her eyes had lifted to sweep the snow field for any sign of the hunters' return. Now, looking out of the window without much expectation of seeing them, her glance fell on a traveler, a speck of black on a sea of white. Her heart began to beat a drum of excitement. She waited, eyes riveted, expecting to see a second figure and a dog-team top the rise and show in silhouette.

None appeared. The man advanced steadily. He did not look backward. Evidently he had no companion. Was this lone traveler West?

Jessie picked up the rifle and made sure that it was in good working order. A tumultuous river seemed to beat through her temples. The pulses in her finger-tips were athrob.

Could she do this dreadful thing, even to save honor and life, though she knew the man must be twice a murderer? Once she had tried and failed, while he stood taunting her with his horrible, broken-toothed grin. And once, in the stress of battle, she had wounded him while he was attacking.

The moving black speck became larger. It came to her presently with certainty that this was not West. He moved more gracefully, more lightly, without the heavy slouching roll. . . . And then she knew he was not Whaley either. One of her friends! A little burst of prayer welled out of her heart.

She left the cabin and went toward the man. He waved a hand to her and she flung up a joyful gesture in answer. For her rescuer was Onistah.

Jessie found herself with both hands in his, biting her lower lip to keep back tears. She could not speak for the emotion that welled up in her.

"You—all well?" he asked, with the imperturbable facial mask of his race that concealed all emotion.

She nodded.

"Good," he went on. "Your father pray the Great Spirit keep you safe."

"Where is Father?"

He looked in the direction from which he had come. "We go Jasper's cabin—your father, red soldier, American trader, Onistah. You gone. Big storm—snow—sleet. No can go farther. Then your father he pray. We wait till Great Spirit he say, 'No more wind, snow.' Then we move camp. All search—go out find you." He pointed north, south, east, and west. "The Great Spirit tell me to come here. I say, 'Sleeping Dawn she with God, for Jesus' sake, Amen.'"

"You dear, dear boy," she sobbed.

"So I find you. Hungry?"

"No. I shot a fox."

"Then we go now." He looked at her feet. "Where your snowshoes?"

"West took them to keep me here. I'm making a pair. Come. We'll finish them."

They moved toward the house. Onistah stopped. The girl followed his eyes. They were fastened on a laden dog-train with two men moving across a lake near the shore of which the cabin had been built.

Her fear-filled gaze came back to the Indian. "It's West and Mr. Whaley. What'll we do?"

Already he was kneeling, fumbling with the straps of his snowshoes. "You go find your father. Follow trail to camp. Then you send him here. I hide in woods."

"No—no. They'll find you, and that West would shoot you."

"Onistah know tricks. They no find him."

He fastened the snow-webs on her feet while she was still

127

protesting. She glanced again at the dog-train jogging steadily forward. If she was going, it must be at once. Soon it would be too late for either of them to escape.

"You will hide in the woods, won't you, so they can't find you?" she implored.

He smiled reassurance. "Go," he said.

Another moment, and she was pushing over the crust along the trail by which the Blackfoot had come.

CHAPTER XXVII

Apache Stuff

THE hunters brought back three caribou and two sacks of rabbits, supplies enough to enable West to reach Lookout. The dogs were stronger than when they had set out, for they had gorged themselves on the parts of the game unfit for human use.

Nothing had been said by either of the men as to what was to be done with Jessie McRae, but the question was in the background of both their thoughts, just as was the growing anger toward each other that consumed them. They rarely spoke. Neither of them let the other drop behind him. Neither had slept a wink the previous night. Instead, they had kept themselves awake with hot tea. Fagged out after a day of hard hunting, each was convinced his life depended on wakefulness. West's iron strength had stood the strain without any outward signs of collapse, but Whaley was stumbling with fatigue as he dragged himself along beside the sled.

The bad feeling between the partners was near the explosion point. It was bound to come before the fugitive started on his long trip north. The fellow had a single-track mind. He still intended to take the girl with him. When Whaley interfered, there would be a fight. It could not come too soon to suit West. His brooding had reached the point where he was morally certain that the gambler meant to betray him to the police and set them on his track.

Smoke was rising from the chimney of the hut. No doubt the McRae girl was inside, waiting for them with a heart of fear fluttering in her bosom. Whaley's thin lips set grimly. Soon now it would be a show-down.

There was a moment's delay at the door, each hanging back under pretense of working at the sled. There was always the chance that the one who went first might get a shot in the back.

West glanced at the big mittens on the other's hands, laughed hardily, and pushed into the cabin. A startled grunt escaped him.

"She's gone," he called out.

"Probably in the woods back here—rabbit-shooting likely. She can't have gone far without snowshoes," Whaley said.

The big man picked up the ski Jessie had made. "Looky here."

Whaley examined it. "She might have made a pair of 'em and got away. Hope so."

The yellow teeth of the convict showed in a snarl. "Think I don't see yore game? Playin' up to McRae an' the red-coats. I wouldn't put it by you to sell me out."

The gambler's ice-cold eyes bored into West. Was it to be now?

West was not quite ready. His hands were cold and stiff. Besides, the other was on guard and the fugitive was not looking for an even break.

"Oh, well, no use rowin' about that. I ain't gonna chew the rag with you. It'll be you one way an' me another pretty soon," he continued, shifty eyes dodging. "About the girl—easy to find out, I say. She sure didn't fly away. Must 'a' left tracks. We'll take a look-see."

Again Whaley waited deferentially, with a sardonic and mirthless grin, to let the other pass first. There were many tracks close to the cabin where they themselves, as well as the girl, had moved to and fro. Their roving glances went farther afield.

Plain as the swirling waters in the wake of a boat stretched the tracks of a snowshoer across the lower end of the lake.

They pushed across to examine them closer, following them a dozen yards to the edge of the ice-field. The sign written there on that white page told a tale to both of the observers, but it said more to one than to the other.

"Some one's been here," West cried with a startled oath.

"Yes," agreed Whaley. He did not intend to give any unnecessary information.

"An' lit out again. Must 'a' gone to git help for the girl."

"Yes," assented the gambler, and meant "No."

What he read from the writing on the snow was this: Some one had come and some one had gone. But the one who had come was not the one who had gone. An Indian had made the first tracks. He could tell it by the shape of the webs and by the way the traveler had toed in. The outward-bound trail was different. Some one lighter of build was wearing the snowshoes, some one who took shorter steps and toed out.

"See. She run out to meet him. Here's where her feet kept sinkin' in," West said.

The other nodded. Yes, she had hurried to meet him but that was not all he saw. There was the impression of a knee in the snow. It was an easy guess that the man had knelt to take off the shoes and adjust them to the girl's feet.

"An' here's where she cut off into the woods," the convict went on. "She's hidin' up there now. I'm hittin' the trail after her hot-foot."

Whaley's derisive smile vanished almost before it appeared. What he knew was his own business. If West wanted to take a walk in the woods, it was not necessary to tell him that a man was waiting for him there behind some tree.

"Think I'll follow this fellow," Whaley said, with a lift of the hand toward the tracks that led across the lake. "We've got to find out where he went. If the Mounted are hot on our trail, we want to know it."

"Sure." West assented craftily, eyes narrowed to conceal the thoughts that crawled through his murderous brain. "We gotta know that."

He believed Whaley was playing into his hands. The man meant to betray him to the police. He would never reach them. And he, Bully West, would at last be alone with the girl, nobody to interfere with him.

The gambler was used to taking chances. He took one now and made his first mistake in the long duel he had been playing with West. The eagerness of the fellow to have him gone was apparent. The convict wanted him out of the way so that he could go find the girl. Evidently he thought that Whaley was backing down as gracefully as he could.

"I'll start right after him. Back soon," the gambler said casually.

"Yes, soon," agreed West.

Their masked eyes still clung to each other, wary and watchful. As though without intent Whaley backed away, still talking to the other. He wanted to be out of revolver range before he turned. West also was backing clumsily, moving toward the sled. The convict wheeled and slid rapidly to it.

Whaley knew his mistake now. West's rifle lay on the sled and the man was reaching for it.

The man on the ice-field did the only thing possible. He

130

bent low and traveled fast. When the first shot rang out he was nearly a hundred fifty yards away. He crumpled down into the snow and lay still.

West's hands were cold, his fingers stiff. He had not been sure of his aim. Now he gave a whoop of triumph. That was what happened to any one who interfered with Bully West. He fired again at the still huddled heap on the lake.

Presently he would go out there and make sure the man was dead. Just now he had more important business, an engagement to meet a girl in the woods back of the house.

"Got him good," he told himself aloud. "He sure had it comin' to him, the damned traitor."

To find the McRae girl could not be difficult. She had left tracks as she waded away in the deep snow. There was no chance for her to hide. Nor could she have gone far without webs. The little catamount might, of course, shoot him. He had to move carefully, not to give her an opportunity.

As he went forward he watched every tree, every stick of timber behind which she might find cover to ambush him. He was not of a patient temperament, but life in the wilds had taught him to subdue when he must his gusty restlessness. Now he took plenty of time. He was in a hurry to hit the trail with his train and be off, but he could not afford to be in such great haste as to stop a bullet with his body.

He called to her. "Where you at, Dawn? I ain't aimin' to hurt you none. Come out an' quit devilin' me."

Then, when his wheedling brought no answer, he made the forest ring with threats of what he would do to her when he caught her unless she came to him at once.

Moving slowly forward, he came to the end of the tracks that had been made in the snow. They ended abruptly, in a thicket of underbrush. His first thought was that she must be hidden here, but when he had beat through it half a dozen times, he knew this was impossible. Then where was she?

He had told Whaley that she could not fly away. But if she hadn't flown, what had become of her? There were no trees near enough to climb without showing the impressions of her feet in the snow as she moved to the trunk. He had an uneasy sense that she was watching him all the time from some hidden place near at hand. He looked up into the branches of the trees. They were heavy with snow which had not been shaken from them.

West smothered a laugh and an oath. He saw the trick now. She must have back-tracked carefully, at each step putting her feet in exactly the same place as when she had moved forward. Of course! The tracks showed where she had brushed the deep drifts occasionally when the moccasin went in the second time.

It was slow business, for while he studied the sign he must keep a keen eye cocked against the chance of a shot from his hidden prey.

Twice he quartered over the ground before he knew he had reached the place where the back-tracking ceased. Close to the spot was a pine. A pile of snow showed where a small avalanche had plunged down. That must have been when she disturbed it on the branches in climbing.

His glance swept up the trunk and came to a halt. With his rifle he covered the figure crouching close to it on the far side.

"Come down," he ordered.

He was due for one of the surprises of his life. The tree-dweller slid down and stood before him. It was not Jessie McRae, but a man, an Indian, the Blackfoot who had ridden out with the girl once to spoil his triumph over the red-coat Beresford.

For a moment he stood, stupefied, jaw fallen and mouth open. "Whad you doin' here?" he asked at last.

"No food my camp. I hunt," Onistah said.

"Tha's a lie. Where's the McRae girl?"

The slim Indian said nothing. His face was expressionless as a blank wall.

West repeated the question. He might have been talking to a block of wood for all the answer he received. His crafty, cruel mind churned over the situation.

"Won't talk, eh? We'll see about that. You got her hid somewheres an' I'm gonna find where. I'll not stand for yore Injun tricks. Drop that gun an' marché—back to the cabin. Un'erstand?"

Onistah did as he was told.

They reached the cabin. There was one thing West did not get hold of in his mind. Why had not the Blackfoot shot him from the tree? He had had a score of chances. The reason was not one the white man would be likely to fathom. Onistah had not killed him because the Indian was a Christian. He had learned from Father Giguère that he must turn the other cheek.

West, revolver close at hand, cut thongs from the caribou skins. He tied his captive hand and foot, then removed his moccasins and duffles. From the fire he raked out a live coal and put it on a flat chip. This he brought across the room.

"Changed yore mind any? Where's the girl?" he demanded.

Onistah looked at him, impassive as only an Indian can be.

"Still sulky, eh? We'll see about that."

The convict knelt on the man's ankles and pushed the coal against the naked sole of the brown foot.

An involuntary deep shudder went through the Blackfoot's body. The foot twitched. An acrid odor of burning flesh filled the room. No sound came from the locked lips.

The tormentor removed the coal. "I ain't begun to play with you yet. I'm gonna give you some real Apache stuff 'fore I'm through. Where's the girl? I'm gonna find out if I have to boil you in grease."

Still Onistah said nothing.

West brought another coal. "We'll try the other foot," he said.

Again the pungent acrid odor rose to the nostrils.

"How about it now?" the convict questioned.

No answer came. This time Onistah had fainted.

CHAPTER XXVIII

"Is A' Well Wi' You, Lass?"

JESSIE'S shoes crunched on the snow-crust. She traveled fast. In spite of Onistah's assurance her heart was troubled for him. West and Whaley would study the tracks and come to at least an approximation of the truth. She did not dare think of what the gorilla-man would do to her friend if they captured him.

And how was it possible that they would not find him? His footsteps would be stamped deep in the snow. He could not travel fast. Since he had become a Christian, the Blackfoot, with the simplicity of a mind not used to the complexities of modern life, accepted the words of Jesus literally. He would not take a human life to save his own.

She blamed herself for escaping at his expense. The right thing would have been to send him back again for her father. But West had become such a horrible obsession with her that the sight of him even at a distance had put her in a panic.

From the end of the lake she followed the trail Onistah had made. It took into the woods, veering sharply to the right. The timber was open. Even where the snow was deep, the crust was firm enough to hold.

In her anxiety it seemed that hours passed. The sun was

133

still fairly high, but she knew how quickly it sank these winter days.

She skirted a morass, climbed a long hill, and saw before her another lake. On the shore was a camp. A fire was burning, and over this a man stooping.

At the sound of her call, the man looked up. He rose and began to run toward her. She snowshoed down the hill, a little blindly, for the mist of glad tears brimmed her eyes.

Straight into Beresford's arms she went. Safe at last, she began to cry. The soldier petted her, with gentle words of comfort.

"It's all right now, little girl. All over with. Your father's here. See! He's coming. We'll not let anything harm you."

McRae took the girl into his arms and held her tight. His rugged face was twisted with emotion. A dam of ice melted in his heart. The voice with which he spoke, broken with feeling, betrayed how greatly he was shaken.

"My bairn! My wee dawtie! To God be the thanks."

She clung to him, trying to control her sobs. He stroked her hair and kissed her, murmuring Gaelic words of endearment. A thought pierced him, like a swordthrust.

He held her at arm's length, a fierce anxiety in his haggard face. "Is a' well wi' you, lass?" he asked, almost harshly.

She understood his question. Her level eyes met his. They held no reservations of shame. "All's well with me, Father. Mr. Whaley was there the whole time. He stood out against West. He was my friend." She stopped, enough said.

"The Lord be thankit," he repeated again, devoutly.

Tom Morse, rifle in hand, had come from the edge of the woods and was standing near. He had heard her first call, had seen her go to the arms of Beresford direct as a hurt child to those of its mother, and he had drawn reasonable conclusions from that. For under stress the heart reveals itself, he argued, and she had turned simply and instinctively to the man she loved. He stood now outside the group, silent. Inside him too a river of ice had melted. His haunted, sunken eyes told the suffering he had endured. The feeling that flooded him was deeper than joy. She had been dead and was alive again. She had been lost and was found.

"Where have you been?" asked Beresford. "We've been looking for days."

"In a cabin on Bull Creek. Mr. Whaley took me there, but West followed."

"How did you get away?"

"We were out of food. They went hunting. West took my snowshoes. Onistah came. He saw them coming back and gave

134

me his shoes. He went and hid in the woods. But they'll see his tracks. They'll find him. We must hurry back."

"Yes," agreed McRae. "I'm thinkin' if West finds the lad, he'll do him ill."

Morse spoke for the first time, his voice dry as a chip. "We'd better hurry on, Beresford and I. You and Miss McRae can bring the sled."

McRae hesitated, but assented. There might be desperate need of haste. "That'll be the best way. But you'll be carefu', lad. Yon West's a wolf. He'd as lief kill ye baith as look at ye."

The younger men were out of sight over the brow of the hill long before McRae and Jessie had the dogs harnessed.

"You'll ride, lass," the father announced.

She demurred. "We can go faster if I walk. Let me drive. Then you can break trail where the snow's soft."

"No. You'll ride, my dear. There's nae sic a hurry. The lads'll do what's to be done. On wi' ye."

Jessie got into the cariole and was bundled up to the tip of the nose with buffalo robes, the capote of her own fur being drawn over the head and face. For riding in the sub-Arctic winter is a freezing business.

"Marché," [1] ordered McRae.

Cuffy led the dogs up the hill, following the trail already broken. The train made good time, but to Jessie it seemed to crawl. She was tortured with anxiety for Onistah. An express could not have carried her fast enough. It was small comfort to tell herself that Onistah was a Blackfoot and knew every ruse of the woods. His tracks would lead straight to him and the veriest child could follow them. Nor could she persuade herself that Whaley would stand between him and West's anger. To the gambler Onistah was only a nitchie.

The train passed out of the woods to the shore of the lake. Here the going was better. The sun was down and the snow-crust held dogs and sled. A hundred fifty yards from the cabin McRae pulled up the team. He moved forward and examined the snow.

With a heave Jessie flung aside the robes that wrapped her and jumped from the cariole. An invisible hand seemed to clutch tightly at her throat. For what she and her father had seen were crimson splashes in the white. Some one or something had been killed or wounded here. Onistah, of course! He

[1] Most of the dogs of the North were trained by trappers who talked French and gave commands in that language. Hence even the Anglo-Saxon drivers used in driving a good many words of that language. (W. M. R.)

135

must have changed his mind, tried to follow her, and been shot by West as he was crossing the lake.

She groaned, her heart heavy.

McRae offered comfort. "He'll likely be only wounded. The lads wouldna hae moved him yet if he'd no' been livin'."

The train moved forward, Jessie running beside Angus. Morse came to the door. He closed it behind him.

"Onistah?" cried Jessie.

"He's been—hurt. But we were in time. He'll get well."

"West shot him? We saw stains in the snow."

"No. He shot Whaley."

"Whaley?" echoed McRae.

"Yes. Wanted to get rid of him. Thought your daughter was hidden in the woods here. Afraid, too, that Whaley would give him up to the North-West Mounted."

"Then Whaley's dead?" the Scotchman asked.

"No. West hadn't time right then to finish the job. Pretty badly hurt, though. Shot in the side and in the thigh."

"And West?"

"We came too soon. He couldn't finish his deviltry. He lit out over the hill soon as he saw us."

They went into the house.

Jessie walked straight to where Onistah lay on the balsam boughs and knelt beside him. Beresford was putting on one of his feet a cloth soaked in caribou oil.

"What did he do to you?" she cried, a constriction of dread at her heart.

A ghost of a smile touched the immobile face of the native. "Apache stuff, he called it."

"But—"

"West burned his feet to make him tell where you were," Beresford told her gently.

"Oh!" she cried, in horror.

"Good old Onistah. He gamed it out. Wouldn't say a word. West saw us coming and hit the trail."

"Is he—is he—?"

"He's gone."

"I mean Onistah."

"Suffering to beat the band, but not a whimper out of him. He's not permanently hurt—be walking around in a week or two."

"You poor boy!" the girl cried softly, and she put her arm under the Indian's head to lift it to an easier position.

The dumb lips of the Blackfoot did not thank her, but the dark eyes gave her the gratitude of a heart wholly hers.

All that night the house was a hospital. The country was

one where men had learned to look after hurts without much professional aid. In a rough way Angus McRae was something of a doctor. He dressed the wounds of both the injured, using the small medical kit he had brought with him.

Whaley was a bit of a stoic himself. The philosophy of his class was to take good fortune or ill undemonstratively. He was lucky to be alive. Why whine about what must be?

But as the fever grew on him with the lengthening hours, he passed into delirium. Sometimes he groaned with pain. Again he fell into disconnected babble of early days. He was back again with his father and mother, living over his wild and erring youth.

". . . Don't tell Mother. I'll square it all right if you keep it from her. . . . Rotten run of cards. Ninety-seven dollars. You'll have to wait, I tell you. . . . Mother, Mother, if you won't cry like that . . ."

McRae used the simple remedies he had. In themselves they were, he knew, of little value. He must rely on good nursing and the man's hardy constitution to pull him through.

With Morse and Beresford he discussed the best course to follow. It was decided that Morse should take Onistah and Jessie back to Faraway next day and return with a load of provisions. Whaley's fever must run its period. It was impossible to tell yet whether he would live or die, but for some days at least it would not be safe to move him.

CHAPTER XXIX

Not Going Alone

"MORSE, I've watched ye through four-five days of near-hell. I ken nane I'd rather tak wi' me as a lone companion on the long traverse. You're canny an' you're bold. That's why I'm trustin' my lass to your care. It's a short bit of a trip, an' far as I can see there's nae danger. But the fear's in me. That's the truth, man. Gie me your word you'll no' let her oot o' your sight till ye hand her ower to my wife at Faraway."

Angus clamped a heavy hand on the young man's shoulder. His blue eyes searched steadily those of the trader.

"I'll not let her twenty yards from me any time. That's a promise, McRae," the trader said quietly.

Well wrapped from the wind, Onistah sat in the cariole.

Jessie kissed the Scotchman fondly, laughing at him the while. "You're a goose, Father. I'm all right. You take good care of yourself. That West might come back here."

"No chance of that. West will never come back except at the end of a rope. He's headed for the edge of the Barrens, or up that way somewhere," Beresford said. "And inside of a week I'll be north-bound on his trail myself."

Jessie was startled, a good deal distressed. "I'd let him go. He'll meet a bad end somewhere. If he never comes back, as you say he won't, then he'll not trouble us."

The soldier smiled grimly. "That's not the way of the Mounted. Get the fellow you're sent after. That's our motto. I've been assigned the job of bringing in West and I've got to get him."

"You don't mean you're going up there alone to bring back that—that wolf-man?"

"Oh, no," the trooper answered lightly. "I'll have a Cree along as a guide."

"A Cree," she scoffed. "What good will he be if you find West? He'll not help you against him at all."

"Not what he's with me for. I'm not supposed to need any help to bring back one man."

"It's—it's just suicide to go after him alone," she persisted. "Look what he did to the guard at the prison, to Mr. Whaley, to Onistah! He's just awful—hardly human."

"The lad's under orders, lass," McRae told her. "Gin they send him into the North after West, he'll just have to go. He canna argy-bargy aboot it."

Jessie gave up, reluctantly.

The little cavalcade started. Morse drove. The girl brought up the rear.

Her mind was still on the hazard of the journey Beresford must take. When Morse stopped to rest the dogs for a few moments, she tucked up Onistah again and recurred to the subject.

"I don't think Win Beresford should go after West alone except for a Cree guide. The Inspector ought to send another constable with him. Or two more. If he knew that man—how cruel and savage he is—"

Tom Morse spoke quietly. "He's not going alone. I'll be with him."

She stared. "You?"

"Yes. Sworn in as a deputy constable."

"But—he didn't say you were going when I spoke to him about it a little while ago."

"He didn't know. I've made up my mind since."

In point of fact he had come to a decision three seconds before he announced it.

Her soft eyes applauded him. "That'll be fine. His friends won't worry so much if you're with him. But—of course you know it'll be a horrible trip—and dangerous."

"No picnic," he admitted.

She continued to look at him, her cheeks flushed and her face vivid. "You must like Win a lot. Not many men would go."

"We're good friends," Morse answered dryly. "Anyhow, I owe West something on my own account."

The real reason why he was going he had not given. During the days she had been lost he had been on the rack of torture. He did not want her to suffer months of such mental distress while the man she loved was facing alone the peril of his grim work in the white Arctic desert.

They resumed the journey.

Jessie said no more. She would not mention the subject again probably. But it would be a great deal in her thoughts. She lived much of the time inside herself with her own imagination. This had the generosity and the enthusiasm of youth. She wanted to believe people fine and good and true. It warmed her to discover unexpected virtues in them.

Mid-afternoon brought them to Faraway. They drove down the main street of the village to McRae's house while the half-breeds cheered from the door of the Morse store.

Jessie burst into the big family room where Matapi-Koma sat bulging out from the only rocking-chair in the North woods.

"Oh, Mother—Mother!" the girl cried, and hugged the Cree woman with all the ardent young savagery of her nature.

The Indian woman's fat face crinkled to an expansive smile. She had stalwart sons of her own, but no daughters except this adopted child. Jessie was very dear to her.

In a dozen sentences the girl poured out her story, the words tumbling pell-mell over each other in headlong haste.

Matapi-Koma waddled out to the sled. "Onistah stay here," she said, and beamed on him. "Blackfoot all same Cree to Matapi-Koma when he friend Jessie. Angus send word nurse him till he well again."

Tom carried the Indian into the house so that his feet would not touch the ground. Jessie had stayed in to arrange the couch where Fergus usually slept.

She followed Morse to the door when he left. "We'll have some things to send back to Father when you go. I'll bring them down to the store to-morrow morning," she said. "And Mother wants you to come to supper to-night. Don't you dare say you're too busy."

He smiled at the intimate feminine fierceness of the injunction. The last few hours had put them on a somewhat different footing. He would accept such largesse as she was willing to offer. He recognized the spirit in which it was given. She wanted to show her appreciation of what he had done for her and was about to do for the man she loved. Nor would Morse meet her generosity in a churlish spirit.

"I'll be here when the gong rings," he told her heartily.

"Let's see. It's nearly three now. Say five o'clock," she decided.

"At five I'll be knockin' on the door."

She flashed at him a glance both shy and daring. "And I'll open it before you break through and bring it with you."

The trader went away with a queer warmth in his heart he had not known for many a day. The facts did not justify this elation, this swift exhilaration of blood, but to one who has starved for long any food is grateful.

Jessie flew back into the house. She had a busy two hours before her. "Mother, Mr. Morse is coming to dinner. What's in the house?"

"Fergus brought a black-tail in yesterday."

"Good. I know what I'll have. But first off, I want a bath. Lots of hot water, and all foamy with soap. I've got to hurry. You can peel the potatoes if you like. And fix some of those young onions. They're nice. And Mother—I'll let you make the biscuits. That's all. I'll do the rest."

The girl touched a match to the fire that was set in her room. She brought a tin tub and hot water and towels. Slim and naked she stood before the roaring logs and reveled in her bath. The sense of cleanliness was a luxury delicious. When she had dressed herself from the soles of her feet up in clean clothes, she felt a new and self-respecting woman.

She did not pay much attention to the psychology of dress, but she knew that when she had on the pretty plaid that had come from Fort Benton, and when her heavy black hair was done up just right, she had twice the sex confidence she felt in old togs. Jessie would have denied indignantly that she was a coquette. None the less she was intent on conquest. She wanted this quiet, self-contained American to like her.

The look she had seen in his red-brown eyes at times tantalized her. She could not read it. That some current of feeling about her raced deep in him she divined, but she did not know what it was. He had a way of letting his steady gaze rest on her disturbingly. What was he thinking? Did he despise her? Was he, away down out of sight, the kind of man toward women that West and Whaley were? She wouldn't believe it. He had never taken an Indian woman to live with him. There was not even a rumor that he had ever taken an interest in any Cree girl. Of course she did not like him—not the way she did Win Beresford or even Onistah—but she was glad he held himself aloof. It would have greatly disappointed her to learn of any sordid intrigue involving him.

Jessie rolled up her sleeves and put on a big apron. She saw that the onions and the potatoes were started and the venison ready for broiling. From a chest of drawers she brought one of the new white linen tablecloths of which she was inordinately proud. She would not trust any one but herself to set the table. Morse had come from a good family. He knew about such things. She was not going to let him go away thinking Angus McRae's family were barbarians, even though his wife was a Cree and his children of the half-blood.

On the table she put a glass dish of wild-strawberry jam. In the summer she had picked the fruit herself, just as she had gathered the saskatoon berries sprinkled through the pemmican she was going to use for the rubaboo.

CHAPTER XXX

"M" For Morse

Two in the village bathed that day. The other was Tom Morse. He discarded his serviceable moccasins, his caribou-skin capote with the fur on, his moose-skin trousers, and his picturesque blanket shirt. For these he substituted the ungainly clothes of civilization, a pair of square-toed boots, a store suit, a white shirt.

This was not the way Faraway dressed for gala occasions, but in several respects the trader did not choose to follow the habits of the North. At times he liked to remind himself that he was an American and not a French half-breed born in the woods.

As he had promised, he was at the McRaes' by the appointed hour. Jessie opened to his knock.

The girl almost took his breath. He had not realized how attractive she was. In her rough outdoor costumes she had a certain naïve boyishness, a very taking quality of vital energy that was sexless. But in the house dress she was wearing now, Jessie was wholly feminine. The little face, cameo-fine and clear-cut, the slender body, willow-straight, had the soft rounded curves that were a joy to the eye. He had always thought of her as dark, but to his surprise he found her amazingly fair for one of the métis blood.

A dimpled smile flashed him welcome. "You did come, then?"

"Is it the wrong night? Weren't you expectin' me?" he asked in pretended alarm.

"I was and I wasn't. It wouldn't have surprised me if you had decided you were too busy to come."

"Not when Miss Jessie McRae invites me."

"She invited you once before," the girl reminded him.

"Then she asked me because she thought she ought. Is that why I'm asked this time?"

She laughed. "You mustn't look a gift dinner in the mouth."

They were by this time in the big family room. She relieved him of his coat. He walked over the couch upon which Onistah lay.

"How goes it? Tough sleddin'?" he asked.

The bronze face of the Blackfoot was immobile. He must still have been in great pain from the burnt feet, but he gave no sign of it.

"Onistah find good friends," he answered simply.

Tom looked round the room, and again there came to him the sense of home. Logs roared and snapped in the great fireplace. The table, set with the dishes and the plated silver McRae had imported from the States, stirred in him a pleasure that was almost poignant. The books, the organ, the quaint old engravings Angus had brought with him when he crossed the ocean: all of these touched the trader nearly. He was in exile, living a bachelor life under the most primitive conditions. The atmosphere of this house penetrated to every fiber of his being. It filled him with an acute hunger. Here were love and friendly intercourse and all the daily, homely routine that made life beautiful.

And here was the girl that he loved, vivid, vital, full of

charm. The swift deftness and grace of her movements enticed him. The inflections of her warm, young voice set his pulses throbbing as music sometimes did. An ardent desire for her flooded him. She was the most winsome creature under heaven —but she was not for him.

Matapi-Koma sat at the head of the table, a smiling and benignant matron finished in copper. She had on her best dress, a beaded silk with purple satin trimmings, brought by a Red River cart from Winnipeg, accompanied with a guarantee from the trader that Queen Victoria had none better. The guarantee was worth what it was worth, but Matapi-Koma was satisfied. Never had she seen anything so grand. That Angus McRae could afford to buy it for her proved him a great chief.

Jessie waited on the table herself. She set upon it such a dinner as neither of her guests had eaten in years. Venison broiled to a turn, juicy, succulent mallard ducks from the cold storage of their larder, mashed potatoes with gravy, young boiled onions from Whoop-Up, home-made rubaboo of delicious flavor, hot biscuits and wild-strawberry jam! And finally, with the tea, a brandy-flavored plum pudding that an old English lady at Winnipeg had taught Jessie how to make.

Onistah ate lying on the couch. Afterward, filled to repletion, with the sense of perfect contentment a good dinner brings, the two young men stuffed their pipes and puffed strata of smoke toward the log rafters of the room. Jessie cleared the table, then sat down and put the last stitches in the gun-case she had been working at intermittently for a month. It was finished, but she had not till now stitched the initials into the cloth.

As the swift fingers of the girl flashed back and forth, both men watched, not too obviously, the profile shadowed by the dark, abundant, shining hair. The picture of her was an intimate one, but Tom's tricky imagination tormented him with one of still nearer personal association. He saw her in his own house, before his own fireside, a baby clinging to her skirt. Then, resolutely, he put the mental etching behind him. She loved his friend Beresford, a man out of a thousand, and of course he loved her. Had he not seen her go straight to his arms after her horrible experience with West?

Matapi-Koma presently waddled out of the room and they could hear the clatter of dishes.

"I told her I'd help her wash them if she'd wait," explained Jessie. "But she'd rather do them now and go to bed. My conscience is clear, anyhow." She added with a little bubble

143

of laughter, "And I don't have to do the work. Is that the kind of a conscience you have, Mr. Morse?"

"If I were you my conscience would tell me that I couldn't go and leave my guests," he answered.

She raked him with a glance of merry derision. "Oh, I know how yours works. I wouldn't have it for anything. It's an awf'lly bossy one. It's sending you out to the Barrens with Win Beresford just because he's your friend."

"Not quite. I have another reason too," he replied.

"Yes, I know. You don't like West. Nobody does. My father doesn't—or Fergus—or Mr. Whaley—but they're not taking the long trail after him as you are. You can't get out of it that way."

She had not, of course, hit on the real reason for going that supplemented his friendship for the constable and he did not intend that she should.

"It doesn't matter much why I'm going. Anyhow, it'll be good for me. I'm gettin' soft and fat. After I've been out in the deep snows a month or so, I'll have taken up my belt a notch or two. It's time I wrestled with a blizzard an' tried livin' on lean rabbit." [1]

Her gaze swept his lean, hard, compact body. "Yes, you look soft," she mocked. "Father said something of that sort when he looked at that door there you came through."

Tom had been watching her stitching. He offered a comment now, perhaps to change the subject. It is embarrassing for a modest man to talk about himself.

"You're workin' that 'W' upside down," he said.

"Am I? Who said it was a 'W'?"

"I guessed it might be."

"You're a bad guesser. It's an 'M.' 'M' stands for McRae, doesn't it?"

"Yes, and 'W' for Winthrop," he said with a little flare of boldness.

A touch of soft color flagged her cheeks. "And 'I' for impudence," she retorted with a smile that robbed the words of offense.

He was careful not to risk outstaying his welcome. After an hour he rose to go. His good-bye to Matapi-Koma and Onistah was made in the large living-room.

Jessie followed him to the outside door.

[1] Rabbit is about the poorest meat in the North. It is lean and stringy, furnishes very little nourishment and not much fat, and is not a muscle-builder. In a country where oil and grease are essentials, such food is not desirable. The Indians ate great quantities of them. (W. M. R.)

He gave her a word of comfort as he buttoned his coat. "Don't you worry about Win. I'll keep an eye on him."

"Thank you. And he'll keep one on you, I suppose."

He laughed. That reversal of the case was a new idea to him. The prettiest girl in the North was not holding her breath till he returned safely. "I reckon," he said. "We'll team together fine."

"Don't be foolhardy, either of you," she cautioned.

"No," he promised, and held out his hand. "Good-bye, if I don't see you in the mornin'."

He did not know she was screwing up her courage and had been for half an hour to do something she had never done before. She plunged at it, a tide of warm blood beating into her face beneath the tan.

" 'M' is for Morse too, and 'T' for Tom," she said.

With the same motion she thrust the gun-case into his hand and him out of the door.

He stood outside, facing a closed door, the bit of fancywork in his mittens. An exultant electric tingle raced through his veins. She had given him a token of friendship he would cherish all his life.

CHAPTER XXXI
The Long Trail

For four days Whaley lay between life and death. There were hours when the vital current in him ebbed so low that McRae thought it was the beginning of the end. But after the fifth day he began definitely to mend. His appetite increased. The fever in him abated. The delirium passed away. Just a week from the time he had been wounded, McRae put him on the cariole and took him to town over the hard crust of the snow.

Beresford returned from Fort Edmonton a few hours later, carrying with him an appointment for Morse as guide and deputy constable.

"Maintiens le droit," said the officer, clapping his friend on the shoulder. "You're one of us now. A great chance for a short life you've got. Time for the insurance companies to cancel any policies they may have on you."

Morse smiled. He was only a deputy, appointed temporarily, but it pleased him to be chosen even in this capacity as a member of the most efficient police force in the world. "Maintiens le droit" was the motto of the Mounted. Tom did not intend that the morale of that body should suffer through him if he could help it.

Angus McRae had offered his dog-train for the pursuit and Beresford had promptly accepted. The four dogs of the Scotch trapper were far and away better than any others that could be picked up in a hurry. They had stamina, and they were not savage and wolfish like most of those belonging to the Indians and even to the Hudson's Bay Company.

Supplies for the trip had been gathered by Morse. From the Crees he had bought two hundred pounds of dried fish for the dogs. Their own provisions consisted of pemmican, dried caribou meat, flour, salt, tea, and tobacco.

All Faraway was out to see the start. The travelers would certainly cover hundreds and perhaps thousands of miles before their return. Even in that country of wide spaces, where men mushed far when the rivers and lakes were closed, this was likely to prove an epic trip.

Beresford cracked the long lash and Cuffy leaned forward in the traces. The tangle of dogs straightened out and began to move. A French voyageur lifted his throat in a peculiar shout that was half a bark. Indians and half-breeds snowshoed down the street beside the sled. At the door of the McRae house stood Angus, his wife, and daughter.

"God wi' you baith," the trapper called.

Jessie waved a scarf, and Beresford, who had spent the previous evening with her, threw up a hand in gay greeting.

The calvacade drew to the edge of the woods. Morse looked back. A slim figure, hardly distinguishable in the distance, still stood in front of the McRae house fluttering the scarf.

A turn in the trail hid her. Faraway was shut out of view.

For four or five miles the trappers stayed with them. It was rather a custom of the North to speed travelers on their way in this fashion. At the edge of the first lake the Indians and half-breeds said good-bye and turned back.

Morse moved onto the ice and broke trail. The dogs followed in tandem—Cuffy, Koona, Bull, and Cæsar. They traveled fast over the ice and reached the woods beyond. The timber was not thick. Beyond this was a second lake, a larger one. By the time they had crossed this, the sun was going down.

The men watched for a sheltered place to camp and as soon as they found one, they threw off the trail to the edge of the woods, drawing up the sledge back of them as a windbreak. They gathered pine for fuel and cut balsam boughs for beds. It had come on to snow, and they ate supper with their backs to the drive of the flakes, the hoods of their furs drawn over their heads.

The dogs sat round in a half-circle watching them and the frozen fish thawing before the fire. Their faces, tilted a little sideways, ears cocked and eyes bright, looked anxiously expectant. When the fish were half-thawed, Morse tossed them by turn to the waiting animals, who managed to get rid of their supper with a snap and a gulp. Afterward they burrowed down in the snow and fell asleep.

On the blazing logs Beresford had put two kettles filled with snow. These he refilled after the snow melted, until enough water was in them. Into one kettle he put a piece of fat caribou meat. The other was to make tea.

Using their snowshoes as shovels, they scraped a place clear and scattered balsam boughs on it. On this they spread an empty flour sack, cut open at the side. Tin plates and cups served as dish.

Their supper consisted of soggy bannocks, fat meat, and tea. While they ate, the snow continued to fall. It was not unwelcome, for so long as this lasted the cold could not be intolerable. Moreover, snow makes a good white blanket and protects against sudden drops in temperature.

They changed their moccasins and duffles and pulled on as night-wear long buffalo-skin boots, hood, mufflers, and fur mits. A heavy fur robe and a blanket were added. Into these last they snuggled down, wrapping themselves up so completely that a tenderfoot would have smothered for lack of air.

Before they retired, they could hear the ice on the lake cracking like distant thunder. The trees back of them occasionally snapped from the cold with reports that sounded like pistol shots.

In five minutes both men were asleep. They lay with their heads entirely covered, as the Indians did. Not once during the night did they stir. To disarrange their bedding and expose the nose or the hands to the air would be to risk being frozen.

Morse woke first. He soon had a roaring fire. Again there were two kettles on it, one for fat meat and the other for strong tea. No fish were thawing before the heat, for dogs are fed only once a day. Otherwise they get sleepy and sluggish, losing the edge of their keenness.

They were off to an early start. There was a cold head

wind that was uncomfortable. For hours they held to the slow, swinging stride of the webs. Sometimes the trail was through the forest, sometimes in and out of brush and small timber. Twice during the day they crossed lakes and hit up a lively pace. Once they came to a muskeg, four miles across, and had to plough over the moss hags while brush tangled their feet and slapped their faces.

Cuffy was a prince of leaders. He seemed to know by some sixth sense the best way to wind through underbrush and over swamps. He was master of the train and ruled by strength and courage as well as intelligence. Bull had ideas of his own, but after one sharp brush with Cuffy, from which he had emerged ruffled and bleeding, the native dog relinquished claim to dominance.

The travelers made about fifteen miles before noon. They came to a solitary tepee, built on the edge of a lake with a background of snow-burdened spruce. This lodge was constructed of poles arranged cone-shaped side by side, the chinks between plastered with moss wedged in to fill every crevice. A thin wisp of smoke rose from an open space in the top.

At the sound of the yelping dogs a man lifted the moose-skin curtain that served as a door. He was an old and wrinkled Cree. His face was so brown and tough and netted with seams that it resembled a piece of alligator leather. From out of it peered two very small bright eyes.

"Ugh! Ugh!" he grunted.

This appeared to be all the English that he knew. Beresford tried him in French and discovered he had a smattering of it. After a good many attempts, the soldier found that he had seen no white man with a dog-train in many moons. The Cree lived there alone, it appeared, and trapped for a living. Why he was separated from all his kin and tribal relations the young Canadian could not find out at the time. Later he learned that the old fellow was an outcast because he had once shown the white feather in a battle with Blackfeet fifty years earlier.

Before they left, the travelers discovered that he knew two more words of English. One was rum, the other tobacco. He begged for both. They left him a half-foot of tobacco. The scant supply of whiskey they had brought was for an emergency.

Just before night fell, Morse shot two ptarmigan in the woods. These made a welcome addition to their usual fare.

Though both the men were experienced in the use of snowshoes, their feet were raw from the chafing of the thongs. Before the camp-fire they greased the sore places with tallow.

In a few days the irritation due to the webs would disappear and the leg muscles brought into service by this new and steady shuffle would harden and grow fit.

They had built a wind-break of brush beside the sled and covered the ground with spruce boughs after clearing away the snow. Here they rested after supper, drying socks, duffles, and moccasins, which were wet with perspiration, before the popping fire.

Beresford pulled out his English briar pipe and Tom one picked from the Company stock. Smoke wreathed their heads while they lounged indolently on the spruce bed and occasionally exchanged a remark. They knew each other well enough for long silences. When they talked, it was because they had something to say.

The Canadian looked at his friend's new gun-case and remarked with a gleam in his eye:

"I spoke for that first, Tom. Had miners on it, I thought."

The American laughed sardonically. "It was a present for a good boy," he explained. "I've a notion somebody was glad I was mushin' with you on this trip. Maybe you can guess why. Anyhow, I drew a present out of it."

"I see you did," Beresford answered, grinning.

"I'm to look after you proper an' see you're tucked up."

"Oh, that's it?"

"That's just it."

The constable looked at him queerly, started to say something, then changed his mind.

CHAPTER XXXII

A Picture In A Locket

It was characteristic of McRae that he had insisted on bringing Whaley to his own home to recuperate. "It's nursin' you need, man, an' guid food. Ye'll get baith at the hoose."

The trader protested, and was overruled. His Cree wife was not just now able to look after him. McRae's wife and daughter made good his promise, and the wounded man thrived under their care.

On an afternoon Whaley lay on the bed in his room smoking. Beside him sat Lemoine, also puffing at a pipe. The trapper had brought to the ex-gambler a strange tale of a locket and a ring he had seen bought by a half-breed from a Blackfoot squaw who claimed to have had it eighteen years. He had just finished telling of it when Jessie knocked at the door and came into the room with a bowl of caribou broth.

Whaley pretended to resent this solicitude, but his objection was a fraud. He liked this girl fussing over him. His attitude toward her was wholly changed. Thinking of her as a white girl, he looked at her with respect.

"No more slops," he said. "Bring me a good caribou steak and I'll say thank you."

"You're to eat what Mother sends," she told him.

Lemoine had risen from the chair on which he had been sitting. He stared at her, a queer look of puzzled astonishment in his eyes. Jessie became aware of his gaze and flashed on him a look of annoyance.

"Have you seen a ghost, Mr. Lemoine?" she asked.

"By gar, maybeso, Miss Jessie. The picture in the locket, it jus' lak you—same hair, same eyes, same smile."

"What picture in what locket?"

"The locket I see at Whoop-Up, the one Pierre Roubideaux buy from old Makoye-kin's squaw."

"A picture of a Blackfoot?"

"No-o. Maybe French—maybe from the 'Merican country. I do not know."

Whaley took the pipe from his mouth and sat up, the chill eyes in his white face fixed and intent. "Go back to Whoop-Up, Lemoine. Buy that locket and that ring for me from Pierre Roubideaux. See Makoye-kin—and his squaw. Find out where she got it—and when. Run down the whole story."

The trapper took off a fur cap and scratched his curly poll. "Mais—pourquois? All that will take money, is it not so?"

"I'll let you have the money. Spend what you need, but account for it to me afterward."

Jessie felt the irregular beat of a hammer inside her bosom. "What is it you think, Mr. Whaley?" she cried softly.

"I don't know what I think. Probably nothing to it. But there's a locket. We know that. With a picture that looks like you, Lemoine here thinks. We'd better find out whose picture it is, hadn't we?"

"Yes, but—Do you mean that maybe it has something to do with me? How can it? The sister of Stokimatis was my mother. Onistah is my cousin. Ask Stokimatis. She knows. What could this woman of the picture be to me?"

150

Jessie could not understand the fluttering pulse in her throat. She had not doubted that her mother was a Blackfoot. All the romance of her clouded birth centered around the unknown father who had died when she was a baby. Stokimatis had not been very clear about that. She had never met the man, according to the story she had told Sleeping Dawn. Neither she nor those of her tribal group knew anything of him. Was there a mystery about his life? In her childish dreams Jessie had woven one. He was to her everything desirable, for he was the tie that bound her to all the higher standards of life she craved.

"I don't know. Likely it's all a mare's nest. Find Stokimatis, Lemoine, and bring her back with you. We'll see what she can tell us. And get the locket and the ring, with the story back of them."

Again Lemoine referred to the cost. He would have to take his dog-train to Whoop-Up, and from there out to the creek where Pierre Roubideaux was living. Makoye-kin and his family might be wintering anywhere within a radius of a hundred miles. Was there any use in going out on such a wild-hare chase?

Whaley thought there was and said so with finality. He did not give his real reason, which was that he wanted to pay back to McRae and his daughter the debt he owed. They had undoubtedly saved his life after he had treated her outrageously. There was already one score to his credit, of course. He had saved her from West. But he felt the balance still tipped heavily against him. And he was a man who paid his debts.

It was this factor of his make-up—the obligation of old associations laid upon him—that had taken him out to West with money, supplies, and a dog-train to help his escape.

Jessie went out to find her father. Her eagerness to see him outflew her steps. This was not a subject she could discuss with Matapi-Koma. The Cree woman would not understand what a tremendous difference it made if she could prove her blood was wholly of the superior race. Nor could Jessie with tact raise such a point. It involved not only the standing of Matapi-Koma herself, but also of her sons.

The girl found McRae in the storeroom looking over a bundle of assorted pelts—marten, fox, mink, and beaver. The news tumbled from her lips in excited exclamations.

"Oh, Father, guess! Mr. Lemoine saw a picture—a Blackfoot woman had it—old Makoye-kin's wife—and she sold it. And he says it was like me—exactly. Maybe it was my aunt —or some one. My father's sister! Don't you think?"

151

"I'll ken what I think better gin ye'll just quiet doon an' tell me a' aboot it, lass."

She told him. The Scotchman took what she had to say with no outward sign of excitement. None the less his blood moved faster. He wanted no change in the relations between them that would interfere with the love she felt for him. To him it did not matter whether she was of the pure blood or of the métis. He had always ignored the Indian in her. She was a precious wildling of beauty and delight. By nature she was of the ruling race. There was in her nothing servile or dependent, none of the inertia that was so marked a mental characteristic of the Blackfoot and the Cree. Her slender body was compact of fire and spirit. She was alive to her finger-tips.

None the less he was glad on her account. Since it mattered to her that she was a half-blood, he would rejoice, too, if she could prove the contrary. Or, if she could trace her own father's family, he would try to be glad for her.

With his rough forefinger he touched gently the tender curve of the girl's cheek. "I'm thinkin' that gin ye find relatives across the line, auld Angus McRae will be losin' his dawtie."

She flew into his arms, her warm, young face pressed against his seamed cheek.

"Never—never! You're my father—always that no matter what I find. You taught me to read and nursed me when I was sick. Always you've cared for me and been good to me. I'll never have any real father but you," she cried passionately.

He stroked her dark, abundant hair fondly. "My lass, I've gi'en ye all the love any yin could gi'e his ain bairn. I doot I've been hard on ye at times, but I'm a dour auld man an' fine ye ken my heart was woe for ye when I was the strictest."

She could count on the fingers of one hand the times when he had said as much. Of nature he was a bit of Scotch granite externally. He was sentimental. Most of his race are. But he guarded the expression of it as though it were a vice.

"Maybe Onistah has heard his mother say something about it," Jessie suggested.

"Like enough. There'll be nae harm in askin' the lad."

But the Blackfoot had little to tell. He had been told by Stokimatis that Sleeping Dawn was his cousin, but he had never quite believed it. Once, when he had pressed his mother with questions, she had smiled deeply and changed the subject. His feeling was, and had always been, that there was some mystery about the girl's birth. Stokimatis either knew what it was or had some hint of it.

His testimony at least tended to support the wild hopes flaming in the girl's heart.

Lemoine started south for Whoop-Up at break of day.

CHAPTER XXXIII
Into The Lone Land

INTO Northern Lights the pursuers drove after a four-day traverse. Manders, of the Mounted, welcomed them with the best he had. No news had come to him from the outside for more than two months, and after his visitors were fed and warmed, they lounged in front of a roaring log fire while he flung questions at them of what the world and its neighbor were doing.

Manders was a dark-bearded man, big for the North-West Police. He had two hobbies. One was trouble in the Balkans, which he was always prophesying. The other was a passion for Sophocles, which he read in the original from a pocket edition. Start him on the chariot race in "Elektra" and he would spout it while he paced the cabin and gestured with flashing eyes. For he was a Rugby and an Oxford man, though born with the wanderlust in his heart. Some day he would fall heir to a great estate in England, an old baronetcy which carried with it manors and deer parks and shaven lawns that had taken a hundred years to grow. Meanwhile he lived on pemmican and sour bannocks. Sometimes he grumbled, but his grumbling was a fraud. He was here of choice, because he was a wild ass of the desert and his ears heard only the call of adventure. Of such was the North-West Mounted.

Presently, when the stream of his curiosity as to the outside began to dry, Beresford put a few questions of his own. Manders could give him no information. He was in touch with the trappers for a radius of a hundred miles of which Northern Lights was the center, but no word had come to him of a lone traveler with a dog-train passing north.

"Probably striking west of here," the big black Englishman suggested.

Beresford's face twisted to a wry, humorous grimace. East,

west, or north, they would have to find the fellow and bring him back.

The man-hunters spent a day at Northern Lights to rest the dogs and restock their supplies. They overhauled their dunnage carefully, mended the broken moose-skin harness, and looked after one of the animals that had gone a little lame from a sore pad. From a French half-breed they bought additional equipment much needed for the trail. He was a gay, good-looking youth in new fringed leather hunting-shirt, blue Saskatchewan cap trimmed with ribbons, and cross belt of scarlet cloth. His stock in trade was dog-shoes, made of caribou-skin by his wife, and while in process of tanning soaked in some kind of liquid that would prevent the canines from eating them off their feet.

The temperature was thirty-five below zero when they left the post and there were sun dogs in the sky. Manders had suggested that they had better wait a day or two, but the man-hunters were anxious to be on the trail. They had a dangerous, unpleasant job on hand. Both of them wanted it over with as soon as possible.

They headed into the wilds. The road they made was a crooked path through the white, unbroken forest. They saw many traces of fur-bearing animals, but did not stop to do any hunting. The intense cold and the appearance of the sky were whips to drive them fast. In the next two or three days they passed fifteen or twenty lakes. Over these they traveled rapidly, but in the portages and the woods they had to pack the snow, sometimes cut out obstructing brush, and again help the dogs over rough or heavy places.

The blizzard caught them the third day. They fought their way through the gathering storm across a rather large lake to the timber's edge. Here they cleared away a space about nine feet square and cut evergreen boughs from the trees to cover it. At one side of this, Morse built the fire while Beresford unharnessed the dogs and thawed out a mess of frozen fish for them. Presently the kettles were bubbling on the fire. The men ate supper and drew the sled up as a barricade against the wind.

The cold had moderated somewhat and it had come on to snow. All night a sleety, wind-driven drizzle beat upon them. They rose from an uncomfortable night to a gloomy day.

They consulted about what was best to do. Their camp was in a poor place, among a few water-logged trees that made a poor, smoky fire. It had little shelter from the storm, and there was no evidence of fair weather at hand.

"Better tackle the next traverse," Morse advised. "Once

we get across the lake we can't be worse off than we are here."

"Righto!" assented Beresford.

They packed their supplies, harnessed the dogs, and were off. Into the storm they drove, head down, buffeted by a screaming wind laden with stinging sleet that swept howling across the lake. All about them they heard the sharp reports of cracking ice. At any moment a fissure might open, and its width might be an inch or several yards. In the blinding gale they could see nothing. Literally, they had to feel their way.

Morse went ahead to test the ice, Cuffy following close at his heels. The water rushes up after a fissure and soon freezes over. The danger is that one may come to it too soon.

This was what happened. Morse, on his snowshoes, crossed the thinly frozen ice safely. Cuffy, a step or two behind the trail-breaker, plunged through into the water. The prompt energy of Beresford saved the other dogs. He stopped them instantly and threw his whole weight back to hold the sled. The St. Bernard floundered in the water for a few moments and tried to reach Morse. The harness held Cuffy back. Beresford ran to the edge of the break and called him. A second or two later he was helping to drag the dog back upon the firm ice.

In the bitter cold the matted coat of the St. Bernard froze stiff. Cuffy knew his danger. The instant the sled was across the crack, he plunged at the load and went forward with such speed that he seemed almost to drag the other dogs with him.

Fortunately the shore was near, not more than three or four miles away. Within half an hour land was reached. A forest came down to the edge of the lake.

From the nearer trees Morse sliced birch bark. An abundance of fairly dry wood was at hand. Before a roaring fire Cuffy lay on a buffalo robe and steamed. Within an hour he was snuggling a contented nose up to Beresford's caressing hand.

Fagged out, the travelers went to bed early. Long before daybreak they were up. The blizzard had died down during the night. It left behind a crusted trail over which the dogs moved fast. The thermometer had again dropped sharply and the weather was bitter cold. Before the lights of an Indian village winked at them through the trees, they had covered nearly forty miles. In the wintry afternoon darkness they drove up.

The native dogs were barking a welcome long before they came jingling into the midst of the tepees. Bucks, squaws, and papooses tumbled out to see them with guttural exclamations of greeting. Some of the youngsters and one or two of the maidens had never before seen a white man.

A fast and furious mêlée interrupted conversation. The wolfish dogs of the village were trying out the mettle of the four strangers. The snarling and yelping drowned all other sounds until the gaunt horde of sharp-muzzled, stiff-haired brutes had been beaten back by savage blows from the whip and by quick thrusts of a rifle butt.

The head man of the group invited the two whites into the largest hut. Morse and Beresford sat down before a smoky fire and carried on a difficult dialogue. They divided half a yard of tobacco among the men present and gave each of the women a small handful of various-colored beads.

They ate sparingly of a stew made of fish, the gift of their hosts. In turn the officers had added to the menu a large piece of fat moose which was devoured with voracity.

The Indians, questioned, had heard a story of a white man traveling alone through the Lone Lands with a dog-train. He was a giant of a fellow and surly, the word had gone out. Who he was or where he was going they did not know, but he seemed to be making for the great river in the north. That was the sum and substance of what Beresford learned from them about West by persistent inquiry.

After supper, since it was so bitterly cold outside, the manhunters slept in the tepee of the chief. Thirteen Indians too slept there. Two of them were the head man's wives, six were his children, one was a grandchild. Who the rest of the party were or what relation they bore to him, the guests did not learn.

The place was filthy and the air was vile. Before morning both the young whites regretted they had not taken chances outside.

"Not ever again," Beresford said with frank disgust after they had set out next day. "I'll starve if I have to. I'll freeze if I must. But, by Jove! I'll not eat Injun stew or sleep in a pot-pourri of nitchies. Not good enough."

Tom grinned. "While I was eatin' the stew, I thought I could stand sleepin' there even if I gagged at the eats, and while I was tryin' to sleep, I made up my mind if I had to choose one it would be the stew. Next time we're wrastlin' with a blizzard, we'll know enough to be thankful for our mercies. We'll be able to figure it might be a lot worse."

That afternoon they killed a caribou and got much-needed fresh meat for themselves and the dogs. Unfortunately, while carrying the hind-quarters to the sled, Beresford slipped and strained a tendon in the left leg. He did not notice it much at the time, but after an hour's travel the pain increased. He found it difficult to keep pace with the dogs.

They were traversing a ten-mile lake. Morse proposed that they camp as soon as they reached the edge of it.

"Better get on the sled and ride till then," he added.

Beresford shook his head. "No, I'll carry on all right. Got to grin and bear it. The sled's overloaded anyhow. You trot along and I'll tag. Time you've got the fires built and all the work done, I'll loaf into camp."

Tom made no further protest. "All right. Take it easy. I'll unload and run back for you."

The Montanan found a good camp-site, dumped the supplies, and left Cuffy as a guard. With the other dogs he drove back and met the officer. Beresford was still limping doggedly forward. Every step sent a shoot of pain through him, but he set his teeth and kept moving.

None the less he was glad to see the empty sled. He tumbled on and let the others do the work.

At camp he scraped the snow away with a shoe while Morse cut spruce boughs and chopped wood for the fire.

Beresford suffered a good deal from his knee that night. He did not sleep much, and when day came it was plain he could not travel. The camp-site was a good one. There was plenty of wood, and the shape of the draw in which they were located was a protection from the cold wind. The dogs would be no worse for a day or two of rest. The travelers decided to remain here as long as might be necessary.

Tom went hunting. He brought back a bag of four ptarmigan late in the afternoon. Fried, they were delicious. The dogs stood round in a half-circle and caught the bones tossed to them. Crunch—crunch—crunch. The bones no longer were. The dogs, heads cocked on one side, waited expectantly for more tender tidbits.

"Saw deer tracks. To-morrow I'll have a try for one," Morse said.

The lame man hobbled down to the lake next day, broke the ice, and fished for jack pike. He took back to camp with him all he could carry.

On the fourth day his knee was so much improved that he was able to travel slowly. They were glad to see that night the lights of Fort Desolation, as one of the Mounted had dubbed the post on account of its loneliness.

CHAPTER XXXIV

The Man-Hunters Read Sign

IN the white North travelers are few and far. It is impossible for one to pass through the country without leaving a record of his progress written on the terrain and in the minds of the natives. The fugitive did not attempt concealment. He had with him now an Indian guide and was pushing into the Barren Lands. There was no uncertainty about his movements. From Fort Chippewayan he had swung to the northwest in the line of the great frozen lakes, skirting Athabasca and following the Great Slave River to the lake of the same name. This he crossed at the narrowest point, about where the river empties into it, and headed for the eastern extremity of Lake La Martre.

On his heels, still far behind, trod the two pursuers, patient, dogged, and inexorable. They had left far in the rear the out-forts of the Mounted and the little settlements of the free traders. Already they were deep in the Hudson's Bay Company trapping-grounds. Ahead of them lay the Barrens, stretching to the inlets of the Arctic Ocean.

The days were drawing out and the nights getting shorter. The untempered sun of the Northland beat down on the cold snow crystals and reflected a million sparks of light. In that white field the glare was almost unbearable. Both of them wore smoked glasses, but even with these their eyes continually smarted. They grew red and swollen. If time had not been so great an element in their journey, they would have tried to travel only after sunset. But they could not afford this. West would keep going as long and as fast as he could.

Each of them dreaded snow-blindness. They knew the sign of it—a dreadful pain, a smarting of the eyeballs as though hot burning sand were being flung against them. In camp at night they bathed their swollen lids and applied a cool and healing salve.

Meanwhile the weeks slipped into months and still they held like bulldogs to the trail of the man they were after.

The silence of the wide, empty white wastes surrounded them, except for an occasional word, the whine of a dog, and the slithering crunch of the sled-runners. From unfriendly frozen deserts they passed, through eternal stillness, into the snow wilderness that seemed to stretch forever. When they came to forests, now thinner, smaller, and less frequent, they welcomed them as they would an old friend.

"He's headin' for Great Bear, looks like," Morse suggested one morning after an hour in which neither of them had spoken.

"I was wondering when you'd chirp up, Tom," Beresford grinned cheerfully. "Sometimes I think I'm fed up for life on the hissing of snowshoe runners. The human voice sure sounds good up here. Yes, Great Bear Lake. And after that, where?"

"Up the lake, across to the Mackenzie, and down it to the ocean, I'd say. He's makin' for the whaling waters. Herschel Island maybe. He's hoping to bump into a whaler and get down on it to 'Frisco."

"Your guess is just as good as any," the Canadian admitted. "He's cut out a man-sized job for himself. I'll say that for him. It's a five-to-one bet he never gets through alive, even if we don't nab him."

"What else can he do? He's got to keep going or be dragged back to be hanged. I'd travel too if I were in his place."

"So would I. He's certainly hitting her up. Wish he'd break his leg for a week or two," the constable said airily.

They swung into a dense spruce swamp and jumped up a half-grown bear. He was so close to them that Tom, who was breaking trail, could see his little shining eyes. Morse was carrying his rifle, in the hope that he might see a lynx or a moose. The bear turned to scamper away, but the intention never became a fact. A bullet crashed through the head and brought the animal down.

An hour later they reached an Indian camp on the edge of a lake. On stages, built well up from the ground, drying fish were hanging out of reach of the dogs. These animals came charging toward the travelers as usual, lean, bristling, wolfish creatures that never had been half-tamed.

Beresford lashed them back with the whip. Indians came out from the huts, matted hair hanging over their eyes. After the usual greetings and small presents had been made, the man-hunters asked questions.

"Great Bear Lake—wah-he-o-che (how far)?"

The head man opened his eyes. Nobody in his right mind went to the great water at this time of year. It was maybe fifteen, maybe twenty days' travel. Who could tell? Were all the fair skins mad? Only three days since another dog-train had passed through driven by a big shaggy man who had left them no presents after he had bought fish. Three whites in as many days, and before that none but voyageur half-breeds in twice that number of years.

The trooper let out a boyish whoop. "Gaining fast. Only three days behind him, Tom. If our luck stands up, he'll never reach the Great Bear."

There was reason back of Beresford's exultant shout. At least one of West's dogs had bleeding feet. This the stained snow on the trail told them. Either the big man had no shoes for the animals or was too careless to use them when needed, the constable had suggested to his friend.

"It's not carelessness," Morse said. "It's his bullying nature. Likely he's got the shoes, only he won't put 'em on. He'll beat the poor brute over the head instead and curse his luck when he breaks down. He's too bull-headed to be a good driver."

On the fourth day after this they came upon one of the minor tragedies of sub-Arctic travel. The skeleton of a dog lay beside the trail. Its bones had been picked clean by its ravenous cannibal companions.

"Three left," Beresford commented. "He'll be figuring on picking up another when he meets any Indians or Eskimos."

"If he does it won't be any good to work with his train. I believe we've got him. He isn't twenty-five miles ahead of us right now."

"I'd put it at twenty. In about three days now the fireworks will begin."

It was the second day after this that they began to notice something peculiar about the trail they were following. Hitherto it had taken a straight line, except when the bad terrain had made a détour advisable. Now it swayed uncertainly, much as a drunken man staggers down a street.

"What's wrong with him? It can't be liquor. Yet if he's not drunk, what's got into him?" the soldier asked aloud, expecting no answer that explained this phenomenon.

Tom shook his head. "See. The Indian's drivin' now. He follows a straight enough line. You can tell he's at the tail line by the shape of the webs. And West's still lurchin' along in a crazy way. He fell down here. Is he sick, d'you reckon?"

"Give it up. Anyhow, he's in trouble. We'll know soon enough what it is. Before night now we'll maybe see them."

Before they had gone another mile, the trail in the snow showed another peculiarity. It made a wide half-circle and was heading south again.

"He's given up. What's that mean? Out of grub, d'you think?" Beresford asked.

"No. If they had been, he'd have made camp and gone hunting. We crossed musk-ox sign to-day, you know."

"Righto. Can't be that. He must be sick."

They kept their eyes open. At any moment now they were likely to make a discovery. Since they were in a country of scrubby brush they moved cautiously to prevent an ambush. There was just a possibility that the fugitive might have caught sight of them and be preparing an unwelcome surprise. But it was a possibility that did not look like a probability.

"Something gone 'way off in his plans," Morse said after they had mushed on the south trail for an hour. "Looks like he don't know what he's doing. Has he gone crazy?"

"Might be that. Men do in this country a lot. We don't know what a tough time he's been through."

"I'll bet he's bucked blizzards aplenty in the last two months. Notice one thing. West's trailin' after the guide like a lamb. He's makin' a sure-enough drunk track. See how the point of his shoe caught the snow there an' flung him down. The Cree stopped the sled right away so West could get up. Why did he do that? And why don't West ever stray a foot outa the path that's broke? That's not like him. He's always boss o' the outfit—always leadin'."

Beresford was puzzled, too. "I don't get the situation. It's been pretty nearly a thousand miles that we've been following this trail—eight hundred, anyhow. All the way Bully West has stamped his big foot on it as boss. Now he takes second place. The reason's beyond me."

His friend's mind jumped at a conclusion. "I reckon I know why he's followin' the straight and narrow path. The guide's got a line round his waist and West's tied to it."

"Why?"

The sun's rays, reflected from the snow in a blinding, brilliant glare, smote Morse full in the eyes. For days the white fields had been very trying to the sight. There had been moments when black spots had flickered before him, when red-hot sand had been flung against his eyeballs if he could judge by the burning sensation.

He knew now, in a flash, what was wrong with West.

To Beresford he told it in two words.

The constable slapped his thigh. "Of course. That's the answer."

Night fell, the fugitives still not in sight. The country was so rough that they might be within a mile or two and yet not be seen.

"Better camp, I reckon," Morse suggested.

"Yes. Here. We'll come up with them to-morrow."

They were treated that evening to an indescribably brilliant pyrotechnic display in the heavens. An aurora flashed across the sky such as neither of them had ever seen before. The vault was aglow with waves of red, violet, and purple that danced and whirled, with fickle, inconstant flashes of gold and green and yellow bars. A radiant incandescence of great power lit the arch and flooded it with light that poured through the cathedral windows of the Most High.

At daybreak they were up. Quickly they breakfasted and loaded. The trail they followed was before noon a rotten one, due to a sudden rise in the temperature, but it still bore south steadily.

They reached the camp where West and his guide had spent the night. Another chapter of the long story of the trail was written here. The sled and the guide had gone on south, but West had not been with them. His webs went wandering off at an angle, hesitant and uncertain. Sometimes they doubled across the track he had already made.

Beresford was breaking trail. His hand shot straight out. In the distance there was a tiny black speck in the waste of white. It moved.

Even yet the men who had come to bring the law into the Lone Lands did not relax their vigilance. They knew West's crafty, cunning mind. This might be a ruse to trap them. When they left the sled and moved forward, it was with rifles ready. The hunters stalked their prey as they would have done a musk ox. Slowly, noiselessly, they approached.

The figure was that of a huge man. He sat huddled in the snow, his back to them. Despair was in the droop of the head and the set of the bowed shoulders.

One of the dogs howled. The big torso straightened instantly. The shaggy head came up. Bully West was listening intently. He turned and looked straight at them, but he gave no sign of knowing they were there. The constable took a step and the hissing of the shoerunner sounded.

"I'm watchin' you, Stomak-o-sox," the heavy voice of the convict growled. "Can't fool me. I see every step you're takin'."

It was an empty boast, almost pathetic in its futility. Morse and Beresford moved closer, still without speech.

West broke into violent, impotent cursing. "You're there, you damned wood Cree! Think I don't know? Think I can't see you? Well, I can. Plain as you can see me. You come here an' get me, or I'll skin you alive like I done last week. Hear me?"

The voice rose to a scream. It betrayed terror—the horrible deadly fear of being left alone to perish in the icy wastes of the North.

Beresford crept close and waved a hand in front of the big man's eyes. West did not know it. He babbled vain and foolish threats at his guide.

The convict had gone blind—snow-blind, and Stomak-o-sox had left him alone to make a push for his own life while there was still time.

CHAPTER XXXV

Snow-Blind

WEST grinned up at the officer, his yellow canines showing like tusks. His matted face was an unlovely sight. In it stark, naked fear struggled with craftiness and cruelty.

"Good you came back—good for you. I ain't blind. I been foolin' you all along. Wanted to try you out. Now we'll mush. Straight for the big lake. North by west like we been going. Un'erstand, Stomak-o-sox? I'll not beat yore head off this time, but if you ever try any monkey tricks with Bully West again—" He let the threat die out in a sound of grinding teeth.

Beresford spoke. His voice was gentle. Vile though this murderer was, there was something pitiable in his condition. One cannot see a Colossus of strength and energy stricken to helplessness without some sense of compassion.

"It's not Stomak-o-sox. We're two of the North-West Mounted. You're under arrest for breaking prison and for killing Tim Kelly."

The information stunned West. He stared up out of sightless eyes. So far as he had known, no member of the Mounted was within five hundred miles of him. Yet the law had stretched out its long arm to snatch him back from this Arctic waste after he had traveled nearly fifteen hundred miles. It was incredible that there could exist such a police force on earth.

"Got me, did you?" he growled. He added the boast that he could not keep back. "Well, you'd never'a' got me if I hadn't gone blind—never in this world. There ain't any two of yore damned spies could land Bully West when he's at himself."

"Had breakfast?"

He broke into a string of curses. "No, our grub's runnin' low. That wood Cree slipped away with all we had. Wish I'd killed him last week when I skinned him with the dog-whip."

"How long have you been blind?"

"It's been comin' on two-three days. This damned burnin' glare from the snow. Yesterday they give out completely. I tied myself by a line to the Injun. Knew I couldn't trust him. After all I done for him too."

"Did you know he was traveling south with you—had been since yesterday afternoon?"

"No, was he?" Again West fell into his natural speech of invective. "When I meet up with him, I'll sure enough fill him full o' slugs," he concluded savagely.

"You're not likely to meet him again. We've come to take you back to prison."

Morse brought the train up and the hungry man was fed. They treated his eyes with the simple remedies the North knows and bound them with a handkerchief to keep out the fierce light reflected from the snow.

Afterward, they attached him by a line to the driver. He stumbled along behind. Sometimes he caught his foot or slipped and plunged down into the snow. Nobody had ever called him a patient man. Whenever any mishap occurred, he polluted the air with his vile speech.

They made slow progress, for the pace had to be regulated to suit the prisoner.

Day succeeded day, each with its routine much the same as the one before. They made breakfast, broke camp, packed, and mushed. The swish of the runners sounded from morning till night fell. Food began to run scarce. Once they left the blind man at the camp while they hunted wood buffalo. It was a long, hard business. They came back empty-handed after a two-day chase, but less than a mile from camp they sighted a half-grown polar bear and dropped it before the animal had a chance to move.

One happy hour they got through the Land of Little Sticks and struck the forests again.

They had a blazing fire again for the first time in six weeks. Brush and sticks and logs went into it till it roared furiously.

Morse turned from replenishing it to notice that West had removed the bandage from his eyes.

"Better keep it on," the young man advised.

"I was changin' it. Too tight. Gives me a headache," the convict answered sulkily.

"Can you see anything at all yet?"

"Not a thing. Looks to me like I never would."

Tom turned his head for him, so that he faced the blaze squarely. "No light at all?"

"Nope. Don't reckon I ever will see."

"Maybe you will. I've known cases of snow-blindness where they couldn't see for a month an' came out all right."

"Hurts like blazes," growled the big fellow.

"I know. But not as bad as it did, does it? That salve has helped some."

The two young fellows took care of the man as though he had been a brother. They bathed his eyes, fed him, guided him, encouraged him. He was a bad lot—the worst that either of them had known. But he was in trouble and filled with self-pity. Never ill before, a giant of strength and energy, his condition now apparently filled him with despair.

He would sit hunched down before the fire, head bowed in his hands, a mountain of dole and woe. Sometimes he talked, and he blamed every one but himself for his condition. He never had had a square deal. Every one was against him. It was a rotten world. Then he would fall to cursing God and man.

In some ways he was less trouble than if he had been able to see. He was helpless and had to trust to them. His safety depended on their safety. He could not strike at them without injuring himself. No matter how much he cringed at the thought of being dragged back to punishment, he shrank still more from the prospect of death in the snow wastes. The situation galled him. Every decent word he gave them came grudgingly, and he still snarled and complained and occasionally bullied as though he had the whip hand.

"A nice specimen of *ursus horribilis*," Beresford murmured to his companion one day. "Thought he was game, anyhow, but he's a yellow quitter. Acts as though we were to blame for his blindness and for what's waiting for him at the end of the journey. I like a man to stand the gaff when it's prodding him."

Morse nodded. "Look out for him. I've got a notion in the back o' my head that he's beginning to see again. He'd kill us in a holy minute if he dared. Only his blindness keeps him from it. What do you say? Shall we handcuff him nights?"

"Not necessary," the constable said. "He can't see a thing. Watch him groping for that stick."

"All his brains run to cunning. Don't forget that. Why should he have to feel so long for that stick? He laid it down himself a minute ago. Tryin' to slip one over on us maybe."

The Canadian looked at the lean, brown face of his friend and grinned. "I've a notion our imaginations too are getting a bit jumpy. We've had one bully time on this trip—with the reverse English. It's all in the day's work to buck blizzards and starve and freeze, though I wouldn't be surprised if our systems were pretty well fed up with grief before we caught Mr. Bully West. Since then—well, you couldn't call him a cheerful traveling companion, could you? A dozen times a day I want to rip loose and tell him how much I don't think of him."

"Still—"

"We'll keep an eye on him. If necessary, it'll be the bracelets for him. I'd hate to have the Inspector send in a report to headquarters, 'Constable Beresford missing in the line of duty.' I've a prejudice against being shot in the back."

"That's one of the reasons I'm here—to see you're not if I can help it."

Beresford's boyish face lit up. He understood what his friend meant. "Say, Faraway isn't New York or London or even Toronto. But how'd you like to be sitting down to one of Jessie McRae's suppers? A bit of broiled venison done to a juicy turn, potatoes, turnips, hot biscuits spread with raspberry jam. By jove, it makes the mouth water."

"And a slice of plum puddin' to top off with," suggested Morse, bringing his own memory into play. "Don't ask me how I'd like it. That's a justifiable excuse for murder. Get busy on that rubaboo. Our guest's howlin' for his dinner."

The faint suspicions of Morse made the officers more wary. They watched their prisoner a little closer. Neither of them quite believed that he was recovering his sight. It was merely a possibility to be guarded against.

But the guess of Morse had been true. It had been a week since flashes of light had first come to West faintly. He began to distinguish objects in a hazy way. Every day he could see better. Now he could tell Morse from Beresford, one dog from another. Give him a few more days and he would have as good vision as before he had gone blind.

All this he hid cunningly, as a miser does his gold. For his warped, cruel brain was planning death to these two men. After that, another plunge into the North for life and freedom.

166

CHAPTER XXXVI

The Wild Beast Leaps

TOM MORSE was chopping wood. He knew how to handle an axe. His strokes fell sure and strong, with the full circling sweep of the expert.

The young tree crashed down and he began to lop off its branches. Halfway up the trunk he stopped and raised his head to listen.

No sound had come to him. None came now. But clear as a bell he heard the voice of Win Beresford calling.

"Help! Help!"

It was not a cry that had issued from his friend's throat. Tom knew that. But it was real. It had sprung out of his dire need from the heart, perhaps in the one instant of time left him, and it had leaped silently across space straight to the heart of his friend.

Tom kicked into his snowshoes and began to run. He held the axe in his hand, gripped near the haft. A couple of hundred yards, perhaps, lay between him and camp, which was just over the brow of a small hill. The bushes flew past as he swung to his stride. Never had he skimmed the crust faster, but his feet seemed to be weighted with lead. Then, as he topped the rise, he saw the disaster he had dreaded.

The constable was crumpling to the ground, his body slack and inert, while the giant slashed at him with a club of firewood he had snatched from the ground. The uplraised arm of the soldier broke the force of the blow, but Morse guessed by the way the arm fell that the bone had snapped.

At the sound of the scraping runners, West whirled. He lunged savagely. Even as Tom ducked, a sharp pain shot through his leg from the force of the glancing blow. The axehead swung like a circle of steel. It struck the convict's fur cap. The fellow went down like an ox in a slaughter-house.

Tom took one look at him and ran to his friend. Beresford was a sorry sight. He lay unconscious, head and face battered, the blood from his wounds staining the snow.

167

The man-hunters had come into the wilderness prepared for emergencies. Jessie McRae had prepared a small medicine case as a present for the constable. Morse ran to the sled and found this. He unrolled bandages and after he had washed the wounds bound them. As he was about to examine the arm, he glanced up.

For a fraction of a second West's wolfish eyes glared at him before they took on again the stare of blindness. The man had moved. He had hitched himself several yards nearer a rifle which stood propped against a balsam.

The revolver of the deputy constable came to light. "Stop right where you're at. Don't take another step."

The convict snarled rage, but he did not move. Some sure instinct warned him what the cold light in the eyes of his captor meant, that if he crept one inch farther toward the weapon he would die in his tracks.

"He—he jumped me," the murderer said hoarsely.

"Liar! You've been shammin' for a week to get a chance at us. I'd like to gun you now and be done with it."

"Don't." West moistened dry lips. "Honest to God he jumped me. Got mad at somethin' I said. I wouldn't lie to you, Tom."

Morse kept him covered, circled round him to the rifle, and from there to the sled. One eye still on the desperado, he searched for the steel handcuffs. They were gone. He knew instantly that some time within the past day or two West had got a chance to drop them in the snow.

He found rawhide thongs.

"Lie in the snow, face down," he ordered. "Hands behind you and crossed at the wrists."

Presently the prisoner was securely tied. Morse fastened him to the sled and returned to Beresford.

The arm was broken above the wrist, just as he had feared. He set it as best he could, binding it with splints.

The young officer groaned and opened his eyes. He made a motion to rise.

"Don't get up," said Morse. "You've been hurt."

"Hurt?" Beresford's puzzled gaze wandered to the prisoner. A flash of understanding lit it. "He asked me—to light—his pipe—and when I—turned—he hit—me—with a club," the battered man whispered.

"About how I figured it."

"Afraid—I'm—done—in."

"Not yet, old pal. We'll make a fight for it," the Montanan answered.

"I'm sick." The soldier's head sank down. His eyes closed.

All the splendid, lithe strength of his athletic youth had been beaten out of him. To Morse it looked as though he were done for. Was it possible for one to take such a terrific mauling and not succumb? If he were at a hospital, under the care of expert surgeons and nurses, with proper food and attention, he might have a chance in a hundred. But in this Arctic waste, many hundred miles from the nearest doctor, no food but the coarsest to eat, it would be a miracle if he survived.

The bitter night was drawing in. Morse drove West in front of him to bring back the wood he had been cutting. He made the man prepare the rubaboo for their supper. After the convict had eaten, he bound his hands again and let him lie down in his blankets beside the fire.

Morse did not sleep. He sat beside his friend and watched the fever mount in him till he was wildly delirious. Such nursing as was possible he gave.

The prisoner, like a chained wild beast, glowered at him hungrily. Tom knew that if West found a chance to kill, he would strike. No scruple would deter him. The fellow was without conscience, driven by the fear of the fate that drew nearer with every step southward. His safety and the desire of revenge marched together. Beresford was out of the way. It would be his companion's turn next.

After a time the great hulk of a man fell asleep and snored stertorously. But Tom did not sleep. He dared not. He had to keep vigilant guard to save both his friend's life and his own. For though West's hands were tied, it would be the work of only a minute to burn away with a live coal the thongs that bound them.

The night wore away. There was no question of travel. Beresford was in the grip of a raging fever and could not be moved. Morse made West chop wood while he stood over him, rifle in hand. They were short of food and had expected to go hunting next day. The supplies might last at best six or seven more meals. What was to be done then? Morse could not go and leave West where he could get at the man who had put him in prison and with a dog-train to carry him north. Nor could he let West have a rifle with which to go in search of game.

There were other problems that made the situation impossible. Another night was at hand, and again Tom must keep awake to save himself and his friend from the gorilla-man who watched him, gloated over him, waited for the moment to come when he could safely strike. And after that there would be other nights—many of them.

What should he do? What could he do? While he sat beside

the delirious officer, Tom pondered that question. On the other side of the fire lay the prisoner. Triumph—a horrible, cruel, menacing triumph—rode in his eye and strutted in his straddling walk when he got up. His hour was coming. It was coming fast.

Once Tom fell asleep for a cat-nap. He caught himself nodding, and with a jerk flung back his head and himself to wakefulness. In the air was a burning odor. Instinct told him what it was. West had been tampering with the rawhide thongs round his wrists, had been trying to burn them away.

He made sure that the fellow was still fast, then drank a tin cup of strong tea. After he had fed the sick man a little caribou broth, persuading him with infinite patience to take it, a spoonful at a time, Morse sat down again to wear out the hours of darkness.

The problem that pressed on him could no longer be evaded. A stark decision lay before him. To postpone it was to choose one of the alternatives. He knew now, almost beyond any possibility of doubt, that either West must die or else he and his friend. If he had not snatched himself awake so promptly an hour ago, Win and he would already be dead men. It might be that the constable was going to die, anyhow, but he had a right to his chance of life.

On the other hand there was one rigid rule of the North-West Mounted. The Force prided itself on living up to it literally. When a man was sent out to get a prisoner, *he brought him in alive*. It was a tradition. The Mounted did not choose the easy way of killing lawbreakers because of the difficulty of capturing them. They walked through danger, usually with aplomb, got their man, and brought him in.

That was what Beresford had done with Pierre Poulette after the Frenchman had killed Buckskin Jerry. He had followed the man for months, captured him, lived with him alone for a fourth of a year in the deep snows, and brought him back to punishment. It was easy enough to plead that this situation was a wholly different one. Pierre Poulette was no such dangerous wild beast as Bully West. Win did not have with him a companion wounded almost to death who had to be nursed back to health, one struck down by the prisoner treacherously. There was just a fighting chance for the officers to get back to Desolation if West was eliminated from the equation. Tom knew he would have a man's work cut out for him to win through—without the handicap of the prisoner.

Deep in his heart he believed that it was West's life or theirs. It wasn't humanly possible, in addition to all the other difficulties that pressed on him, to guard this murderer and bring

170

him back for punishment. There was no alternative, it seemed to Tom. Thinking could not change the conditions. It might be sooner, it might be later, but under existing circumstances the desperado would find his chance to attack, *if he were alive to take it.*

The fellow's life was forfeit. As soon as he was turned over to the State, it would be exacted of him. Since his assault on Beresford, surely he had lost all claim to consideration as a human being.

Just now there were only three men in the world so far as they were concerned. These three constituted society. Beresford, his mind still wandering with incoherent mutterings, was a non-voting member. He, Tom Morse, must be judge and jury. He must, if the prisoner were convicted, play a much more horrible rôle. In the silence of the cold sub-Arctic night he fought the battle out while automatically he waited on his friend.

West snored on the other side of the fire.

CHAPTER XXXVII

Near The End Of A Long Crooked Trail

WHEN West awoke, Morse was whittling on a piece of wood with his sharp hunting-knife. It was a flat section from a spruce, and it had been trimmed with an axe till it resembled a shake in shape.

The outlaw's curiosity overcame his sullenness at last. It made him jumpy, anyhow, to sit there in silence except for the muttering of the sick man.

"Whajamakin'?" he demanded.

Morse said nothing. He smoothed the board to his satisfaction, then began lettering on it with a pencil.

"I said whajadoin'," growled West, after another silence.

The special constable looked at him, and in the young man's eyes there was something that made the murderer shiver.

"I'm making a tombstone."

"What?" West felt a drench of ice at his heart.

"A marker for a grave."

"For—for him? Maybe he won't die. Looks better to me. Fever ain't so high."

"It's not for him."

West moistened his dry lips with his tongue. "You will have yore li'l' joke, eh? Who's it for?"

"For you."

"For me?" The man's fear burst from him in a shriek. "Whajamean for me?"

From the lettering Morse read aloud. " 'Bully West, Executed, Some Time late in March, 1875.' " And beneath it, " 'May God Have Mercy on His Soul.' "

Tiny beads of sweat gathered on the convict's clammy forehead. "You aimin' to—to murder me?" he asked hoarsely.

"To execute you."

"With—without a trial? My God, you can't do that! I got a right to a trial."

"You've been tried—and condemned. I settled all that in the night."

"But—it ain't legal. Goddlemighty, you got no *right* to act thataway. All you can do is to take me back to the courts." The heavy voice broke again to a scream.

Morse slipped the hunting-knife back into its case. He looked steadily at the prisoner. In his eyes there was no anger, no hatred. But back of the sadness in them was an implacable resolution.

"Courts and the law are a thousand miles away," he said. "You know your crimes. You murdered Tim Kelly treacherously. You planned to spoil an inncent girl's life by driving her to worse than death. You shot your partner in the back after he did his best to help you escape. You tortured Onistah and would have killed him if we hadn't come in time. You assaulted my friend here and he'll probably die from his wounds. It's the end of the long trail for you, Bully West. Inside of half an hour you will be dead. If you've anything to say—if you can make your peace with heaven—don't waste a moment."

The face of West went gray. He stared at the other man, the horror-filled eyes held fascinated. "You—you're tryin' to scare me," he faltered. "You wouldn't do that. You couldn't. It ain't allowed by the Commissioner." One of the bound arms twitched involuntarily. The convict knew that he was lost. He had a horrible conviction that this man meant to do as he had said.

The face of Morse was inexorable as fate itself, but inside he was a river of rushing sympathy. This man was bad. He himself had forced the circumstances that made it impossible to let him live. None the less Tom felt like a murderer. The thing he had to do was so horribly cold-blooded. If this had been a matter between the two of them, he could at least have given the fellow a chance for his life. But not now—not with Win Beresford in the condition he was. If he were going to save his friend, he could not take the chances of a duel.

"Ten minutes now," Morse said. His voice was hoarse and low. He felt his nerves twitching, a tense aching in the throat.

"I always liked you fine, Tom," the convict pleaded desperately. "Me'n' you was always good pals. You wouldn't do me dirt thataway now. If you knew the right o' things—how that Kelly kep' a-devilin' me, how Whaley was layin' to gun me when he got a chanct, how I stood up for the McRae girl an' protected her against him. Goddlemighty, man, you ain't aimin' to kill me like a wolf!" The shriek of uncontrollable terror lifted into his voice once more. "I ain't ready to die. Gimme a chance, Tom. I'll change my ways. I swear I will. I'll do like you say every minute. I'll nurse Beresford. Me, I'm a fine nurse. If you'll gimme a week—jus' one more week. That ain't much to ask. So's I can git ready."

The man slipped to his knees and began to crawl toward Morse. The young man got up, his teeth set. He could not stand much of this sort of thing without collapsing himself.

"Get up," he said. "We're going over the hill there."

"No—no—no!"

It took Morse five minutes to get the condemned man to his feet. The fellow's face was ashen. His knees shook.

Tom was in almost as bad a condition himself.

Beresford's high voice cut in. In his delirium he was perhaps living over again his experience with Pierre Poulette.

"Maintiens le droit. Get your man and bring him in. Tough sledding. Never mind. Go through, old fellow. Bring him in. That's what you're sent for. Hogtie him. Drag him with a rope around his neck. Get him back somehow."

The words struck Tom motionless. It was as though some voice were speaking to him through the sick man's lips. He waited. ᐧ ᐧ

"Righto, sir," the soldier droned on. "See what I can do, sir. Have a try at it, anyhow." And again he murmured the motto of the Mounted Police.

Tom had excused himself for what he thought it was his duty to do on the ground that it was not humanly possible to save his friend and bring West back. It came to him in a flash that the Mounted Police were becoming so potent a power for law and order because they never asked whether the job assigned them was possible. They went ahead and did it or died trying to do it. It did not matter primarily whether Beresford and he got back alive or not. If West murdered them, other red-coats would take the trail and get him.

What he, Tom Morse, had to do was to carry on. He could not choose the easy way, even though it was a desperately hard one for him. He could not make himself a judge over this murderer, with power of life and death. The thing that had been given him to do was to bring West to Faraway. He had no choice in the matter. Win or lose, he had to play the hand out as it was dealt him.

CHAPTER XXXVIII

Over a Rotting Trail

Tom believed that Beresford's delirious words had condemned them both to death. He could not nurse his friend, watch West night and day, keep the camp supplied with food, and cover the hundreds of miles of bleak snow fields which stretched between them and the nearest settlement. He did not think that any one man lived who was capable of succeeding in such a task.

Yet his first feeling was of immediate relief. The horrible duty that had seemed to be laid upon him was not a duty at all. He saw his course quite simply. All he had to do was to achieve the impossible. If he failed in it, he would go down like a soldier in the day's work. He would have, anyhow, no torturings of conscience, no blight resting upon him till the day of his death.

"You're reprieved, West," he announced simply.

The desperado staggered to the sled and leaned against it faintly. His huge body swayed. The revulsion was almost too much for him.

"I—I—knowed you couldn't treat an old pardner thataway, Tom," he murmured.

Morse took the man out to a fir tree. He carried with him a blanket, a buffalo robe, and a part of the dog harness.

"Whad you aimin' to do?" asked West uneasily. He was not sure yet that he was out of the woods.

"Roll up in the blankets," ordered Morse.

The fellow looked at his grim face and did as he was told. Tom tied him to the tree, after making sure that his hands were fast behind him.

"I'll freeze here," the convict complained.

The two officers were lean and gaunt from hard work and insufficient nourishment, but West was still sleek and well padded with flesh. He had not missed a meal, and during the past weeks he had been a passenger. All the hard work; the packing at portages, the making of camp, the long, wearing days of hunting, had fallen upon the two whose prisoner he was. He could stand a bit of hardship, Tom decided.

"No such luck," he said brusquely. "And I wouldn't try to break away if I were you. I can't kill you, but I'll thrash you with the dog-whip if you make me any trouble."

Morse called Cuffy and set the dog to watch the bound man. He did not know whether the St. Bernard would do this, but he was glad to see that the leader of the train understood at once and settled down in the snow to sleep with one eye watchful of West.

Tom returned to his friend. He knew he must concentrate his efforts to keep life in the battered body of the soldier. He must nurse and feed him judiciously until the fever wore itself out.

While he was feeding Win broth, he fell asleep with the spoon in his hand. He jerkily flung back his head and opened his eyes. Cuffy still lay close to the prisoner, evidently prepared for an all-night vigil with short light naps from which the least movement would instantly arouse him.

"I'm all in. Got to get some sleep," Morse said to himself, half aloud.

He wrapped in his blankets. When his eyes opened, the sun was beating down from high in the heavens. He had slept from one day into the next. Even in his sleep he had been conscious of some sound drumming at his ears. It was the voice of West.

"You gonna sleep all day? Don't we get any grub? Have I gotta starve while you pound yore ear?"

Hurriedly Tom flung aside his wraps. He leaped to his feet, a new man, his confidence and vitality all restored.

The fire had died to ashes. He could hear the yelping of the dogs in the distance. They were on a private rabbit hunt of their own, all of them but Cuffy. The St. Bernard still lay in the snow watching West.

Beresford's delirium was gone and his fever was less. He was very weak, but Tom thought he saw a ghost of the old boyish grin flicker indomitably into his eyes. As Tom looked at the swathed and bandaged head, for the first time since the murderous attack he allowed himself to hope. The never-say-die spirit of the man and the splendid constitution built up by a clean outdoor life might pull him through yet.

"West was afraid you never were going to wake up, Tom. It worried him. You know how fond of you he is," the constable said weakly.

Morse was penitent. "Why didn't you wake me, Win? You must be dying of thirst."

"I could do with a drink," he admitted. "But you needed that sleep. Every minute of it."

Tom built up the fire and thawed snow. He gave Beresford a drink and then fed more of the broth to him. He made breakfast for the prisoner and himself.

Afterward, he took stock of their larder. It was almost empty. "Enough flour and pemmican for another mess of rubaboo. Got to restock right away or our stomachs will be flat as a buffalo bull's after a long stampede."

He spoke cheerfully, yet he and Beresford both knew a hunt for game might be unsuccessful. Rabbits would not do. He had to provide enough to feed the dogs as well as themselves. If he did not get a moose, a bear, or caribou, they would face starvation.

Tom redressed the wounds of the trooper and examined the splints on the arm to make sure they had not become disarranged during the night in the delirium of the sick man.

"Got to leave you, Win. Maybe for a day or more. I'll have plenty of wood piled handy for the fire—and broth all ready to heat. Think you can make out?"

The prospect could not have been an inviting one for the wounded man, but he nodded quite as a matter of course.

"I'll be all right. Take your time. Don't spoil your hunt worrying about me."

Yet it was with extreme reluctance Tom had made up his mind to go. He would take the dog-train with him—and West, unarmed, of course. He had to take him on Beresford's account, because he dared not leave him. But as he looked at his friend, all the supple strength stricken out of him, weak and helpless as a sick child, he felt a queer tug at the heart. What assurance had he that he would find him still alive on his return?

Beresford knew what he was thinking. He smiled, the gentle, affectionate smile of the very ill. "It's all right, old fellow. Got to buck up and carry on, you know. Look out—for West. Don't give him any show at you. Never trust him—not for a minute. Remember he's—a wolf." His weak hand gripped Tom's in farewell.

The American turned away hurriedly, not to show the tears that unexpectedly brimmed his lids. Though he wore the hard surface of the frontier, his was a sensitive soul. He was very fond of this gay, gallant youth who went out to meet adventure as though it were a lover with whom he had an appointment. They had gone through hell together, and the fires of the furnace had proved the Canadian true gold. After all, Tom was himself scarcely more than a boy in years. He cherished, deep hidden in him, the dreams and illusions that long contact with the world is likely to dispel. At New Haven and Cambridge lads of his age were larking beneath the elms and playing childish pranks on each other.

West drove the team. Tom either broke trail or followed. He came across plenty of tracks, but most of them were old ones. He recognized the spoor of deer, bear, and innumerable rabbits. Toward noon fresh caribou tracks crossed their path. The slot pointed south. Over a soft and rotting trail Morse swung round in pursuit.

They made heavy going of it. He had to break trail through slushy snow. His shoes broke through the crust and clogged with the sludgy stuff so that his feet were greatly weighted. Fatigue pressed like a load on his shoulders. The dogs and West wallowed behind.

By night probably the trail would be much better, but they dared not wait till then. The caribou would not stop to suit the convenience of the hunters. This might be the last shot in the locker. Every dragging lift of the webs carried Morse farther from camp, but food had to be found and in quantity.

It was close to dusk when Tom guessed they were getting near the herd. He tied the train to a tree and pushed on with West. Just before nightfall he sighted the herd grazing on muskeg moss. There were about a dozen in all. The wind was fortunately right.

Tom motioned to West not to follow him. On hands and knees the hunter crept forward, taking advantage of such cover as he could find. It was a slow, cold business, but he was not here for pleasure. A mistake might mean the difference between life and death for him and Win Beresford.

For a stalker to determine the precise moment when to shoot is usually a nice decision. Perhaps he can gain another dozen yards on his prey. On the other hand, by moving closer he may startle them and lose his chance. With so much at stake Tom felt for the second time in his life the palsy that goes with buck fever.

177

A buck flung up his head and sniffed toward the hidden danger. Tom knew the sign of startled doubt. Instantly his trembling ceased. He aimed carefully and fired. The deer dropped in its tracks. Again he fired—twice—three times. The last shot was a wild one, sent on a hundredth chance. The herd vanished in the gathering darkness.

Tom swung forward exultant, his webs swishing swiftly over the snow. He had dropped two. A second buck had fallen, risen, run fifty yards, and come to earth again. The hunter's rifle was ready in case either of the caribou sprang up. He found the first one dead, the other badly wounded. At once he put the buck out of its pain.

West came slouching out of the woods at Tom's signal. Directed by the officer, he made a fire and prepared for business. The stars were out as they dressed the meat and cooked a large steak on the coals. Afterward they hung the caribou from the limb of a spruce, drawing them high enough so that no prowling wolves could reach the game.

With the coming of night the temperature had fallen and the snow hardened. The crust held beneath their webs as they returned to the sled. West wanted to camp where the deer had been killed. He protested, with oaths, in his usual savage growl, that he was dead tired and could not travel another step.

But he did. Beneath the stars the hunters mushed twenty miles back to camp. They made much better progress by reason of the frozen trail and the good meal they had eaten.

It was daybreak when Morse sighted the camp-fire smoke. His heart leaped. Beresford must have been able to keep it alive with fuel. Therefore he had been alive an hour or two ago at most.

Dogs and men trudged into camp ready to drop with fatigue. Beresford, from where he lay, waved a hand at Tom. "Any luck?" he asked.

"Two caribou."

"Good. I'll be ready for a steak to-morrow."

Morse looked at him anxiously. The glaze had left his eyes. He was no longer burning up with fever. Both voice and movements seemed stronger than they had been twenty-four hours earlier.

"Bully for you, Win," he answered.

CHAPTER XXXIX

A Cree Runner Brings News

"DON'T you worry about that lad, Jessie. He's got as many lives as a cat—and then some. I've knew him ever since he was knee-high to a grasshopper."

Brad Stearns was talking. He sat in the big family room at the McRae house and puffed clouds of tobacco smoke to the rafters.

"Meaning Mr. Beresford?" asked Jessie demurely. She was patching a pair of leather trousers for Fergus and she did not raise her eyes from the work.

"Meanin' Tom Morse," the old-timer said. "Not but what Beresford's a good lad too. Sand in his craw an' a kick like a mule in his fist. But he was brought up somewhere in the East, an' o' course he's a leetle mite less tough than Tom. No, sir. Tom'll bob up one o' these here days good as ever. Don't you worry none about that. Why, he ain't been gone but—lemme see, a week or so better'n four months. When a man's got to go to the North Pole an' back, four months—"

Beneath her long lashes the girl slanted a swift look at Brad. "That makes twice you've told me in two minutes not to worry about Mr. Morse. Do I look peaked? Am I lying awake nights thinking about him, do you think?" She held up the renewed trousers and surveyed her handiwork critically.

Brad gazed at her through narrowed lids. "I'll be doggoned if I know whether you are or you ain't. I'd bet a pair o' red-topped boots it's one of them lads. 'Course Beresford's got a red coat an' spurs that jingle an' a fine line o' talk. Tom he ain't got ary one o' the three. But if it's a man you're lookin' for, a two-fisted man who—"

A wave of mirth crossed Jessie's face like a ripple on still water. Her voice mimicked his. "Why do you want to saw off an old maid on that two-fisted man you've knew ever since he was knee-high to a grasshopper? What did he ever do to you that was so doggoned mean?"

"Now looky here, you can laugh at me all you've a mind to. All I'm sayin is—"

"Oh, I'm not laughing at you," she interposed hurriedly with an assumption of anxiety her bubbling eyes belied. "If you could show me how to get your two-fisted man when he comes back—or even the one with the red coat and the spurs and the fine line of talk—"

"I ain't sayin' he ain't a man from the ground up too." Brad broke in. "Considerin' his opportunities he's a right hefty young fellow. But Tom Morse he—"

"That's it exactly. Tom Morse he—"

"Keep right on makin' fun o' me. Tom Morse he's a man outa ten thousand, an' I don't know as I'm coverin' enough population at that."

"And you're willing to make a squaw-man of him. Oh, Mr. Stearns!"

He looked at her severely. "You got no license to talk thataway, Jessie McRae. You're Angus McRae's daughter an' you been to Winnipeg to school. Anyways, after what Lemoine found out—"

"What did he find out? Pierre Roubideaux couldn't tell him anything about the locket and the ring. Makoye-kin said he got it from his brother who was one of a party that massacred an American outfit of trappers headed for Peace River. He doesn't know whether the picture of the woman in the locket was that of one of the women in the camp. All we've learned is that I look like a picture of a white woman found in a locket nearly twenty years ago. That doesn't take us very far, does it?"

"Well, Stokimatis may know something. When Onistah comes back with her, we'll get the facts straight."

McRae came into the room. "News, lass," he cried, and his voice rang. "A Cree runner's just down frae Northern Lights. He says the lads were picked up by some trappers near Desolation. One o' them's been badly hurt, but he's on the mend. Which yin I dinna ken. What wi' starvation an' blizzards an' battles they've had a tough time. But the word is they're doing fine noo."

"West?" asked Brad. "Did they get him?"

"They got him. Dragged him back to Desolation with a rope round his neck. Hung on to him while they were slam-bangin' through blizzards an' runnin' a race wi' death to get back before they starved. Found him up i' the Barrens somewhere, the story is. He'll be hangit at the proper time an' place. It's in the Word. 'They that take the sword shall perish with the sword.' Matthew 26:52."

Brad let out the exultant rebel yell he had learned years before in the Confederate army. "What'd I tell you about that boy? Ain't I knowed him since he was a li'l' bit of a tad? He's a go-getter, Tom is. Y'betcha!"

Jessie's heart was singing too, but she could not forbear a friendly gibe at him. "I suppose Win Beresford wasn't there at all. He hadn't a thing to do with it, had he?"

The old cowpuncher raised a protesting hand. "I ain't said a word against him. Now have I, McRae? Nothin' a-tall. All I done said was that I been tellin' everybody Tom would sure enough bring back Bully West with him."

The girl laughed. "You're daffy about that boy you brought up by hand. I'll not argue with you."

"They're both good lads," the Scotchman summed up, and passed to his second bit of news. "Onistah and Stokimatis are in frae the Blackfoot country. They stoppit at the store, but they'll be alang presently. I had a word wi' Onistah. We'll wait for him here."

"Did he say what he'd found out?" Jessie cried.

"Only that he had brought back the truth. That'll be the lad knockin' at the door."

Jessie opened, to let in Onistah and his mother. Stokimatis and the girl gravitated into each other's arms, as is the way with women who are fond of each other. The Indian is stolid, but Jessie had the habit of impetuosity, of letting her feelings sweep her into demonstration. Even the native women she loved were not proof against it.

McRae questioned Stokimatis.

Without waste of words the mother of Onistah told the story she had traveled hundreds of miles to tell.

Sleeping Dawn was not the child of her sister. When the attack had been made on the white trappers bound for Peace River, the mother of a baby had slipped the infant under an iron kettle. After the massacre her sister had found the wailing little atom of humanity. The Indian woman had recently lost her own child. She hid the babe and afterward was permitted to adopt it. When a few months later she died of smallpox, Stokimatis had inherited the care of the little one. She had named it Sleeping Dawn. Later, when the famine year came, she had sold the child to Angus McRae.

That was all she knew. But it was enough for Jessie. She did not know who her parents had been. She never would know, beyond the fact that they were Americans and that her mother had been a beautiful girl whose eyes laughed and danced. But this knowledge made a tremendous difference to

181

her. She belonged to the ruling race and not to the métis, just as much as Win Beresford and Tom Morse did.

She tried to hide her joy, was indeed ashamed of it. For any expression of it seemed like a reproach to Matapi-Koma and Onistah and Stokimatis, to her brother Fergus and in a sense even to her father. None the less her blood beat fast. What she had just found out meant that she could aspire to the civilization of the whites, that she had before her an outlook, was not to be hampered by the limitations imposed upon her by race.

The heart in the girl sang a song of sunshine dancing on grass, of meadowlarks flinging out their care-free notes of joy. Through it like a golden thread ran for a motif little melodies that had to do with a man who had staggered into Fort Desolation out of the frozen North, sick and starved and perhaps wounded, but still indomitably captain of his soul.

CHAPTER XL

"Malbrouck S'en Va-t-en Guerre"

INSPECTOR MACLEAN was present in person when the two man-hunters of the North-West Mounted returned to Faraway. Their reception was in the nature of a pageant. Gayly dressed voyageurs and trappers, singing old river songs that had been handed down to them from their fathers, unharnessed the dogs and dragged the cariole into town. In it sat Beresford, still unfit for long and heavy mushing. Beside it slouched West, head down, hands tied behind his back, the eyes from the matted face sending sidling messages of hate at the capering crowd. At his heels moved Morse, grim and tireless, an unromantic figure of dominant efficiency.

Long before the worn travelers and their escort reached the village, Jessie could hear the gay lilt of the chantey that heralded their coming:

"Malbrouck s'en va-t-en guerre,
Mironton-ton-ton, mirontaine."

The girl hummed it herself, heart athrob with excitement. She found herself joining in the cheer of welcome that rose joyously when the cavalcade drew into sight. In her cheeks fluttered eager flags of greeting. Tears brimmed the soft eyes, so that she could hardly distinguish Tom Morse and Win Beresford, the one lean and gaunt and grim, the other pale and hollow-eyed from illness, but scattering smiles of largesse. For her heart was crying, in a paraphrase of the great parable, "He was dead, and is alive again; he was lost, and is found."

Beresford caught sight of the Inspector's face and chuckled like a schoolboy caught in mischief. This gay procession, with its half-breeds in tri-colored woolen coats, its gay-plumed voyageurs suggesting gallant troubadours of old in slashed belts and tassels, was not quite the sort of return to set Inspector MacLean cheering. Externally, at least, he was a piece of military machinery. A trooper did his work, and that ended it. In the North-West Mounted it was not necessary to make a gala day of it because a constable brought in his man. If he didn't bring him in—well, that would be another and a sadder story for the officer who fell down on the assignment.

As soon as Beresford and Morse had disposed of their prisoner and shaken off their exuberant friends, they reported to the Inspector. He sat at a desk and listened dryly to their story. Not till they had finished did he make any comment.

"You'll have a week's furlough to recuperate, Constable Beresford. After that report to the Writing-on-Stone detachment for orders. Here's a voucher for your pay, Special Constable Morse. I'll say to you both that it was a difficult job well done." He hesitated a moment, then proceeded to free his mind. "As for this Roman triumph business—victory procession with prisoners chained to your chariot wheels—quite unnecessary, I call it."

Beresford explained, smilingly. "We really couldn't help it, sir. They were bound to make a Roman holiday out of us whether we wanted to or not. You know how excitable the French are. Had to have their little frolic out of it."

"Not the way the Mounted does business. You know that, Beresford. We don't want any fuss and feathers—any fol-de-rol—this mironton-ton-ton stuff. Damn it, sir, you liked it. I could see you eat it up. D'you s'pose I haven't eyes in my head?"

The veneer of sobriety Beresford imposed on his countenance refused to stay put.

MacLean fumed on. "Hmp! Malbrouck's s'en va-t-en guerre, eh? Very pretty. Very romantic, no doubt. But damned sentimental tommyrot, just the same."

"Yes, sir," agreed the constable, barking into a cough just in time to cut off a laugh.

"Get out!" ordered the Inspector, and there was the glimmer of a friendly smile in his own eyes. "And I'll expect you both to dine with me to-night. Six o'clock sharp. I'll hear that wonderful story in more detail. And take care of yourself, Beresford. You don't look strong yet. I'll make that week two or three if necessary."

"Thank you, sir."

"Hmp! Don't thank me. Earned it, didn't you? What are you hanging around for? Get out!"

Constable Beresford had his revenge. As he passed the window, Inspector MacLean heard him singing. The words that drifted to the commissioned officer were familiar.

> "Malbrouck s'en va-t-en guerre,
> Mironton-ton-ton, mirontaine."

MacLean smiled at the irrepressible youngster. Like most people, he responded to the charm of Winthrop Beresford. He could forgive him a touch of debonair impudence if necessary.

It happened that his heart was just now very warm toward both these young fellows. They had come through hell and had upheld the best traditions of the Force. Between the lines of the story they had told he gathered that they had shaved the edge of disaster a dozen times. But they had stuck to their guns like soldiers. They had fought it out week after week, hanging to their man with bulldog pluck. And when at last they were found almost starving in camp, they were dividing their last rabbit with the fellow they were bringing out to be hanged.

The Inspector walked to the window and looked down the street after them. His lips moved, but no sound came from them. The rhythmic motion of them might have suggested, if there had been anybody present to observe, that his mind was running on the old river song.

> "Malbrouck s'en va-t-en guerre,
> Mironton-ton-ton, mirontaine."

CHAPTER XLI

Sense And Nonsense

BERESFORD speaking, to an audience of one, who listened with soft dark eyes aglow and sparkling:

"He's the best scout ever came over the border, Jessie. Trusty as steel, stands the gaff without whining, backs his friends to the limit, and plays the game out till the last card's dealt and the last trick lost. Tom Morse is a man in fifty thousand."

"I know another," she murmured. "Every word you've said is true for him too."

"He's a wonder, that other," admitted the soldier dryly. "But we're talking about Tom now. I tell you that iron man dragged West and me out of the Barrens by the scruff of our necks. Wouldn't give up. Wouldn't quit. The yellow in West came out half a dozen times. When the ten-day blizzard caught us, he lay down and yelped like a cur. I wouldn't have given a plugged sixpence for our chances. But Tom went out into it, during a little lull, and brought back with him a timber wolf. How he found it, how he killed it, Heaven alone knows. He was coated with ice from head to foot. That wolf kept us and the dogs alive for a week. Each day, when the howling of the blizzard died down a bit, Tom made West go down with him to the creek and get wood. It must have been a terrible hour. They'd come back so done up, so frozen, they could hardly stagger in with their jags of pine for the fire. I never heard the man complain—not once. He stood up to it the way Tom Sayers used to."

The girl felt a warm current of life prickling swiftly through her. "I love to hear you talk so generously of him."

"Of my rival?" he said, smiling. "How else can I talk? The scoundrel has been heaping on me those coals of fire we read about. I haven't told you half of it—how he nursed me like a woman and looked after me so that I wouldn't take cold, how he used to tuck me up in the sled with a hot stone at my feet and make short days' runs in order not to wear out my

185

strength. By Jove, it was a deucedly unfair advantage he took of me."

"Is he your rival?" she asked.

"Isn't he?"

"In business?"

"How demure Miss McRae is," he commented. "Observe those long eyelashes flutter down to the soft cheeks."

"In what book did you read that?" she wanted to know.

"In that book of suffering known as experience," he sighed, eyes dancing.

"If you're trying to tell me that you're in love with some girl—"

"Haven't I been trying to tell you for a year?"

Her eyes flashed a challenge at him. "Take care, sir. First thing you know you'll be on thin ice. You might break through."

"And if I did—"

"Of course I'd snap you up before you could bat an eye. Is there a girl living that wouldn't? And I'm almost an old maid. Don't forget that. I'm to gather rosebuds while I may, because time's flying so fast, some poet says."

"Time stands still for you, my dear," he bowed, with a gay imitation of the grand manner.

"Thank you." Her smile mocked him. She had flirted a good deal with this young man and understood him very well. He had no intention whatever of giving up the gay hazards of life for any adventure so enduring as matrimony. Moreover, he knew she knew it. "But let's stick to the subject. While you're proposing—"

"How you help a fellow along!" he laughed. "Am I proposing?"

"Of course you are. But I haven't found out yet whether it's for yourself or Mr. Morse."

"A good suggestion—novel, too. For us both, let's say. You take your choice." He flung out a hand in a gay debonair gesture.

"You've told his merits, but I don't think I ever heard yours mentioned," she countered. "If you'd recite them, please."

"It's a subject I can do only slight justice." He bowed again. "Sergeant Beresford, at your service, of the North-West Mounted."

"Sergeant! Since when?"

"Since yesterday. Promoted for meritorious conduct in the line of duty. My pay is increased to one dollar and a quarter a day. In case happily your choice falls on me, don't squander it on silks and satins, on trips to Paris and London—"

"If I choose you, it won't be for your wealth," she assured him.

"Reassured, fair lady. I proceed with the inventory of Sergeant Beresford's equipment as a future husband. Fond, but, alas! fickle. A family black sheep, or if not black, at least striped. Likely not to plague you long, if he's sent on many more jobs like the last. Said to be good-tempered, but not docile. Kind, as men go, but a ne'er-do-well, a prodigal, a waster. Something whispers in my ear that he'll make a better friend than a husband."

"A twin fairy is whispering the same in my ear," the girl nodded. "At least a better friend to Jessie McRae. But I think he has a poor advocate in you. The description is not a flattering one. I don't even recognize the portrait."

"But Tom Morse——"

"Exactly, Tom Morse. Haven't you rather taken the poor fellow for granted?" She felt an unexpected blush burn into her cheek. It stained the soft flesh to her throat. For she was discovering that the nonsense begun so lightly was embarrassing. She did not want to talk about the feelings of Tom Morse toward her. "It's all very well to joke, but——"

"Shall I ask him?" he teased.

She flew into a mild near-panic. "If you dare, Win Beresford!" The flash in her eyes was no longer mirth. "We'll talk about something else. I don't think it's very nice of us to—to——"

"Tom retired from conversational circulation," he announced. "Shall we talk of cats or kings?"

"Tell me your plans, now you've been promoted."

"Plans? Better men make 'em. I touch my hat, say, 'Yes, sir,' and help work 'em out. Coming back to Tom for a minute, have you heard that the Colonel has written him a letter of thanks for the distinguished service rendered by him to the Mounted and suggesting that a permanent place of importance can be found for him on the Force if he'll take it?"

"No. Did he? Isn't that just fine?" The soft glow had danced into her eyes again. "He won't take it, will he?"

"What do you think?" His eyes challenged hers coolly. He was willing, if he could, to discover whether Jessie was in love with his friend.

"Oh, I don't think he should," she said quickly. "He has a good business. It's getting better all the time. He's a coming man. And of course he'd get hard jobs in the Mounted, the way you do."

"That's a compliment, if it's true," he grinned.

"I dare say, but that doesn't make it any safer."

"They couldn't give him a harder one than you did when you sent him into the Barrens to bring back West." His eyes, touched with humor and yet disconcertingly intent on information, were fixed steadily on hers.

The girl's cheeks flew color signals. "Why do you say that? I didn't ask him to go. He volunteered."

"Wasn't it because you wanted him to?"

"I should think you'd be the last man to say that," she protested indignantly. "He was your friend, and he didn't want you to run so great a risk alone."

"Then you didn't want him to go?"

"If I did, it was for you. Maybe he blames me for it, but I don't see how *you* can. You've just finished telling me he saved your life a dozen times."

"Did I say I was blaming you?" His warm, affectionate smile begged pardon if he had given offense. "I was just trying to get it straight. You wanted him to go that time, but you wouldn't want him to go again. Is that it?"

"I wouldn't want either of you to go again. What are you driving at, Win Beresford?"

"Oh, nothing!" He laughed. "But if you think Tom's too good to waste on the Mounted, you'd better tell him so while there's still time. He'll make up his mind within a day or two."

"I don't see him. He never comes here."

"I wonder why."

Jessie sometimes wondered why herself.

CHAPTER XLII

The Imperative Urge

THE reason why Tom did not go to see Jessie was that he longed to do so in every fiber of his being. His mind was never freed for a moment from the routine of the day's work that it did not automatically turn toward her. If he saw a woman coming down the street with the free light step only one person in Faraway possessed, his heart would begin to beat faster. In short, he suffered that torment known as being in love.

He dared not go to see her for fear she might discover it.

She was the sweetheart of his friend. It was as natural as the light of day that she turn to Win Beresford with the gift of her love. Nobody like him had ever come into her life. His gay courage, his debonair grace, the good manners of that outer world such a girl must crave, the affectionate touch of friendliness in his smile: how could any woman on this forsaken edge of the Arctic resist them?

She could not, of course, let alone one so full of the passionate longing for life as Jessie McRae.

If Tom could have looked on her unmoved, if he could have subdued or concealed the ardent fire inside him, he would have gone to call occasionally as though casually. But he could not trust himself. He was like a volcano ready for eruption. Already he was arranging with his uncle to put a subordinate here and let him return to Benton. Until that could be accomplished, he tried to see her as little as possible.

But Jessie was a child of the imperative urge. She told herself fifty times that it was none of her business if he did accept the offer of a place in the North-West Mounted. He could do as he pleased. Why should she interfere? And yet—and yet—

She found a shadow of excuse for herself in the fact that it had been through her that he had offered himself as a special constable. He might think she wanted him to enlist permanently. So many girls were foolish about the red coats of soldiers. She had noticed that among her school-girl friends at Winnipeg. If she had any influence with him at all, she did not want it thrown on that side of the scale.

But of course he probably did not care what she thought. Very likely it was her vanity that whispered to her he had gone North with Win Beresford partly to please her. Still, since she was his friend, ought she not to just drop an offhand hint that he was a more useful citizen where he was than in the Mounted? He couldn't very well resent that, could he? Or think her officious? Or forward?

She contrived little plans to meet him when he would be alone and she could talk with him, but she rejected these because she was afraid he would see through them. It had become of first importance to her that Tom Morse should not think she had any but a superficial interest in him.

When at last she did meet him, it was by pure chance. Dusk was falling. She was passing the yard where his storehouse was. He wheeled out and came on her plumply face to face. Both were taken by surprise completely. Out of it neither could emerge instantly with casual words of greeting.

Jessie felt her pulses throb. A queer consternation paralyzed the faculties that ought to have come alertly to her rescue. She stood, awkwardly silent, in a shy panic to her pulsing finger-tips. Later she would flog herself scornfully for her folly, but this did not help in the least now.

"I—I was just going to Mr. Whaley's with a little dress Mother made for the baby," she said at last.

"It's a nice baby," was the best he could do.

"Yes. It's funny. You know Mr. Whaley didn't care anything about it before—while it was very little. But now he thinks it's wonderful. I'm so glad he does."

She was beginning to get hold of herself, to emerge from the emotional crisis into which this meeting had plunged her. It had come to her consciousness that he was as perturbed as she, and a discovery of this nature always brings a woman composure.

"He treats his wife a lot better too."

"There was room for it," he said dryly.

"She's a nice little thing."

"Yes."

Conversation, which had been momentarily brisk, threatened to die out for lack of fuel. Anything was better than significant silences in which she could almost hear the hammering of her heart.

"Win Beresford told me about the offer you had to go into the Mounted," she said, plunging.

"Yes?"

"Will you accept?"

He looked at her, surprised. "Didn't Win tell you? I said right away I couldn't accept. He knew that."

"Oh! I don't believe he did tell me. Perhaps you hadn't decided then." Privately she was determining to settle some day with Winthrop Beresford for leading her into this. He had purposely kept silent, she knew now, in the hope that she would talk to Tom Morse about it. "But I'm glad you've decided against going in."

"Why?"

"It's dangerous, and I don't think it has much future."

"Win likes it."

"Yes, Win does. He'll get a commission one of these days."

"He deserves one. I—I hope you'll both be very happy."

He was walking beside her. Quickly her glance flashed up at him. Was that the reason he had held himself so aloof from her?

"I think we shall, very likely, if you mean Win and I. He's always happy, isn't he? And I try to be. I'm sorry he's leaving this part of the country. Writing-on-Stone is a long way from here. He may never get back. I'll miss him a good deal. Of course you will too."

This was plain enough, but Tom could not accept it at face value. Perhaps she meant that she would miss him until Win got ready to send for her. An idea lodged firmly in the mind cannot be ejected at an instant's notice.

"Yes, I'll miss him. He's a splendid fellow. I've never met one like him, so staunch and cheerful and game. Sometime I'd like to tell you about that trip we took. You'd be proud of him."

"I'm sure all his friends are," she said, smiling a queer little smile that was lost in the darkness.

"He was a very sick man, in a great deal of pain, and we had a rather dreadful time of it. Of course it hit him far harder than it did either West or me. But never a whimper out of him from first to last. Always cheerful, always hopeful, with a little joke or a snatch of a song, even when it looked as though we couldn't go on another day. He's one out of ten thousand."

"I heard him say that about another man—only I think he said one in fifty thousand," she made comment, almost in a murmur.

"Any girl would be lucky to have such a man for a husband," he added fatuously.

"Yes. I hope he'll find some nice one who will appreciate him."

This left no room for misunderstanding. Tom's brain whirled. "You—you and he haven't had any—quarrel?"

"No. What made you think so?"

"I don't know. I suppose I'm an idiot. But I thought—"

He stopped. She took up his unfinished sentence.

"You thought wrong."

They had come to Whaley's house. She made as though to turn in.

He caught at her coat. "Wait," he said huskily. "Let's—let's walk to the end of the street."

Her heart flung out panic signals again. The pulse in her soft throat drummed. "I—don't think I'd better," she protested in a small voice.

"Yes," he said. "I've something to say to you."

She meant to go into the house, but her feet did not obey. Before she knew it they were keeping step with those of Morse.

If he had anything to say, he appeared to have trouble in finding words to express himself. They walked in silence. Once a wolf in the forest howled mournfully. Their moccasins crunched on the snow crystals. No other sound broke the stillness.

They reached the end of the street.

Caught in the tide of an emotional stress, the girl made one attempt to escape. "I must hurry back," she murmured.

He ignored her words, if he heard them. A world of cold wonderful moonlight surrounded them. Above them twinkled a million other worlds. And in all this universe of space were just two people, the man and the woman.

"I'm a presumptuous fool," he broke out. "After what's between us—after that first night when I made you hate me—but I can't help it—I'd better tell you and be done with it. I love you—always have—always shall. Now tell me that you hate me, and I'll never trouble you again. I'm going away—soon."

"Can I tell you that—when I don't?" she asked, so low he just caught the words.

"You are good. You've tried to be friendly to me, but deep down in you—"

Her eyes met his—wonderful eyes, soft and radiant and dewy, with the light in them it is given only one man to see. "A girl forgives a man everything he has done—when she loves him. There isn't room for anything else. It just fills her."

His heart sang. It was impossible, of course. Yet it was true. She loved him. Had she not just said so? He looked at her, dazed, his soul full of her slender sweetness, of the sense of the amazing gift he dared not reach out his hands to take.

Then—how neither of them knew—she was in his arms, warm, trembling, close to tears, her whole being exquisitely happy.

When he looked up into the sky again, the moonlight was no longer chill. The stars twinkled warm benedictions. A miracle had transformed the night.

THE END